To my daughter and nephews
who will carry on the solution to the equation of life.
– J.I.

To García Márquez, Cortázar, and Borges,
all of whom set my mind reeling many years ago.
– L.A.

THE EDGE OF THE WORLD

JULIAN IRAGORRI
AND LOU ARONICA

The Story Plant
Studio Digital CT, LLC
PO Box 4331
Stamford, CT 06907

Print ISBN-13: 978-1-61188-273-5
E-book ISBN-13: 978-1-945839-32-0

Visit our website at www.TheStoryPlant.com
Visit Lou Aronica's website at www.LouAronica.com

Originally published under the title *Differential Equations*:
First Fiction Studio printing: April 2012
First Story Plant printing: September 2013
First publication under the title *The Edge of the World*: March 2019
Printed in the United States of America

PRAISE FOR THE EDGE OF THE WORLD

"A fascinating character study that digs deep into individuals in different eras but tied together by the colors emulating from others."
– Genre Go Round Reviews

"Like eating a fresh lime sorbet with saltwater in your (sex-tousled) hair."
– Smallgood Hearth

"Reminds us how intricately we are all tethered together."
– Lazy Day Books

"One of those books where you can't stop reading. It was an amazing read and I think you should give it a try."
– Ruby's Books

THE EDGE OF THE WORLD

Maria,

I hope one day
you discover the
"Ashram" that
changed Alex
Soberano's path.

Julián

NYC — May 18, 2023

ACKNOWLEDGMENTS

From Julian Iragorri:

Thanks to Lou Aronica who really understands the magical realism that literature can bring to life. He is a genius at understanding the intricacies in different cultures that create all the variables of the world.

Also to my family and friends for supporting this endeavor.

From Lou Aronica:

Thanks to Julian Iragorri for inviting me into this project and for being a true Renaissance man. You are remarkable in so many ways.

Thanks to my wife Kelly and my four children, Molly, David, Abigail, and Tigist, for giving my life meaning.

Thanks to Jackie Baron McCue for her copyediting help.

Watch your thoughts, for they become words.
Watch your words, for they become actions. Watch
your actions, for they become habits. Watch your
habits, for they become character. Watch your
character, for it becomes your destiny.

– Margaret Thatcher

1.

The weight of the cufflinks was palpable. The Tateossian gold squares with mother-of-pearl inlay exerted a faintly noticeable pressure on his Ascot Chang-draped wrists. Alex Soberano preferred it that way. He appreciated the confirmation that his efforts had generated for him the treasure of Tateossian and Ascot Chang, in the same way that they'd netted him Hermes ties, custom Saville Row suits and, for that matter, the mahogany table in the conference room of his 24th floor Park Avenue offices where he now sat, and the calfskin tablet and Waterman pen that lay upon it. Alex Soberano liked regular reminders that, at age forty-two, he'd done very, very well with his life.

The deal he was about to consummate had required little of his attention over the past six months. His due diligence people had completed their usual exhaustive vetting, uncovering only one hiccup in the books that they'd promised him was inconsequential. His acquisition staff hired industry experts to project growth for the sector and the numbers were promising. The company profiled well and allowed him to add a new component – social media – to his collection, and its executive staff seemed to require few changes beyond the usual streamlining of the back office. The current owner, Tom Waxman, was extraordinarily smart and he was going to be attached to the operation for the conceivable future, but Alex felt that the number two at the company, Richard Plum, might have the stronger leadership skillset. Even the price seemed reasonable. In all, buying this majority stake was little more than a matter of going through the motions for Alex. It would be his third such deal this year. Growing the corporation was important, as Alex had charged the senior members of his organization with an aggressive budget goal, and he knew they could only reach that goal through acquisitions of this sort.

Lawyers on both sides chattered as Alex leaned forward slightly. He knew that his legal team had gained a reputation for fighting aggressively to maintain his interests and he knew that the reputation alone was usually enough to keep the lawyers on the other side honest. Alex didn't need to listen to what they said to each other. The chattering was ceremonial now, anyway. Every deal point was already in place and it would be folly for those he was acquiring to try to renegotiate in the final stage.

Alex needed to concern himself with only one more thing. He glanced at Plum for a moment, finding him relaxed and engaged. He shifted his eyes quickly to Waxman. He'd met the man twice during the acquisition process. The president of Sandbank Media had started the company in his living room and managed to grow it to $500 million in revenue in eleven years, nearly all of which came from advertisers who liked the demographics of the members who used the Sandbank site. No one in Waxman's segment of the industry questioned his vision or his dedication, and Waxman seemed earnest enough and dedicated enough in the conversations Alex had had with him. This setting was different though. Tom Waxman's life was about to change and Alex understood that people revealed much when they knew their lives were about to veer into new territory. Whatever Waxman was feeling right now would be perhaps the greatest indicator of how he would handle himself and the company he would continue to run after they completed this deal.

Alex leaned forward an imperceptible bit more and studied Waxman. The man smiled at him, then turned his attention to a document one of his attorneys handed him. Waxman seemed nervous, but Alex considered that a good sign. A man should be nervous when he is about to entrust majority ownership in his creation to someone else. Alex watched as Waxman read the document, initialed it, and then glanced up at him, seemingly surprised that Alex was still looking at him. Alex barely noticed, though, because by that point his eyes rested elsewhere.

One of Alex's lawyers attempted to hand him a piece of paper, but Alex didn't take it. He wanted just one more moment.

Something was appearing.

"Alex, I need your signature here," the lawyer said, understandably oblivious to what Alex was doing. He placed the sheet on Alex's tablet.

Alex broke his gaze from Waxman and looked down at the document, not bothering to read it. Instead, he moved his hands to the surface of the conference table, feeling his cufflinks glide forward.

"I'm sorry, but we won't be making this deal," Alex said, rising.

Waxman sputtered, suddenly seeming like a flustered teenager at his first high school debate rather than an entrepreneurial visionary. "I...I'm not sure I understand."

Alex didn't owe the man an explanation. Not now. Still, his own people had worked long hours on this acquisition. It was for them that he said to Waxman, "Every decision I make is in the best interests of my organization. I have just made such a decision here."

Plum stood. "Mr. Soberano, there must be something we can do to address any concerns you have."

Alex waved off the overture and glanced at Waxman one more time. The man seemed ready to speak again, but the words were stillborn. That confirmed everything Alex sensed about this deal. Removing his suit jacket from the back of his chair, gathering his tablet and his pen, Alex walked from the room and into the hallway of his offices. The only sound he heard was that of his executive assistant Mark Kamen pulling his materials together and trailing behind him.

"Um, what just happened in there?" Mark said as the conference room door closed behind them.

"Did I really leave anything to the imagination, Mark?"

"We're walking away from this deal?"

"I'll assume that was a rhetorical question."

Mark appeared flummoxed. He seemed even more rattled by this than Waxman had. "The numbers were great. The projections were better. We checked these guys out upside down and backward."

"And then the boss goes and pulls a crazy-ass stunt and a blockbuster acquisition vanishes into thin air. I assume the phrase, 'I don't get paid enough for this crap' is going through your head right about now."

"Will you fire me if I say you read my mind?"

Alex chuckled, the laughter causing the tension he always felt when he made a last-second reversal to abate slightly. "You're safe for now. Look, Mark, this isn't the first time I've walked away from a deal."

Alex glanced over at his assistant to see the young man shrugging. "It's the first time you've walked away from a deal this good, though."

"Maybe it wasn't as good as everyone assumed. I'm never going to deny my instincts. They have served this organization very well. They may give me the reputation of being an unpredictable lunatic, but they've contributed in a major way to the bottom line."

Alex knew that Mark wanted to say more. He appreciated the fact that the man seemed unafraid to challenge him. At twenty-four, Mark wasn't concerned about feeding a family or paying a mortgage. Alex hoped that Mark never let such concerns gag him. At the same time, though, he was glad that

Mark had the good judgment to let this lie. After all, what Alex had just said to him was true; his instincts had produced the foundation of the corporation, put up the walls, and kept both of them well dressed, well fed, and extremely well compensated. Even if he hadn't spent the past two-plus decades honing his other professional skills, his instincts alone would have made him and everyone associated with him very successful.

They reached Alex's suite and Mark peeled off to go to his office.

"Mark, come on in for a minute."

As Mark pivoted to follow him, Alex turned to his administrative assistant Kathy, who seemed completely baffled by his presence. "I know; I'm not supposed to be here. I'm supposed to be in the conference room signing documents. Let's pretend you didn't see me just now. If anyone wants me, I'll be available in about an hour."

Kathy still seemed confused, though she'd been through this with Alex before. After looking at him blankly for a couple of seconds, she said, "You got it," and returned to her computer screen.

Alex gestured Mark into his office and closed the door behind them.

"Explain to me how much of a nightmare I just caused for you," Alex said when they both sat down.

Mark put up his hands. "It's cool; I can handle it."

"I know you can handle it. That's not the point. I'm giving you the rare opportunity to let me have it. Vent."

Mark's eyes glittered and his mouth turned the slightest bit upward. "You mean I should tell you that you just negated four months of the best work I've ever done in my life, that I'm going to have to apologize on your behalf to nearly every department head in the company, and that no one is ever going to believe me again when I tell them that my project is of the highest priority? Is that what you had in mind?"

"Something like that."

"Or that the legal people are going to be all over my ass and that I'll probably have to offer up my first born to get the IT people to drop everything to run a report for me the next time I ask?"

"That too."

"Or that I will *never* get the chance to date a woman anywhere near as hot as the woman I could have dated if I weren't pulling all-nighters for you?"

"Okay, I hadn't anticipated that one. Feel better?"

Mark seemed to exhale for the first time since they left the conference room. "Little bit."

"Good. If you don't have a voodoo doll for me already, feel free to make one now. At the same time, though, watch Sandbank. Watch Waxman. See what happens over the next year. If it's nothing, you can call me on it."

Mark grinned at him appreciatively. "I'm not going to get to call you on it, am I?"

"Highly unlikely."

Mark looked down at the reports and files in his lap. "I liked this one."

"I know you did. I really wish we could have gone through with it. You never know, though. Maybe we needed to walk away from this deal because there's a better one out there."

"If you say it, I'll believe it."

Alex stood at that point and Mark followed suit. They both walked out, Mark continuing on to his office while Alex stopped at Kathy's desk, picking up a couple of messages waiting for him.

"Are you still not here?" Kathy said.

"Yeah; I'm going to take a little time."

"Sandbank was a nonstarter?"

Alex nodded. "Things came up short. You know the drill."

Kathy smiled at him. She'd been at this desk for five years and she knew that no deal was truly closed for Alex until the final meeting. "That's too bad, Alex. It seemed that you kinda wanted this one."

"It was a good fit. Not good enough to make me look in the other direction, though."

"I get it."

Alex closed his office door again, removed his jacket, and sat at his desk. The desk had been hand made by a master carpenter in Vermont. Alex had wandered into the carpenter's studio during one of his last good weekends with Opal. By the time the desk had arrived on Park Avenue, the sparring with his soon-to-be-ex-wife had turned to open hostility. Before the desk had its first scratch, Alex knew that, if it were a Tuesday, his divorce lawyer's daughter would be going to ballet class after school.

Alex took another deep breath and tried to get his blood pressure down to normal levels. He had realized last night that there was the distinct chance the Sandbank deal might break down this morning. He could have warned Mark, maybe even suggested a private meeting with Waxman before everyone gathered. It would have diminished the high drama and unnecessary theatre that had just taken place in the conference room. How many people were still sitting there mutely? How many of Waxman's lawyers were trying to salvage the deal? Had Waxman suggested renegotiating the terms yet, or was he smart enough to realize that he needed to move on, to find another suitor who wouldn't study him the way Alex had studied him?

Alex swung his eyes around the room, landing on the sideboard. He'd never had a place for personal objects in his office until he got married. Before then, the seal presented to him by the city of Anhelo in South America for building a hospital in his mother's name and five "tombstones" from blockbuster transactions he'd made during his years as a mergers-and-acquisitions banker in London were the only items from home he felt he needed. The sideboard was Opal's idea, somewhere to put pictures of her, trinkets from their vacations, some of the Indian artifacts she loved to collect, and other endearments they'd gathered in their time together. There was little on the sideboard now. The pictures of Opal had disappeared instantly when they split, as did the artifacts (except for the statue of Ganesh, the elephant-headed Hindu deity known for removing obstacles); Alex gave away most of the trinkets methodically to those he thought might enjoy them.

Alex felt himself sink into his chair, as though he were becoming physically heavier while he sat there. So many long hours lately; even more than usual. He was convinced that the company would make their goal this year, though it would be tougher than ever before. Some might have said he was foolish for being so aggressive in a still recuperating economy, but he felt the need to push. It was only September; they might be able to close one of the other acquisitions before then, and it was still possible for an opportunity to materialize that he could leap on. Maybe he could finalize his divorce agreement by the end of the year as well. If that were the case, he'd sing "Auld Lang Syne" until the middle of the next week.

He tugged on his left cufflink and absently gave it a quarter twirl. Realizing the backs of the two cufflinks were now out of line, he twirled the left one back to its original position.

Walking away from Sandbank was the right decision. Alex never extricated himself from a business transaction with any regrets. Still, this one had left him feeling tired; it had drained more out of him than these last-minute reversals usually did.

Alex awakened his computer from sleep mode and checked his e-mail. He didn't want to deal with most of these now, but he did click on a message from his sister Daniela.

> Just wanted you to know that I'm not going to be able to get out to buy the present for Aunt Lorena today. Christina is a little under the weather, so I kept her out of preschool. I'll try to get it tomorrow – unless you want to get it instead. Just kidding.

D

Alex picked up the phone and speed-dialed Daniela.

"What's up with Chrissy?"

"Oh, nothing that can't be cured by repeated viewings of *Finding Nemo*."

"So she's not going to be out of commission, right?"

"This isn't going to mess up your 'date,' if that's what you're asking."

Alex smiled. First real one of the day. "Can I say hi to her?"

"Yeah, she's right here."

A few seconds later, Christina's squeaky three-year-old chirp was on the other end. "Hi, Uncle Alex."

"Hey, Chrissy. I hear you're not feeling so good."

"My tummy hurts a little."

"Oh, that's too bad. Is Mommy making you feel better?"

"We're cuddling on the couch watching *Nemo*."

"Sounds perfect. I wish I could be there with you. You're going to be all better by Saturday, right?"

"You bet."

"I sure hope so, because I would hate to miss out on one of our special days together."

"I'll be all better, Uncle Alex, don't worry."

"I'm counting on it. Well, watch lots and lots of movies today and snuggle really close to Mom. Love you."

"Love you."

Alex hung up the phone and sat back in his chair, realizing how much of a balm that brief conversation with his niece had been. Something about Christina's voice made the world seem right.

Glancing back at his computer to the other e-mail messages awaiting him threw him right off his axis again. Something really had to be wrong if he couldn't even get a few minutes of bliss after talking with Chrissy.

Rather than tackling any of the many challenges in his inbox, he picked up his phone and called his travel manager. Marina was on the other end within two rings. Fifty-thousand-dollar annual retainers guaranteed that kind of service.

"I need to recharge," Alex said to her. "I'm thinking about that place you mentioned the last time we spoke."

"The ashram?" Marina said brightly. "It'll be perfect for you. I'm so glad you're finally thinking about it. You won't believe how good you'll feel afterward. As I told you, though, they usually book up six months in advance. You weren't thinking of going sometime this year, were you?"

"I was thinking of going next week."

Marina hesitated. "Oh. Next week." Alex knew she was calculating how to make this happen. She would never tell him that she couldn't do it. Her company had the reputation for getting their clients wherever they wanted to go, even if it meant making extraordinary arrangements. Hence the huge retainers that their clients gratefully paid. "Let me call them right now, then."

Marina asked Alex a number of questions about accommodations and then a few more about his intended flight plans. She would handle all the remaining details herself. Before signing off, she told him about an upgrade she'd gotten for him for a meeting he had in São Paulo in November.

Alex thanked Marina for her help, hung up, and pressed Kathy's intercom button.

"Yes, Alex."

"I need you to cancel my appointments for the next two weeks starting on Monday."

"Did you say two weeks?"

"I did."

She was silent for ten seconds. Unlike Marina, Kathy said no to him all the time. Of course, he paid her to say no just as he paid Marina to say yes. "That's an awful lot to cancel," she said after the long pause. "I don't think I've ever done more than three days for you before. People might be a little freaked about this."

"They're going to be out of their minds, I know. And you're going to take all the grief over this. I'm sorry."

"That's why I bring in the big bucks, boss."

Alex chuckled. "Remember to bring this up at your next performance review. Meanwhile, I have a feeling that you're going to need a nice dinner out by the time this day is over. Why don't you make a reservation for you and your husband at one of our corporate accounts?"

"Are we talking about the deli around the corner or The Four Seasons?"

"For two weeks of cancellations, you can go wherever you want. Never mind, I'll call. I can get you into Masa."

"Works for me. Let me get started, though. I just got an e-mail from Meg trying to *add* a meeting next week."

"Thanks, Kath."

Alex put the phone down and glanced around the room again. Maybe he'd come back from this trip with something to put on Opal's sideboard. Maybe adding rather than subtracting would improve his energy.

He still had some time before his next appointment. He knew he should probably check in with Mark or his Head Counsel to talk about how to manage the ramifications of leaving Sandbank behind. There were, after all, always loose ends to deal with and egos to soothe.

Instead, he turned to his computer and typed in the URL for the ashram's website.

&

ANHELO, LEGADO, SOUTH AMERICA, 1928

With her eyes closed, all she could see were waves of brown. The woman sitting across the table from her wasn't troubled or damaged in any particular way, as that color sometimes indicated; her spirit and her future simply seemed featureless.

"Vidente, you have been quiet for a long time," the woman said tentatively. "If you see bad things, you must tell me. I must prepare."

People had been calling her "Vidente" for so long that she couldn't recall the last time she heard her real name spoken aloud. Some in the community preferred to call her "Tia Vidente" as a form of endearment. Even her sons called her "Madre Vidente" now, having long ago accepted their mother's place in the lives of the townspeople. After these many years, she had even come to think of herself by that name.

She opened her eyes slowly and her vision began to fill again with color. The violet and red of the tapestry that hung on the far wall. The ochre and bronze of the pottery on the shelf. The cobalt and white of the figurines on the cupboard. The terra cotta of the antique cazuela and the copper of the chafing dish, both presents from a grateful recipient of her services, neither of which had felt fire in Vidente's home. The saffron of the sash that billowed over the window. The crystals and pewters and golds and greens; the room was a rainbow visible nowhere else in the world – a Vidente rainbow. A rainbow for a woman who sensed color beyond her eyes and who liked those colors expressed in the finest things available. Vidente's home was her palace, a testament to her station as one of Anhelo's most prominent and prosperous citizens.

Finally, Vidente focused on Ana, the woman seeking her help who, in contrast to the brown that Vidente saw with eyes closed, wore a bright orange frock with lemon embroidery. Ana had called on Vidente several times in the past year and she'd encountered her at church and in the shops. At all times, Ana wore brilliant clothing. *She wants color in her life*, Vidente thought. *How sad that she doesn't seem able to hold any in her soul.*

"I am not seeing bad things, Ana," Vidente said, tipping her head toward the woman.

"But you have been so quiet."

Vidente patted the woman's hand. "Sometimes the images come very slowly. That doesn't mean you have anything to fear."

Vidente truly believed that Ana had nothing to worry about regarding her future – except that it was likely to be a life without incident. The brown was everywhere. Sometimes darker, sometimes lighter, but always brown. The color of inconsequentiality and an abundance of self-doubt. For reasons Vidente couldn't discern, Ana wouldn't absorb the colors she wore so boldly in her clothing, though she seemed entirely capable of doing so. There were places Vidente didn't plumb, for the sake of Ana's privacy, but she guessed that if she looked there she might find why the woman avoided what she so wanted.

Ana's brow furrowed and she looked down at her hands. Vidente wanted to offer her something, some suggestion that days more vibrant lay ahead. Vidente never lied to anyone during a reading, even when she believed the person wanted to hear a lie. However, she had many times kept searching and searching until she found a way to offer something promising.

"I am not finished, Ana," she said as the woman looked up at her. "I will use another technique with you today. I need to look farther with this technique. I may not open my eyes or speak with you for several minutes."

"I will be patient, Vidente."

Vidente closed her eyes again. Usually, what she saw in colors was enough to give her useful messages for those who requested readings from her. The colors had always been reliable to her. Sometimes, though, she needed to extend her vision. If she sent herself deeply enough into the space outside of herself, she could see actual images. Occasionally, entire scenes played out in front of her. Vidente had come to learn that these visions weren't nearly as reliable as the colors; unlike the colors, they were mutable. Still, they sometimes offered direction when none other was available.

The waves of brown appeared again. Like molten chocolate wending its way through a sea of caramel. It was necessary for Vidente to look past the color. She focused intently on the darkest of the brown and in doing so made the message of the brown drop away. It was like stepping through the fog and coming to a clear space. Here, though, the space offered only shadow. She could see the faintest movement. Was that a man? Ana wanted a man so badly; one who would finally erase Oscar's humiliation of her. The image Vidente saw here was so indistinct, though, that it could as easily be a deer, a sloth, or even a vegetable cart.

Vidente concentrated further, pushing her soul toward the shadow, encouraging her will to be in the same place as the shadow. Something was definitely moving around and she could now see that the shape was human. Male? Female? Young? Old? None of that was clear. Nor was it clear why there was such a veil over Ana's future. This had nothing to do with the woman's health. Vidente would have seen that in the colors. For some reason, the spirits did not want to offer the images they usually gave so generously.

She so didn't want to disappoint Ana. Once a month Ana came to her, gaily dressed and bearing a tray of the delicious pastries she made, eyes gleaming with hope but shaded by desperation. Vidente always found a vision to encourage her; the visit of a favorite nephew, a celebration Ana would attend, the birth of a neighbor's child. These visions were never what Ana truly wanted, but she always left Vidente's house viewing the world with a little less desperation. And she always came back.

Several minutes passed, but the images remained indistinct. *I must go beyond sight*, Vidente thought. She rarely used the process she was considering, and she was not entirely comfortable with it, but she knew it was possible to close her eyes completely. To allow her other senses to tell her what her vision did not.

Vidente tipped her head slightly and felt herself falling backward. With this sensation of falling came absolute blackness. There were no colors here, no shadows, nothing nearly so brilliant as brown. It was as though she had never seen anything at all, ever in her life. The feeling of unease that always accompanied this technique rippled her skin. Vidente had never stayed long in this place and she knew she could not linger here now. However, there had to be a reason why the other techniques eluded her, and she would spend a few sightless moments here for Ana's sake. She liked the woman too much to let her go away with nothing.

She felt cooler suddenly, as though someone had opened all the doors and windows of her home at once. The air was different. It was crisper and thinner. It smelled of loam and oak. Vidente knew, though she wasn't sure how she knew, that she was somewhere very far away. Was Ana going on a trip? Maybe to some distant mountains in Europe or even America? The only thing Vidente knew for sure was that no place in Anhelo or anywhere near it had air that felt this way.

Just on the edges of her hearing, Vidente found the sound of moaning. These were not moans of pleasure. Nor were they moans of pain or suffering. The moans held a sense of sadness and loss, but not the dissonance of true grief. As she extended herself to try to make more of this sound, Vidente felt a moist softness on her forehead followed by a silken brush across her face and then warm pressure. Moments passed and she felt the same series of sensations again. More moments passed and the experience repeated itself. Each iteration felt slightly different but materially the same.

As this happened for the fifth time, Vidente caught the scent of perfume. A floral and consciously unrefined smell, one that announced itself as its bearer entered a room and lingered for many minutes after the visit was over. It was unmistakably Ana's latest perfume. No one else in Anhelo wore it. But the scent was not coming from the Ana who sat across the table from Vidente. It came instead from the scene Vidente sensed in her temporary blackness and it grew stronger as Vidente again felt the pressure on her body. Vidente heard a sob and then the pressure lessened. Soon the smell of Ana's perfume diminished. It was then that Vidente realized that Ana was a part of this scene, but she was not the focus of it.

Vidente was.

Kisses on the forehead. Unreturned embraces. Repeated multiple times.

Vidente's eyes opened involuntarily, causing the colors in the room to close on her vertiginously.

"Vidente, your expression; it frightens me."

Vidente tried to stop the swirling of colors, tried to fix her eyes on Ana without scaring her further. "You have no reason to be frightened," she said.

As her vision corrected, Vidente saw Ana's hand go to the cross at her neck. "How can I believe that when you go into your trance for a long time and then come back looking like the devil was chasing you?"

Vidente took Ana's free hand and clasped it with both of hers. "Believe me when I say that I didn't see anything that should cause you fear. I just couldn't get a clear image for you and this frustrated me." Vidente stood abruptly, holding the side of the table to guarantee that she wouldn't stumble. "I am sorry, Ana, that I could not do better. Maybe next month."

Ana rose slowly, thanked Vidente, and left, her eyes more clouded and confused than when she entered. As soon as the woman was gone, Vidente sat down again, feeling the need to close her own eyes once more, but worried about what she would experience if she did so. If what she'd already felt was true – and it was important for her to remember that only the colors were always true – she would soon take a journey that would send her to a place of crisp, oaken air.

And then, before Ana changed her perfume again, Vidente would die.

&

JOYA DE LA COSTA, LEGADO, SOUTH AMERICA, 1920

If he could complete this sale, this would turn out to be a very good day. Khaled Hebron had spent every possible minute of the past nine weeks introducing himself to the merchants of Joya de la Costa. He'd come to this burgeoning port city from his homeland in Bethlehem, suffering through more than a month of seasickness, bedsores, and a ceaselessly bland diet.

Back home, he'd left Nahla, the woman he'd been arranged to marry sixteen years earlier. Nahla took care of the household and raised their three children with affectionate attention. He couldn't really blame her that she'd never offered the same affectionate attention to him. He'd seen men and women walking hand in hand in Legado. He'd heard the local songs of magical love and devastating heartbreak. The people here were very public in their sentiments, and Khaled found it all very curious. Where he came from, marriages were business arrangements and romance was something left to the ancient poets. He ascribed the little ache in his heart when he watched the lovers here to nothing more than his ongoing confusion over the local customs.

He'd made this journey because he heard that the people of Legado were fascinated with the exotic and that Joya de la Costa in particular was a commercial paradise. Such notions had sent a ship

from Palestine to Legado every few months for the
past three years and had led him to learn Spanish,
even though he spoke it with a heavy Arabic accent.
However, the reality was something far less ideal.
Yes, Joya de la Costa's shops were busy, but the customers defined "exotic" as originating from nearby
countries in South America. Few of them had even
heard of Palestine, and fewer still seemed willing
to consider the goods he'd brought with him on the
long journey in three large suitcases.

His circumstances had begun to change over the
past few days, though. Perhaps it was his growing familiarity with the language and customs of this land
he had entered. Perhaps it was that word had begun
to travel of sales of his wares in the few shops that
had been willing to carry them. Perhaps it was that
the friends he'd made in the neighborhood where he
took a small apartment had begun to endorse him to
others in the community. Whatever the reason, he'd
placed an order of six pieces on Wednesday, two orders of five items apiece yesterday, and, if he completed this sale, orders in four different shops today.

"What kind of wood is this?" the shopkeeper
asked, running his fingers over the smooth planes of
the small statue of a mother and child that he held
in front of him with fascination.

"It is olivewood. The cuttings are from trees
that are thousands of years old and it takes an artist many steps over two months to make each piece.
Olivewood carvings are considered treasures in
my homeland." Khaled knew he was embellishing
the truth here, but not in a deceitful way. In reality, most homes in Bethlehem had several pieces of

olivewood on display, so one could hardly consider them rare. However, the artists who created them did require years of apprenticeship and each piece took much time to complete because of the curing process, though an artist could work on several dozen pieces at once.

The shopkeeper held up an embroidered basket. "And this?"

Though Khaled had only recently decided to pursue his fortune by brokering crafts, he took special pride in attending to even the smallest details before he embarked on this venture. "Ah, very, very special. I'm glad you asked me about it. The process is known as tatreez. Village women in Palestine learn this craft from their grandmothers at a very young age, but they can only create cross-stitching of this quality when they have practiced for an extremely long time and have many children of their own."

The shopkeeper nodded appreciatively and commented on the delicacy of the interleaving. Then he stopped his examination of Khaled's products to attend to a customer. While he did, Khaled surveyed the array of items he'd laid out for the shopkeeper's perusal. Vessels, figurines, trays, and pillows in olivewood, mother of pearl, tatreez, tahriri, and tashreem. Khaled had put so many things out on the table because the shopkeeper remained interested with each new addition, even though customers continually drew away his attention.

The sale completed, the shopkeeper answered the question of another customer before returning to Khaled. At last, he came back, lifted a small wooden vase, and examined its grain.

"Yes, I'll take this," he said.

"The vases?" Khaled said, hoping his use of the plural would make the shopkeeper think about taking more than one vase.

The shopkeeper swept his hand across the table. "All of it. These will look good in my shop. I've noticed some of the women glancing toward these items while we've been speaking. They had the look of buyers." He laughed. "Unless, of course, they were examining *you* instead."

Khaled chuckled at the shopkeeper's compliment and tried to conceal how startled he felt. There were easily two dozen of his pieces on display in front of them. It had taken him weeks and many, many solicitations to sell a total of this many pieces before. Inside, he was dancing, though he was confident that he managed to keep the celebration contained.

"Would you like me to help you arrange these items on a shelf?" he said, remaining outwardly composed.

"That won't be necessary. I like to live with my new pieces for a day or so before I make them available for sale. It gives me a better sense of how to present them to my customers."

With no further discussion about the purchase, the shopkeeper paid Khaled for the goods and gathered them up to bring to his back room. Khaled put the money in his pocket, enjoying the thought that he would eat very well tonight. Maybe he'd even buy his neighbors a bottle of rum to share later in the evening. He'd rarely been able to contribute much to their gatherings in the past, and he was growing increasingly enamored with the way the people down

here liked to celebrate whenever possible. It thrilled
him to think that he could lead the toasts tonight –
and provide the drink as well.

Thanking the shopkeeper, Khaled returned to
the busy street. He began to head toward home and
then stopped midstride to consider the change in
his fortunes. He had left his family behind to come
here because he knew there was no future for him at
home. Many people had questioned why he needed
to travel so far away – surely there were opportunities in other Palestinian towns or perhaps in the
neighboring countries – but something inside of him
told him to do so, that he needed to do something
dramatic if his life were ever going to be anything
but desperate. Now, for the first time, he felt wise
in listening to that voice. If business continued this
way, he would soon write to his brother to send
another large shipment. And he would send some
money back to Nahla for the children. She'd been
so nervous about this new venture, though she accepted his need to make this attempt. It would be a
pleasure to offer her some evidence that he could be
a real provider. The fortune that had always eluded
him in Bethlehem seemed, with the promise of this
good day, within reach at last.

Khaled decided to stop at the butcher on the way
back to his apartment. The meat here was unlike any
he'd eaten at home, succulent, tender, and flavorful.
He only allowed himself to indulge in meat rarely
because he needed to keep a careful watch on his
money, but if any night were one for celebration, it
was this one. He ordered a steak, already feeling the
richness of its juices warming his throat. If today's

business were any indication of his future transactions, he would soon be feasting this way every night and inviting his neighbors to join him for that as well. He would throw parties to celebrate good fortune and an adopted home that had embraced him.

Paper-wrapped steak in one hand and gloriously depleted sample case in the other, Khaled stepped out onto the street again. After his first few weeks in Joya de la Costa, he'd begun to wonder if he would need to move elsewhere in Legado to find a home for his wares. He began to consider the possibility that he'd even need to be an itinerant, wandering all over the country or even the continent to make a living. Recently, though, this town, with its rapid talkers and people in constant motion had begun to feel like a place where he could settle. Now, if the money were indeed beginning to flow, he could finally call a place home for the first time in his life.

"Khaled?"

Khaled turned toward the sound of the voice, not distinguishing its source.

"It *is* you," the speaker said. Khaled could now see that it was a dark man who'd called his name, and that the man was approaching him rapidly from the other side of the street. "What a remarkable thing to find you here."

Khaled squinted as though to bring the man's features into greater focus. The man spoke as a friend and, as he closed the distance between them and embraced him, handled him as a friend as well.

"Can you believe it?" the man said in Arabic. "Khaled and Samih on the same street an ocean away from our homeland."

The name registered faintly with Khaled. Yes, he and Samih had met before. They'd spoken on one or two occasions. The man's father had something to do with horses, or maybe it was mules.

"How long have you been here?" Khaled said.

"I arrived two weeks ago. Your face is the first familiar thing I've seen." Samih chuckled softly. "This place is not like home."

"It is certainly not like home. But maybe that's a good thing, no?"

Samih's face fell. Khaled could not recall ever before seeing such a rapid swing in emotions from an adult.

"Of course," Samih said. "I should have given you my condolences the moment I saw you. It must have been devastating to hear about your wife and children when you were so far away. And to have them die in such a horrible way."

Khaled set his sample case down on the ground, suddenly feeling dizzy. "My wife and children are dead?"

Samih's expression shifted again, this time to dismayed bewilderment. "Please don't tell me you didn't know." His head shook rapidly. "Please don't tell me that I am the bearer of this awful news."

Khaled tried to summon the faces of his wife, son, and two daughters. The little girls were so sweet. They loved it when he let them ride on his back. "When?" was the only word he could speak, barely getting that out.

"It was only days before my journey. I don't re-call who told me about it, but it came up because they knew I was going to Legado. Oh, Khaled, I am so sorry to be the person to bring this to you."

The man started crying then, leaving Khaled in the ridiculous position of needing to console him. Samih embraced him again at that point, which Khaled found awkward and unwelcome. They weren't friends. They weren't even really acquaintances. They simply happened to share a place of birth.

"I need to go," Khaled said, patting the man on the back.

"Of course, of course. Is there anything I can do for you, my dear brother?"

Khaled picked up his sample case. "I appreciate your offer, but no."

Without engaging Samih further, Khaled began to walk down the street. The wrapped steak in his hand felt heavier now. His meal tonight would have a different purpose from the one he'd originally intended.

He would certainly get that bottle of rum he'd been planning, but he would not be sharing it with his neighbors. He would cook the steak and open the bottle and he would consume both alone. In memory of good Nahla and his children. In memory of their spirits, so rarely shared with him, but vibrant and real all the same.

He could barely believe they were gone.

࿔

CAMBRIDGE, MA, UNITED STATES OF AMERICA, 1985

As Dro took his first step onto the campus, he focused all of his concentration on his feet. He wanted to remember this feeling, this sense of rooting in the place where he knew he belonged. He'd been reading about the Massachusetts Institute of Technology since he was a young teen. From then, he'd targeted MIT as the school that would cultivate his mind. The rigorousness of curriculum, the unparalleled faculty, and the international network of connections the school provided made it his only choice. Now, at last, he'd arrived.

He had spent a very long time getting here. The overnight flight from Legado into Miami had been delayed on the runway. Then, the wait to go through customs had been tedious and so slow that he nearly missed his connecting flight to Logan Airport, which itself arrived nearly an hour behind schedule. When he finally landed, he got a taxi as quickly as possible, left his bags in the room he'd rented in Boston from a retired dean of a local women's college, and took the T into Cambridge.

Dro surveyed the campus, which seemed so familiar to him from the dozens of catalogs, brochures, and articles he'd read about the university. The stately dome and columns of the main building. The sprawling setting along the Charles River. The vast expanses of lawn.

There were very few students visible now. Dro had anticipated as much. Within a few weeks, the path he stood on would be bustling. Right now, though, it was virtually untrod, allowing the majesty of the structures to have no competition for his attention. The Massachusetts Institute of Technology: a dream become real in front of him. His first in America, but far from his last.

He enjoyed the relative solitude and the sense that the campus was his alone for at least a brief juncture. Then, he started toward the steps before stopping again. The building was enormous; which of the multitude of doors should he enter?

The sound of a bicycle coming up on his right caused him to turn in that direction. The female bicyclist stopped next to him.

"May I help you?" she said.

"Admissions?" Dro said in response. Though he'd been studying English for the past few years, he still found the grammar confusing and inconsistent. He figured it would be better if he spoke as few words as possible until he became accustomed to American cadences. He didn't want anyone here to mistake him for stupid or uneducated.

The woman pointed up the stairs. "Right in there, first floor."

Dro followed her finger and then turned back to her. "Thank you."

She smiled. "Peru?"

Dro had been hoping he wouldn't be so quickly tabbed as a foreigner. He tipped his head toward her. "Legado. Do you know South America?"

"Nah, ex-boyfriend. He came from Peru and your accent seemed similar. I hope I didn't just offend you. I mean, I do realize it's a very big continent with lots of different cultures."

Dro nodded. "No problem." He took a step in the direction the woman had pointed, anxious to get on with his quest, even though the woman was diverting. "Thank you again."

The woman smiled once more. She was very attractive when she smiled. Actually, she was quite attractive even when she wasn't smiling, especially when strands of her hair tickled her face. Dro could tell she was an athlete; she had that kind of body. A swimmer, maybe. Their lines were different from those of runners or gymnasts, for instance. "You're welcome," she said, mounting her bicycle. "See ya around campus." She waved and pedaled away.

Dro watched her go for a few seconds. Definitely a swimmer. Then he turned and headed into the building and up toward the admissions office. There was more activity over here, many students and quite a few adults who he assumed to be faculty or administrators. He stood in the hallway for several minutes watching people enter and exit, imagining himself as part of the flow of the university, as an active member of its community, realizing in that moment that he'd truly staked everything on being in this place. It was now time to do what he needed to do to make that a reality.

He headed into a set of offices fronted by four cubicles, three of which were unoccupied. The furthest and largest office had the name Susan Roemer, Associate Admissions Director stenciled on the

door. Ignoring the gaze of the man at the one occupied cubicle, Dro headed toward the back office.
There, he found a woman he guessed to be in her
mid-thirties reading from a report of some sort and
taking notes.

Dro knocked on the door softly and the woman
looked up from her work. "Yes?"

"I would like to start coming to this school," he
said confidently.

"Okay," the woman said, glancing over at the
calendar on her desk. "Are you here on a tour? I
don't seem to have anything scheduled with you."

Dro took a step into the office. "I came from Legado today."

"Legado in South America?"

"Yes. I arrived at Logan Airport four hours ago.
I came here as soon as I could."

The woman said nothing for a long time. Dro
knew his English was weak and that his accent was
strong. Had he said something wrong?

"Are you considering MIT for your college education?" she said at last.

"There is nothing to consider. I only want this
school."

The woman looked down at her report and
then up at Dro again. "That's very flattering. If you
would like, I'd be happy to have one of our aides
give you a tour and talk to you about applying for
admission in the fall of '86."

Dro began to feel uncomfortable standing near
the woman's desk. He decided to sit in an open chair.
"I would prefer to come this year. I flew here from
Legado for this reason."

The woman shook her head and seemed a little ruffled. "I'm afraid that isn't possible. The fall semester starts in less than a month, and our freshman class has been full since March. Most of it was full by last December."

Dro leaned forward. "I have wanted to come to MIT since I was a young teenager."

The woman picked up a pencil and tapped it against her left forefinger. "You'll need to go through the application process. I'm sure it is the same in Legado."

Dro honestly didn't know about the college application process in Legado. He'd never considered going to school there. "I can't start right away?"

The woman's eyebrows arched. "To be honest, you might never be able to start here. I don't know how much you know about MIT, but our admissions standards are extremely high."

"Eight Nobel Prizes, I know."

Her expression softened. "Yes, our former students have won eight Nobel Prizes. Our faculty, of course, has won many others."

"Including Samuelson and Modigliani in Economics, which is what I will study. I want them to teach me. That is why I am here." Dro felt desperation in his voice. He didn't like it when he sounded desperate, but he needed to let Ms. Roemer understand just how essential this was to him.

"But you need to accept that you may not –"

"– My English is not good yet, but my mind is very good. I had the second highest scores in our national exams – good for any school in South America. My calculus scores were the highest. I am proficient at differential equations and as you know, that is the essence of any science at MIT – even Economics."

That caused her to tilt her head. "You can do differential equations at your age? How old are you? Eighteen?"

"Nineteen. I know differential equations very well."

He knew he would never be able to explain this with his current grasp of English. He pulled out the sheet of paper upon which he'd written the address of the campus, though he'd memorized it before he boarded the plane in Legado – years before, actually. Then, taking a pencil from the woman's desktop, he sketched out an example, showing the impact the multiple variables in the equation had on the equation itself. When he finished, he immediately started another without looking up. He loved the complexity of this form of mathematics, how the constant shifting of one variable or another changed everything.

When he finished the second example, he put the pencil back on the woman's desk. He glanced anxiously toward the woman and noticed that she was studying him. It was as though her eyes held all of him and everything around him at once. He wasn't sure how to respond to such scrutiny, but he felt surprisingly naked. It was as though this woman was seeing him in a way that no one ever had before.

"I can do another," he said. "I can show you many more if you want."

She finally moved her eyes away and picked up the paper. "That won't be necessary. I'm not a mathematician, but I can identify mastery."

"So I can come here?"

She sat back in her chair and steepled her fingers, her expression thoughtful. She no longer seemed as though she were ready to rush him out of her office, and for that, Dro was tremendously grateful. "Not yet. I can't do anything to get you into a school like this for this academic year. But we might be able to put some kind of plan together. Has any other American college accepted you?"

Dro shook his head. "I have not tried."

"I want you to try as soon as you can. Boston is one of the best collegiate cities in the country. We have many excellent institutions here. Some might be open to a foreign student with your mind, even at this late date." She looked at him again as she did earlier and didn't speak for several seconds and then offered him the closest thing to a smile he'd seen on her face. "I might even be able to make some phone calls for you."

Dro knew Ms. Roemer was reaching out to him, and he appreciated that more than he could express. However, this was not how he had planned things. "I would prefer not to go to another school."

"Your only other alternative is to wait to apply here next year. What I'm suggesting makes more sense. Go to another school for a year. Do *sensationally* well – I don't want you to set your sights on anything less than an A in any class. You'll need to take physics, calculus, chemistry, and at least one humanities class. Nothing else will work. Then we'll see what we can do about accepting you as a transfer student."

Dro had imagined this conversation going completely differently and he struggled in his mind to think of some way to turn things around. At the same time, he had the innate sense that what Ms. Roemer was saying was the best he was going to hear. Others had suggested as much, but Dro believed in the quality of his vision and the substance of his skill. He'd always been able to do the impossible. Still, if this were the only alternative, he would pursue it.

He stayed with Ms. Roemer for twenty minutes longer. She explained the process of applying to and being accepted into American colleges. She indeed did "make some phone calls" on his behalf, including one to Boston College that led to his scheduling an interview for the next day.

As he stood to leave, Susan stood to shake his hand. He turned to go and she held out the paper to him upon which he'd written the two differential equations.

"You should show this to the person who conducts your interview at BC."

Dro held up a hand. "I can do others. You keep that paper. One day, we will look at it together again."

Susan looked down at the equations, reading them as though they formed some kind of map. "I think I'll do that," she said, and then pointed at him with the hand holding the paper. "Do well out there. You'll be a great story if you do."

2.

NEW YORK, 2010

Business warfare had been Alex's crucible. He'd contended with hostile competitors, untrustworthy colleagues, and an unmerciful marketplace. He'd seen emotion cripple very talented associates and he'd learned from their mistakes. Therefore, very few people could get under his skin.

Unfortunately, Opal was one of those who could. Simply seeing her name on his caller ID sent adrenaline coursing through his system. There was a time when he welcomed this, when he embraced the charge that came within him from their every interaction, when he thrilled to the sound of her lightly Indian-accented voice. There was a time when Opal could take him out of his element so pleasurably that he welcomed the way she turned his world upside down.

That ended when the lawyers entered the picture.

"We've discussed the paintings already," he said into the phone as he paced the living room of his loft in the meatpacking district. "They're investment properties of the corporation and you have no access to the holdings of the corporation."

"I compromised on the London apartment," Opal said tersely. "I think that opens everything up to negotiation."

Alex willed himself to speak calmly. "First of all, your version of 'compromise' involved my buying the apartment from you at above-market value. Second, if you want to negotiate anything, we'll do it through the lawyers. I believe that is why both of them are getting so much of my money. However, if you think that anything regarding my business – *my* business, Opal – is a deal point, you haven't been paying attention."

Opal's response was flat. "Everything is a deal point, honey. That's what my lawyer tells me, and I believe him. *Your* money is paying for the best. I could leave this to him, but I thought I'd save us both a little ugliness by discussing the subject with you directly."

Opal had in fact been employing this method of negotiation for more than eighteen months now. Alex's one critical mistake in the divorce proceedings had been to acquiesce to one of her approaches in the early stages, believing it would get him out of the marriage more quickly. Now, though he'd long since stiffened his resolve, she seemed to feel that the trick was always worth trying. Alex knew she had no legal footing here; he'd started the company long before they met and he'd always insulated it from his personal affairs. He knew he could keep their divorce agreement at its currently negotiated state and, if Opal forced it to go to court, he wouldn't lose. The issue was how much his intransigence would cost him in time, headaches, and extra fees to the lawyers. More often, recently, he'd been wondering about the value of playing hardball with this woman he once loved. But if he'd learned anything about Opal – and there were plenty of times when he wondered if he understood her at all – it was that she would always want more from him. She blamed him for caring more about his corporation than he did about her. Alex tried to convince her this wasn't the case, that he truly was giving her every bit of himself that he could, but their arguments about this became increasingly bitter, culminating in her sudden departure from their home and the escalating acrimony that filled the space they once shared.

"The paintings are not in play, Opal."

His estranged wife sighed. It was the same kind of sigh she used to release in the languid minutes at the end of their long bouts of lovemaking. Opal had many sighs. Her forlorn sigh. Her impatient sigh. Her wistful sigh. She even had a sigh to indicate her disappointment that Alex wasn't bending to her will, but she chose not to employ that one here – and he knew that sending him echoes of their long treks to sexual satisfaction was a calculated move on her part.

"Why do we need to keep going down this road, Alex? You know that I can put the paintings in play if I want to. Wesson is a wizard. Your own lawyer admits this."

Alex had nearly fired his attorney for saying such a thing about Opal's attorney within her earshot. It had been their other huge mistake during this grotesquely extended affair.

At that moment, Alex heard Angélica's key in the door, causing him a disquieting conflict of emotions. It was like bathing in a hot spring and being pelted with ice cubes at the same time. His eyes shifted in that direction as he said to Opal, "Trust me when I say that you don't want to open this up again."

Angélica stepped into the foyer, saw him standing stiffly on the Persian rug, and mouthed, "Opal?" Alex nodded and then let his head roll toward the ceiling. His girlfriend smiled at him grimly.

"We've known each other for more than five years, Alex," Opal said with measured casualness. "Have you ever known me to shrink from a fight? Certainly you know that you aren't going to intimidate me with idle threats."

Angélica kissed his temple, then took his hand and guided him toward the couch. Alex sat, but could only settle as far as the edge of the cushion. "We're *not* going to go through this again. Every time we settle one point, you reopen another. That stops now, Opal. Keep this up and I'll shut down negotiations entirely. We'll take it straight to a judge. I like my chances with that."

Opal didn't answer for several seconds. While waiting for her next ploy, Alex felt Angélica's nimble fingers stroking his arm. The hot springs were getting warmer.

And then the ice assault returned. "You've become more of a bastard in the last year," Opal said after several seconds of silence. "Do you realize that? What the hell has happened to you? You've forgotten everything. I'll instruct Wesson to set up a meeting. If you want to get this over with, we'll get it over with."

Such a concession would have meant more to Alex if he hadn't heard similar declarations from Opal several times in the past year and a half. This was simply more gamesmanship, and Alex didn't feel like playing. "The meeting will have to wait. I won't be around for the next two weeks."

Alex felt Angélica's massage stop.

"Two weeks?" Opal said. "You're never gone on business that long."

"This isn't business."

"Not business? Are you taking the new love of your life with you?"

Alex placed a hand on Angélica's knee and squeezed. He flicked his eyes away from the question in hers. "My personal business is my personal business, Opal. Like the corporation, it is not your plaything."

"I'll take that as a no. Well, that rose certainly didn't stay in bloom very long."

Alex nearly stood again, but he didn't want Angélica to feel as though he were tearing himself away from her. "Get Wesson to put a meeting on our calendars. I have nothing more to say to you."

Alex clicked off the phone and threw it to the other side of the couch. He drew Angélica softly toward him, trying as he did to quiet his mind. He noticed that Angélica didn't flow into his arms as easily as she usually did.

"I need her out of my life," he said.

Angélica softened and finally melted into him in the way that was inimitably hers. "What did she want this time?"

Alex laughed at the absurdity of the conversation he'd just finished with his ex. "The Boteros. Can you believe that?"

Angélica stared up at him from his chest. "You adore those paintings. She can't get those, can she?"

Alex kissed her forehead. "There's not a chance in hell. She knows that. She's doing this to get something else, something she hasn't mentioned yet. That's the way she works."

Angélica nestled into him and didn't say anything for nearly a minute. Alex felt no need to talk to fill in the space. Holding Angélica next to him settled him; he could practically feel his blood pressure dropping. He could have easily spent the next hour doing nothing more than this.

"You're going somewhere?" she said faintly.

"To an ashram in Southern California. Marina has been trying to convince me to do this for a long time. She thinks I'll find it restorative. I finally decided to go with her recommendation."

"Did you decide to do this today?"

"Yesterday morning. Things came to a head after I pulled the plug on the Sandbank deal. Suddenly an ashram sounded like a very good idea."

Angélica sat up and tilted her head toward him. Her ebony hair flicked his arm as she did so. "We were together last night."

She lowered her lashes. On many women, these dark arches would be their most appealing feature. In Angélica's case, though, the lashes couldn't compete with the delicate planes of her face, the downy cushions of her lips, the gradual taper of her thighs, the smooth cinch of her waist, or any of a number of other attributes. Long glances at Angélica led Alex to a variety of contemporaneous physical responses, some of which he had only fleeting familiarity with before he began to love her.

Angélica lowered her eyes when the world gave her less than she expected. In their eight months as lovers, as well as in the years they'd spent together as schoolmates in Anhelo, Alex had seen her react that way to the indifference of friends, cruelty on the street, even an artlessly prepared meal. He'd rarely seen her eyes drop for him, though. He would have preferred that she find out about his trip to California a different way, and he was going to tell her this afternoon. He should have mentioned it last night, but he knew that his being gone so long was going to bother her. He hated upsetting her, so he forestalled it. It was a childish approach – something he would never have allowed himself in business – and something he was going to have to improve with Angélica.

Now it had proven painfully awkward. Nearly any scenario would have been better than his letting her know via a standoff with his wife.

He ran a fingertip through her hair. "We were together last night. I could have told you then."

She turned toward him slightly, eyes still downcast. "When are you leaving?"

"Sunday morning. I'm completely yours tonight and tomorrow night."

"Did you say you were going to an ashram?"

"In Southern California. It's likely at least one movie star will be there at the same time." She leaned back into him. "Then you'll have to get me an autograph." Alex kissed the top of her head. "Maybe I'll even come back with some salacious information; something you could write about pseudonymously." Angélica smiled softly. "I don't like to dirty myself that way."

"You're right, of course," Alex said, reaching for her hand. "If I discover something spicy, we'll keep it as our little secret."

Angélica nestled against him and, in doing so, ran her leg up his thigh. Alex reacted to this as he always had. As he adjusted to hold her closer, he noticed the phone he'd tossed to the other side of the couch. For an instant, he allowed his conversation with Opal to embed its barbs in his spirit. But as he felt Angélica's pillowy lips upon his neck, he let the memory dissolve. Soon, he hoped, the pains of his marriage would follow.

&

ANHELO, 1928

Every Sunday, Calle Adorar became the most beautiful street in all of Anhelo. Its residents placed clay pots of brilliant flowers on the sidewalks. They draped the porticos of their houses in fabrics of azure and gold. Even the people themselves came magnificently decorated, the men in shirts of woven silk, the women in scarves of delicate lace, carrying fans they didn't need to keep cool but which made lovely props, the children clean, pressed, and combed. The church at the end of the street was what inspired such displays. The building itself was always resplendent, the stone edifice pristine and welcoming, the fifteen-foot statue of the Blessed Virgin on its roof serene and inviting.

Vidente attended Iglesia de la Santa Madre each Sunday without fail, wearing one of her dozens of opulent, colorful dresses, her hair pulled back straight in a bun. Her arrival, in fact, was a ceremony more eagerly anticipated than the oratory of Padre Antonio or the bestowal of the sacraments. Seated in the tufted and brocaded chair that a neighbor and his son carried to the church for her weekly and placed along the first of the too-hard pews, she received the attentions of the community's worshippers. She was difficult to miss, as she was the only one sitting in a different type of seat.

"Good morning, Tia Vidente."

"Vidente, what a magnificent shawl."

"God be with you, Vidente."

As the priest, who Vidente had envisioned would be leaving within a few months for a larger assignment, began services, she sat upright reverently, her eyes fixed on the pulpit. Still, this did not prevent her from hearing the whispers of those behind and around her. They were always whispering and Vidente was always interested in hearing what they said.

"She saw us when she entered, didn't she?"

"Did you compliment her hair?"

"Maybe I'll offer to carry the chair back for her. It looks heavy, but I can do it."

Padre Antonio spoke today about the virtues of work. Vidente knew he was directing his sermon toward the young men of the community, many of whom spent far too many hours in idle pursuits, choosing play over the foundations of a career. Such laziness was hardly new to this generation. Vidente's own youngest son Mauricio had done little more than sleep, eat, and drink Carménère until his mid-twenties when his future wife Luisa dazzled him with her beauty and used that beauty to inspire him to find the kind of work a real man did.

Vidente enjoyed Padre Antonio's sermons regardless of their subject. He spoke with eloquence and earnestness. He had so much more fire and dedication in him than Padre Alvaro had before him. That priest had been so uninspiring that Vidente actually felt herself drifting off to sleep on a few occasions, even though she knew many eyes watched her and that her sleeping would cause the kinds of whispering she didn't want to hear. She could only hope that the church found a priest as gifted as the current one when Padre Antonio received his calling to a larger flock.

Not that Vidente would be here to experience it.

Vidente thought of little else since she received the vision of her death and the strange journey that would precede it. The thoughts occluded her sight of the colors in others and left her so preoccupied that she'd sometimes find herself hunched in the middle of a task with no memory of having started it. This was the first Sunday since the vision and Vidente vowed to push her fateful thoughts aside for this one festive and holy day of the week, but still they sought to dominate her.

She'd considered talking to Padre Antonio about what she saw and what it meant to her. She didn't want to burden him with thoughts of her mortality, though. In the coming weeks, he would face a vexing decision about leaving parishioners who embraced him for the honor of serving a much bigger community. He didn't need to carry Vidente's worries with him as well.

So lost was she in these thoughts that Vidente didn't notice the sermon had ended and that her fellow parishioners were lining up for communion. A woman named Sonia touched her on the elbow, bringing Vidente's attention back to the moment.

"Do you need help going to the pulpit, Tia Vidente?" Sonia said, offering an arm for Vidente to hold.

Vidente smiled at her and took the proffered arm. "Thank you. I'm afraid my mind was wandering." She stood and moved in front of the woman in the line awaiting the holy wafers. Tipping her head toward Sonia conspiratorially, she said, "Would you be so kind as to join me for lunch today?"

The woman beamed. "I would like that very much, Tia Vidente. If it is not too much to ask, could I have my boyfriend come with me? We have only been together a few weeks and I know he would enjoy it quite a bit."

"Then he is very welcome," Vidente said, turning back toward the head of the line. It was time to set aside the thoughts of her destiny. She would have guests this afternoon and they deserved her fullest sense of revelry.

By the time she stood again on the steps of the church, Vidente had invited seven others to join her for lunch. Along with Sonia, her new boyfriend, and the two who carried her chair to and from church, that added up to her usual total of eleven.

When she returned home, the serving girl had already set the table with a dozen places, as she did every Sunday afternoon. Vidente could smell the *chivo al coco* simmering on the stove before she even entered the house, the sweetness of the coconut brightening her spirits further and heightening her appetite. She removed her shawl and twirled with it in a graceful pirouette. At fifty-nine, she was still as delicate on her feet as she'd ever been.

Within twenty minutes, the first of the revelers had arrived. They were Carlos, who owned the finest flower shop in Anhelo along with his wife Ximena, who had a gift for making the miniature knitted dolls that were a signature of Legado artisans. Ten minutes later, the table was full and the serving girl presented the stew.

At the head of the table, Vidente stood from the same seat she'd used at the church. She raised her glass of wine, a bright and fruity white made from the Pedro Giménez grape in Legado's northern hills. "My friends, you do me honor of joining me for this meal. May we always cherish the time we have together."

"The honor is ours, Vidente," said Jairo, the thrice-widowed banker. "No matter how many times you welcome me to your Sunday table, it always feels like a blessing and I always appreciate it as such."

They all toasted Vidente then, causing her to wave her arms to fend off the adulation. "Let's eat," she said above the din. "The *chivo* does not like to wait for us."

A salad of tomatoes, cucumbers, and maracuya followed, and then *pastel de tres leches* for dessert. And more wine, of course. Much, much more wine. Vidente knew that some of the people didn't drink wine in their own homes, so she made sure they had as much as they desired while they were here.

By mid-afternoon, the party had moved from the dining room to the living room and the musicians had begun to arrive. One of them, playing guitar, was Jairo's brother, so Vidente could only assume that the banker had made the arrangements. She noticed just now Jairo handing his brother several British pounds (that being the preferred currency), and gesturing to the other members of the group. Vidente never ordered music for her parties, yet singing and dancing filled her house on most Sundays.

Sonia and her new boyfriend danced fervently and then closely, Sonia's eyes revealing both hunger and ardor. Vidente watched the couple for several minutes and then glanced away satisfied. The couple's first child would be a girl with her mother's auburn ringlets.

In the corner, her neighbor Edgar was trying to romance Isabella, the schoolteacher. Edgar's wife had disappeared suddenly eight months earlier and the talk about her around town ranged from her taking a mysterious Venezuelan lover to her having been kidnapped by bandits. Several townspeople tried to petition Vidente to use her sight to find the woman, but Vidente knew enough about what happened to avoid discussing it. Besides, Edgar had never asked, which either meant that he knew more than he suggested or that he was too afraid to find out. A few months ago, around the time that he and her son started carrying her chair to church every Sunday, Edgar also began flirting with every single woman at the parties. Vidente considered letting him know that he stood no chance of earning Isabella's affections, but she realized it was better to let things follow their natural course.

The band now included two guitarists, a trumpeter, and the milkman on mandolin. The music became raucous for some time with the revelers dancing, clapping, and shouting appreciatively. Then, for the past several minutes, the music had grown first romantic and then wistful and melancholy. Most of Vidente's guests listened quietly, drinking their wine, and nodding softly to the beautiful bittersweet melodies. When the latest song ended, Carlos stood, thanked the musicians, and said, "I believe it is time for our host to grace us with her singing."

Several people sat forward at that point. A couple of them clapped. Vidente smiled demurely and tried to suggest to those that encouraged her that she didn't need to subject her guests to her warbling this night. But of course, she knew that they would continue to exhort her, just as they knew that she wanted them to do so.

Vidente rose from the settee, where she had been sipping brandy. Without asking the musicians if they knew the tune, she sang the first few words of "Mi Noche Triste," a melodramatic tango number made popular a few years earlier by Carlos Gardel. The musicians caught up with her quickly and several in the crowd joined her for the chorus.

> The moment I did surrender
> my heart to you, I remember
> with love and kisses so tender,
> you promised you never lied,
> knowing that my heart was lonely
> and your promises were only,
> an excuse to get my love...
> and since then my life is broken
> and I find myself just walking
> never knowing where to go.
> In the room where we were lovers,
> on the floor pillows and covers,
> sweet "momentos" of our passion,
> memories which make me cry.
> On the table there's your picture
> that reminds me of our future
> which has now become a lie...
>
> Half awake I hear your footsteps,
> I always leave my door open
> assuming your heart is broken
> and you'll come back to my side...
> I keep buying from the corner
> every cake you used to order,
> pie and "mate" to enjoy...
> I can feel our bed complaining
> it misses you every morning
> 'cause she used to watch our joy.

I don't see over your dresser
that feminine touch of beauty,
perfume bottles tied with ribbons,
only a woman can display
and the mirror... faithful witness,
of your beauty and my sickness
is missing you night and day.

I remember in the evenings
all the poems and your singing.
The guitar now's in the closet,
no one else will sing or play...
even the light on the ceiling
seems to be losing its power,
every moment... every hour...
it's a torture... I must say...

At the end, the group burst into applause, filling Vidente with gratefulness for her guests' appreciation. She never tired of singing for a crowd even though she knew her singing voice was far below professional standards. She bowed toward her audience and then toward the musicians. Then she retrieved her brandy and seated herself on a couch next to Sonia and her boyfriend.

"That was a striking song, Tia Vidente," Sonia said.

Vidente smiled at the woman. "I'm delighted you enjoyed it." She patted the boyfriend on the knee without taking her eyes from Sonia. "Is this one treating you well?"

Sonia cast her eyes down and blushed. "Very well, Tia Vidente."

Vidente turned so she had a clearer look at the man's face and locked her gaze on him for several seconds.

"Are you trying to read my mind?" he asked nervously.

"I don't need to read your mind," she said, giving his leg a little squeeze. "I only need to tell you that our Sonia deserves very good things."

"Yes, Vidente." He glanced at Sonia and a bit of color came to his face. "I believe that as well."

Vidente stood and kissed his cheek. She'd seen what she needed to see, and now she'd heard it as well. "Good. Then you are welcome here any time."

After that, Vidente went to sit with Ximena. Of all the people in the room, she'd known Ximena the longest. They'd shared many secrets over the years. Vidente was the first to learn of the illness that nearly took Carlos' life a few years back, and Vidente had confided her concerns about her youngest son to Ximena on multiple occasions.

Vidente would not be sharing her newest secret, though. It would upset Ximena too much. Nearly as much as the thought of it rattled Vidente herself. *Fifty-nine years is not a full life*, she thought, as she had so many times in the past few days.

The musicians struck up another tango and Edgar put a hand on her shoulder and asked her to dance. Casting away her dark thoughts, Vidente twirled into his arms. Though it had been running for hours at this point, the party was still in its early stages. The dancing would continue until well into the morning. And Vidente would dance as often as she could until she left for her journey.

JOYA DE LA COSTA, 1920

W ord had gotten around about the death of Khaled's family in Bethlehem. Samih had turned out to be quite adept at spreading information, even with his limited mastery of the language and few contacts. Khaled's neighbors had come to his aid as though he'd been living there for decades. It seemed that someone was always making him dinner, distracting him with card games, or sipping rum with him late into the night. They'd even arranged a memorial service for Nahla, Tarek, May, and Mona. It amazed Khaled that people could cry over the passing of those they never knew and he appreciated it deeply.

It embarrassed Khaled that some of the women at the memorial service shed more tears than he did. What had happened to Nahla and the children was a terrible thing; no one should ever have to die that way. As Khaled tried to summon their memories, though, he found that his vision of them wasn't nearly as crisp he'd expected it to be. He had to accept that he had shared very little with Nahla over the years. She was always with the women and he was always with the men. Even when they were alone in the bedroom, they didn't share much. He had little to do with May and Mona; he couldn't teach them any of the female things they needed to know. Tarek should have been a different story, but they had never been right together as Khaled had seen with so many other fathers and sons.

Maybe this was all a matter of fate. Maybe Khaled was never supposed to share with his family because it was predestined that they would meet a sudden end. It was impossible for him to know. The only thing he understood was that the news of their death had left him feeling empty in a way that had very little to do with loss.

In contrast, his business had never been fuller. Khaled sometimes wondered if shopkeepers bought his goods out of some sense of pity. That seemed to be the kind of thing that the people of Joya de la Costa would do. However, when he began to receive reorders from customers, he allowed himself to believe that it had nothing to do with the tragic story with which he was associated. Instead, he believed that he'd tapped into some vein of fascination with the crafts he sold. Just yesterday, he'd sent his brother a telegram requesting he put a new quantity of goods on the next ship. Khaled thought about making some mention of Nahla and the children in his message, but he thought better of it. It was not cheap to send a telegram from Legado to Palestine, and they charged by the word.

Having made two successful sales in the morning, Khaled left his sample case with a shopkeeper and walked across the street to an outdoor café for lunch. As always, the midday temperature was balmy, in the low 30s, and Khaled wiped away a thin sheen of perspiration as he sat down. The winters were so much warmer here than they were in Bethlehem. Foolishly, Khaled had packed a coat in his luggage; he'd never even unfolded it. He regretted this because he could have used that space for more items to sell. He only hoped that his brother's shipment arrived before he ran out.

He had just received a glass of water from the waiter when an extraordinary looking woman entered the café. She appeared to be in her early twenties and she was very possibly the most beautiful image he'd ever had the chance to behold. She was tall – likely as tall as he was – her posture was straight without being rigid, and the curve of her ankle suggested lean, supple legs. The vision of her caused Khaled's breath to catch in his throat, something he never remembered happening before.

Hoping she didn't spy him staring, Khaled followed those legs up to the roundness of her hips and bosom, set off by the narrowness of her waist. Her hair flowed inky and straight down to the small of her back and her eyes glimmered like cinnamon crystal. Khaled felt his mouth go dry simply looking at her, and he reached for his water glass without altering his gaze, hoping that he didn't spill down the front of his shirt and make himself appear to be a fool.

A short while later, she sat at a table a few feet away from him. Two older women whose voices seemed intent on carrying all the way to the Gulf of Mexico now blocked his view of her with the fluttering fans they swished rapidly in front of them while they spoke. Khaled tried to angle his chair to get a clearer view of the captivating woman, but he couldn't do so without making his intentions too obvious.

He wondered who she was meeting for lunch. In all likelihood, it was one of the trim, darkly handsome men who seemed to exist everywhere in Joya de la Costa. Maybe she was a young wife meeting her enamored husband for some moments of handholding and endearments. Perhaps a somewhat older man would soon be joining her for a quick meal before a midday tryst.

When Khaled's food arrived, he took the opportunity to stretch his neck to get another look at the woman. No man was with her. No woman, either. Nothing but a sandwich and a cup of coffee. How did a woman who looked like that ever eat alone?

He stood without even realizing he was doing it, as though someone else were operating his body. He passed the yammering women, and as he did, they glanced up at him, their fans stopping in unison. Wanting nothing of their attention, Khaled did something on impulse that he'd never remembered doing to another person before – he winked. One woman's eyes shot open, and they both turned back to each other, their fans flapping again.

Before he truly grasped what he was doing, Khaled stood in front of the beautiful woman's table. "I notice you are dining by yourself," he said, suddenly conscious of the heavy accent he'd nearly forgotten in his daily exchanges. "I am eating alone as well." He pointed to his table. "Would you care to join me?"

The way her dusky eyes narrowed at first suggested that she was going to reject him. How foolish was he going to feel walking back to his meal? But then her expression softened.

"Do you often invite unattended women to eat with you?" she said with a hint of lightness in her voice.

"To be truthful, I have never done anything like this before," he said, hoping his Arabic inflection hid the nervousness he suddenly felt.

She arched her eyebrows. "Then why do it now?"

Khaled was feeling unsteady. His conversations with women rarely went this way. He suddenly realized how unaccustomed he was to speaking in a conversational way with women. "Because one shouldn't have a meal without company," he said.

She reached for her coffee. "I believe you are right. Why don't you bring your lunch over here?"

She was toying with him – yet another thing he had little reference for – and he surprisingly found that he liked it. Rather than continuing to attempt to cajole her to his spot, he retrieved his plate and his cutlery. On his way back, he caught the eye of one of the loud women. She wasn't speaking now and she regarded him amusedly. He couldn't tell if she thought he was impressive or an ass.

"My name is Lina," the beautiful woman said as he settled in his seat and placed his napkin on his lap.

"Khaled," he said, reaching a hand out to her.

"You are not local, I assume."

"My accent announces me," he said wryly.

"It's a lovely accent."

She smiled, which made her face more radiant, and he smiled back at her. "Joya de la Costa is not my original home. But it is my home now."

She nodded, as though he had said something terribly important. "And where was home before this."

"I came from Palestine."

Her eyes widened. "Palestine. It sounds very exotic. *Was* it very exotic?"

Khaled shrugged. "I was born there. It never seemed exotic to me. *Here*, now," he swept the room with his arms, "*this* seems exotic. Legado holds many mysteries for me."

"Really? Like what?"

Her posture encouraged him. She was leaning toward him and he found himself pulled in her direction, feeling a little dizzy over the entire experience. "Like what causes a woman like you to come to this café by herself."

She chuckled. "I wasn't supposed to be by myself. I was supposed to be meeting my aunt here, but she sent word that she couldn't make it. Since I was already here, I decided to sit down to eat. The coffee is very good at this café." She paused to bring her cup to her lips, but she did not drink. The gesture focused attention on her magnificent eyes. "And you never know when you are going to meet someone from Palestine."

Khaled watched as she drank her coffee and then took a delicate bite from her sandwich. Her every movement was graceful, as though a fine artist had rendered each one of them. Long, slender fingers cradling the bread. Jaw muscles giving added definition to her sculpted face. Khaled's own food had become an afterthought. He was feasting on Lina instead. Was this what all those Latin songs were about?

"Tell me about Palestine," she said, dabbing the corner of her mouth with a napkin.

He looked down at his hands. "There isn't that much to tell. My country has been many things over the centuries and we are something else now."

"Is it pretty?"

"The mountains are nice. I lived in Bethlehem, which is quite an historic place, as you might know. It was pleasant enough. I got to the water a few times. The beaches here put it to shame."

Lina seemed to consider this for some time. "What did you do there?"

Khaled shrugged. "Many things. A number of enterprises with my brothers. Some were more successful than others were. I decided to come here because I thought I could do better."

"And have you?"

Khaled let his eyes linger on Lina for several seconds before saying, "Yes, I think I have." Feeling the dryness come back to his mouth, he reached for his water and drank again. "Let's talk about you. I'm sure you are much more interesting than I am."

She laughed at that suggestion. "Oh, I don't know how interesting I am."

Khaled reached for a wedge of tomato and chewed it quickly. "Something tells me that you are very interesting. Go ahead, please. Tell me three interesting things about yourself right now."

Lina cocked her head sideways, as though he'd presented her with a great challenge and that this was going to require considerable thought. Then her eyes brightened and she said, "I am very good at making flowers grow."

"Ah, well that's very interesting indeed. Please continue."

"I was a very good student in school, especially with languages. I learned to speak Latin, Portuguese, and a little bit of English. Maybe you can teach me your language so I can add it to my collection."

The idea of teaching this woman anything seemed very appealing to him. "Well, that's two interesting things." He tipped his water glass to her. "You still owe me a third."

Lina looked away from him toward some spot outside of the café. Khaled thought about following her gaze, but preferred watching her instead. While she was turned, he could stare at her shamelessly.

Perhaps half a minute passed before she focused on him again. She smiled shyly, almost girlishly. "I think I might be a witch."

Khaled hoped he masked the complete surprise he felt at that declaration. Khaled not only didn't believe in witches, but he'd always felt a level of contempt for anyone who played with such fanciful notions. "A witch?"

She ran a finger around the rim of her coffee cup. "Does that make me sound crazy?"

Khaled shook his head briskly, hoping to shake away his prejudices at the same time. "Crazy? No. It makes you sound...intriguing."

She smiled broadly, again seeming like a teenager. "Really? I haven't told many people about this. I can *see* things."

"Like ghosts?"

"No, not ghosts. 'See' is probably the wrong word. I get impressions of things. Strong sensations about the future and about situations. I can't always tell what they mean, but I'm starting to become better at that as well. For instance, when I learned that my aunt wouldn't be joining me here, I thought about going home. But then I got one of my sensations telling me that I was supposed to stay." She looked down at the table for a moment and then back up at him with an invitation he'd never read in a woman's eyes before. "I *was* supposed to stay, wasn't I?"

Khaled didn't believe in witches or "sensations." And he knew virtually nothing about the relationships between men and women. But what he was feeling right now went beyond any belief or feeling.

Leaning as close to Lina as the table would allow, he said softly, "Yes, you were definitely supposed to stay."

CAMBRIDGE, MASSACHUSETTS, 1986

Melanie was having trouble keeping up with Dro as they walked up Massachusetts Avenue, which was saying something.

"Do you get extra credit if you make it there in less than seven minutes? You know, if you break into a sprint, I'm going for coffee instead."

Dro slowed his pace. Melanie was right, of course. The building would still be there five minutes from now.

"That's better," she said as she sidled next to him. "Now take a few deep breaths and dial back the intensity a little. I don't know this Susan Roemer from Adam, but I'm pretty sure serial killer eyes isn't one of the things she's looking for from applicants."

Dro veered to his right to bump Melanie lightly on the shoulder. She responded by throwing a hip at him so hard that he nearly ran into an oncoming bicyclist.

"Sorry, don't know my own strength," she said with an outsized grin. Melanie of course knew her "own strength" very, very well. As a power forward for Boston College's women's basketball team, she used it mercilessly on her competition. Dro had first gotten to know her as a lonely Colorado girl who missed her boyfriend terribly and liked to talk about eighteenth century philosophers. When she shredded through the Providence front line in the first game he saw her play, though, he became fascinated with Melanie's contradictions. Though they hung out together three or four times a week, he was still trying to figure her out.

"Do you bang Neal around like this at home?"

"Why would I do that? I *like* Neal."

That got a laugh out of Dro. He welcomed the laughter. He'd been so anxious about this meeting that he felt as though he hadn't smiled in a week.

They walked onto the MIT campus and along the path that Dro had traveled several times in the past year. When they got to the stairs of the main building, though, Melanie stopped.

"I'm gonna work on my tan while you're in there sweating your ass off," she said.

"You can come in if you want."

"Nah, it'll just screw things up for you. She'll look at you, then she'll look at me and be so impressed by my radiance that she'll forget all about you."

"Yes, good point."

Melanie took his face in both of her hands, surprising him with the gesture, if not with her power. "Be brilliant in there. I'm counting on you."

Dro shook his head, which was difficult since Melanie was still holding it.

"And remember," she said, "we're going for ice cream after this. No matter what happens. Good news: ice cream. Bad news: ice cream. That's all I have to say."

She kissed his forehead and started to walk away.

"Hey, Mel, thanks for coming with me. It's good to know you'll be here no matter how this turns out."

She turned around, her eyes soft. For a second, they just looked at each other and Dro could swear it made him feel stronger. Then Melanie arched an eyebrow and said, "Don't you have to be somewhere?"

Dro hadn't been to admissions since his first trip. Still, he had no trouble finding Susan Roemer's office without any help. As before, the campus was relatively quiet, but there was a languid nature to the proceedings this time, a sense of winding down in the middle of May rather than winding up at the beginning of August.

One of the assistants in the cubicles attempted to stop him, but Dro let her know that he had an appointment with the associate admissions director. The assistant waved him on without any resistance.

As he got to the door, Susan stood up from her desk and came to greet him, extending her hand. "Very good to see you again, Dro."

"Thank you," Dro said, meeting her handshake, "it's nice to be back here. As I'm sure you can imagine, it has been an eventful year."

Susan patted his hand with her free one. "Yes, I would imagine that it has been." She walked back behind her desk gesturing him to an open chair. "Your English seems stronger."

Dro nodded. "I'm glad you think so. I've been taking night classes to improve my vocabulary and syntax."

Susan reached for a file folder and opened it. "Really? In addition to all of the classes we discussed?"

"I don't need much sleep."

"No, I suppose people your age rarely do. It's good to see that you're putting your waking hours to productive use, though. One doesn't necessarily follow the other." She looked down at her desk, and then looked up at him brightly. "So tell me about your experience at Boston College."

Dro leaned forward and steepled his fingers. "Well, I took two semesters each of Physics, Chemistry, and Calculus, as you suggested, along with some other math classes and a couple of humanities classes. One of them was an American literature class, which I thought would help me get a better sense of my bearings."

"And how did you do?"

"A+ in both semesters of Calculus and my second semester of Physics. A's in all the other classes."

Susan closed the folder and tapped a pencil on it twice. "I don't suppose you could have done any better than that."

"I could have, actually. I think I really should have gotten an A-plus in Chemistry this semester, but the professor and I had a disagreement on one of my labs."

Susan laughed softly. "Yes, I heard."

The comment surprised Dro. "You heard?"

Susan tapped the folder again. "I did. To tell you the truth, I've heard from a few of your professors. I found our conversation last August fascinating. I followed up with the person who interviewed you at BC and I knew they'd accepted you. I hope this doesn't seem like prying to you, but I've been keeping track of your progress."

Dro didn't feel as though the woman had been prying at all. He'd hoped to have made enough of an impression on her that she would remember him. Obviously, he'd succeeded. "Does that mean you knew about my grades when we made this appointment?"

"Several of them, but not all. I didn't know about the American literature class, for instance. By the way, you could probably push for that A-plus in Chemistry if it is really important to you. The professor isn't as rigid as he might have appeared. My sense was that he was coming around to your point of view."

Dro thought back to the lengthy debate he'd had with his Chemistry professor early in the semester. He never believed that the professor's arguments made sense; they seemed built on some assumption of authority rather than hard scientific reasoning. "Maybe I'll do that. So I did what you told me to do. Does that mean I can come to MIT next year?"

Susan opened the folder again. "Frankly, you did more than I told you to do – including the English classes. I can admit you as a provisional student in September."

Dro's eyes narrowed. "Why provisional?"

"It's a matter of logistics. It doesn't have any real bearing on your status as a student except in ways that won't matter to you as long as you keep your grades up." She pointed toward the folder with her pencil. "Realistically, if you keep *these* grades up, we'll be talking about scholarships in the future, which I know would be useful to you."

Dro wondered if Susan had done some investigative work about his finances as well as his academic achievements. A scholarship would be a huge help indeed. Dro had saved money from jobs he worked during high school, he'd gotten financial aid from Boston College, and his parents had contributed what they could. His family made it clear, though, that there wouldn't be any additional assistance with tuition. "All I can give you, my son, is my blessing," his mother had said when Dro mentioned that his cash reserves were dwindling quickly.

That was a worry for another day, though. He sat back in his chair, allowing himself to absorb what Susan had told him. He was finally going to live the dream he'd been dreaming since he was a young teen. "Just tell me where you want my signature."

"It's a little more involved than that. We're going to have to fill out quite a bit of paperwork and we'll need to get you registered for classes – we're already late there." She pulled some papers from the file open on her desk. "We'll start with these."

Dro listened attentively as Susan guided him through the paperwork. She told him he'd be receiving more materials in the mail within a few days. More than an hour later, he rose from his chair and shook Susan's hand. "Thank you for all of your help."

Susan smiled. "This doesn't happen, you know, Dro. People don't just knock on my office door and get accepted to this university. You've accomplished some impressive things already. Keep that up, okay?"

"I promise. You won't ever have to worry about that."

Dro thanked her again and exited the office. When he got outside, Melanie was sunning herself on the lawn, just as she suggested she would. Her eyes were closed and her face was tilted toward the sky when he reached her.

"I don't let just anyone get a tan on my campus, you know. You should consider yourself lucky."

Melanie's eyes flew open and she stood quickly. "*Your* campus?"

"It is now."

She flung her arms around him with so much force that he nearly toppled backward. Dro hugged her tight, thrilled that he could share this moment with her. "You were saying something about ice cream, weren't you?"

"You just interrupted me from an ice cream dream, if you want to know the truth."

They headed back onto Massachusetts Avenue and started walking toward one of Cambridge's numerous homemade ice cream shops. It seemed as though ice cream was a religion in this town, and Melanie was one of its most fervent followers. As they walked, Dro recounted his meeting with Susan, and Melanie peppered him with questions.

When they got to the storefront, Melanie squealed like a little child at the prospect of her afternoon treat. For the first time, Dro realized that he wouldn't have as many opportunities to spend time with her now that they would be going to different schools, and this caused his chest to tighten a bit.

"Hey, you're not going to quit hanging around with me now that I'm an MIT geek, are you?" he said as he opened the door for them.

"Nah, I'll still hang out with you. You'll bore the hell out of me, but I'll do it for the good of humanity."

That night, Dro attended a lecture by Viviana Emisario at the Kennedy School of Government at Harvard. Emisario was Legado's ambassador to the U.S. and something of an international celebrity. Some of this was because she achieved the post a few years ago while she was still in her late thirties – unheard of for most diplomats and especially unusual for a woman. Some of this was because she was a passionate and eloquent writer and speaker; her appearance at Harvard coincided with the release of her second international bestseller, *From Terror to Triumph: Answering the Cries of all of the World's People.* And a considerable portion of it was because she looked like and carried herself like a movie star. Viviana Emisario was as mediagenic as any figure to rise from Legado in decades. Outside of the country, she was better known than the president of Legado was. Inside the country, she was more beloved than the president had ever been.

Dro had seen Emisario on television numerous times. Until now, though, he'd never seen her in person. What struck him as soon as he saw her stand behind the podium was how much presence she had. Though she couldn't have been much more than 5'5" and he guessed her weight at somewhere around one hundred and twenty pounds, she filled the stage. While she spoke, Dro didn't hear a whisper or a cough from any of the hundreds of people gathered for the lecture.

The other thing that struck him instantly was that the camera wasn't nearly as kind to her as he'd always assumed. In person, Emisario's good looks were electrifying. Hers was the kind of beauty that overloaded the senses. Dro found his attentions flitting from her cheekbones to her lips to her small yet incredibly expressive fingers. Between her physical appearance and the stirring nature of her words, Dro felt dizzy.

"We can never condone the acts of brutality that take place across Africa, Asia, and South America, including my home country," she said from the podium in perfect, unaccented English. "At the same time, we need to strive to understand the root causes of this brutality. There are few genuinely evil people in the world. There is a far larger number of desperate people. These people, through their acts, as reprehensible as the acts themselves might be, are crying out to us. If we fail to answer these cries, we destine ourselves to decades and even centuries of continued and escalating violence."

The attendees in the hall rose as one at the end of the lecture. Dro found the ambassador's words motivational and he felt a surprising level of national pride over the fact that such potent and avidly received words came from a fellow citizen of Legado. Afterward, Emisario signed copies of her new book in the lobby outside of the lecture hall. Several dozen people lined up for an autograph, many offering effusive thanks and commentary. Dro waited until the line formed before joining it. He wanted to be the last person to speak with the star diplomat.

It was nearly an hour later when he finally brought his copy of Emisario's book to the table.

"You inspired me tonight," he said as he handed her the book.

She regarded him with shimmering blue eyes. "Thank you."

"I am also from Legado," he said in Spanish.

This brought a smile. She truly was considerably more beautiful than the television made her appear. "Really?" she said in her native tongue. "From where?"

"Anhelo."

"Ah. It's beautiful country there. Are you here to go to college?"

"Yes, MIT. I'm starting Economics. I learned today that I'm the only student from Legado in my class." Dro didn't mention that he'd also learned that he would be attending MIT today. The ambassador didn't need to be bothered with these trivialities.

Emisario nodded and finished signing Dro's book. She closed the cover, but she didn't give it back to him. "Economics. I hope you're graduating soon.

We could use your help solving the problems of Legado's economy."

"The problems of Legado's economy have at least as much to do with guerilla warfare as they do with economics, no?"

Emisario straightened in her chair a bit. "Sadly, that is true. But that doesn't mean that we can't find creative solutions from a variety of sectors. We just need to tap our most valuable resources."

"Yes, I agree. I look forward to being part of the solution."

The ambassador picked up the copy of the book she signed for Dro, but still did not hand it to him. Instead, she looked at Dro appraisingly, with a hint of fascination in her eyes. "I'm going back to my hotel from here. I'm staying at the Ritz-Carlton in Boston. Would you care to join me for a drink? I believe my security detail can find room for you in my limo."

For the second time that night, Dro felt an electric charge from the words of this stunning and brilliant woman. "I would like that very much."

Forty-five minutes later, they were sitting at the opulent parlor of Emisario's suite drinking XO brandy. It was Dro's first taste of brandy and he reveled in the mellow heat that bathed his throat. The alcohol he purchased for himself couldn't offer such sensual pleasure. Now that he knew the difference, he would have to change that as soon as humanly possible.

There was luxury everywhere he turned in the room. The sofa on which he sat was crushed gold velvet. Original sculptures stood in two corners.

He had no idea what the fabric was that made the drapes or how to describe the delicate pattern that ran through it, but he could tell by their weight and their fold that they had to be extremely expensive. Being an ambassador clearly had its advantages.

Of course, the greatest luxury from Dro's perspective was the presence of the ambassador herself. The woman exuded such energy that he could feel the air shift when she crossed her legs or reached for the telephone. Dro loved being around beautiful women, but they rarely held him in thrall. In this case, though, Dro not only felt himself captivated, but he found himself willingly so. Viviana Emisario was an experience he would gladly entertain repeatedly.

For the first half hour of the evening, they spoke about Legado and about the political conditions that threatened the peace of their land. The ambassador admitted that fear over the ongoing terrorist strikes was having a dampening effect on their country's financial health. When Dro countered this by saying that without a full-fledged effort to achieve economic growth there would always be guerrillas, the ambassador actually stopped the conversation to make a note.

Then the conversation shifted toward the personal, with Viviana (somewhere during this time, she'd asked him to call her by her first name) asking Dro about his decision to come to America for college and about his course of study.

"So your intention is to become a professor?" she asked, putting her snifter down and then tucking one beautifully curved leg under the other.

Dro took another sip of his drink. "I don't think so. I had my sights on something...bigger. When I am older, though, I do think I would like to teach, perhaps even at MIT."

"But what does one do with a Ph.D. in Economics other than teach?"

Dro found it difficult to believe that this worldly woman didn't know the answer to that question. "I think I would like to be involved in public policy. I also think I would like to do research and bring something new to the world."

Viviana gestured softly with her right hand. "Dro, do you really believe that your greatest contributions will come through academic pursuits?"

The question caught him up short. He didn't answer.

"I spent many years in academia," she continued. "I have my Ph.D. in Political Science. Do you know how much that helped me to get where I am now?"

"I would think it would have helped quite a bit."

Viviana closed her eyes and shook her head slowly. "If anything, I would say it was a detriment. I learned a great deal in college. But I didn't really understand how to do something real with my life until I got out into the world."

She leaned forward suddenly, resting her hands on her legs. Dro could swear he felt a rush of wind from the move.

"Don't get a Ph.D. now, Dro. The world already has too many Ph.D.s. If you think you won't be able to go to God peacefully unless you have one, get it in your old age. Get your B.S. in Economics and then get yourself an MBA. If you really want to make an impact on the world, master Wall Street; become a financial leader."

Dro considered the finery of the room. He had no taste for politics, but he was quickly beginning to realize how much he enjoyed the embrace of extravagance. "You might be right about that," he said gently.

Viviana sat back again. "You will never regret this advice, Dro. I realize we've only been speaking for a short while, but I think I can see who you are – and I like what I see very much." She paused and offered Dro a smile that set his nerves pulsing. "You're someone who is going to accomplish huge things. The only way you will do less than that is if you set your sights too low."

Dro had never once considered himself a person who set his sights low. Susan Roemer probably thought of him as the most ambitious student she'd ever met. But Viviana made him wonder if he'd only begun to envision the type of person he should become.

Dro chuckled. "This is proving very illuminating."

"I'm glad you think so," she said with another devastating smile. "I'm very happy that I met you, Dro. You've made this trip to Boston much more interesting than I expected it to be – no offense to the lovely people at Harvard."

She looked down at the brandy snifter she'd left on the coffee table and seemed to consider it for several seconds before lifting her eyes to him again. "I'm afraid I'm going to have to bring our evening to a close. I have a six a.m. flight back tomorrow."

Viviana stood and Dro followed her to the door. He wasn't ready for the night to end; in fact, he felt as though they'd only completed the prelude. When they got to the door, Dro reached out a hand. Viviana took it and then leaned toward him to kiss him on both cheeks.

"I want you to visit me in Washington," she said, still holding his hand. "I believe we are supposed to get to know one another."

"I would be happy to do that."

She held his hand a few seconds more and then let it go. "Thank you for visiting with me."

A suite of desires coursed through Dro. He wanted to say something memorable, something that would bridge this moment to their next moment, if there was to be another moment. But nothing came to him. At last, he simply said, "It was a great pleasure."

As he walked the corridor to the elevator, Dro felt enchanted. This had been quite a day. Rather than heading back to his apartment, he decided to stop at the hotel bar for another brandy. Such an expense hardly fit his budget.

Tonight, though, he wasn't going to let that be a factor.

3.
NEW YORK, 2010

S unday brunch was a longstanding tradition in Manhattan. By midmorning, often bleary-eyed and moderately hungover, New Yorkers would queue up outside of many of the city's most celebrated white tablecloth restaurants in anticipation of twenty-seven-dollar omelets and fourteen-dollar Bellinis.

Alex Soberano had a brunch tradition of his own, though it took place on Saturday and involved neither white tablecloths nor effervescent drinks. It did on occasion involve an omelet chef, though Alex found this distracting and preferred calling Zabar's for bagels and lox. His Saturday brunch was a mandatory eight-to-eleven meeting of his executive staff at the offices. Alex knew that the brunch interfered with sleep-in days and kids' soccer games, but if you were invited, you knew you were on the fast track in the organization, and some of his team's most creative ideas came when they could talk in casual clothes without the phone ringing. As a concession to the weekend, he made every effort to prevent the meetings from going a minute past eleven.

Alex had an especially compelling reason to make sure the meeting ended in a timely fashion this week: he had a playdate with his niece. When Alex's younger sister, Daniela, had Christina three years ago, he found the idea of the first member of the next generation cheering, but nothing to get overly excited about. He'd never had any real interest in having children of his own. They seemed like an overwhelmingly large responsibility and Alex already had more responsibilities than he could count. When he got serious with Opal and she told him that she was completely opposed to the idea of having kids, this just seemed to confirm that they were right for each other.

At first, Chrissy seemed like nothing more than a curiosity to him – a crying, crapping, spitting-up curiosity. She was certainly cute, especially when she was chuckling, which seemed to be often, but she seemed very delicate and best admired from a distance. Then, when Chrissy was about six months old, Alex came to Daniela's apartment to visit. When she saw him, the baby practically leapt from her mother's arms to jump into his. This caught Alex completely by surprise, as he'd never even held the child before. When he reached for her, though, she laughed and buried her head in his chest. Alex felt something utterly unidentifiable at that moment. Something he definitely wanted to keep feeling. He vowed right then to have Chrissy think of him as the best uncle ever. He even fantasized about her teenage years when she thought her parents were intolerable but introduced Alex to all of her friends because he was so cool.

Every now and then, Alex would urge Daniela to have some "alone time" with her husband, volunteering to take care of Chrissy for them. Daniela saw through this rather quickly, but she seemed happy to play along. Today, Alex was taking Chrissy to Serendipity for her first taste of frozen hot chocolate. He was picking her up at 12:00, so the brunch absolutely had to end on time.

Alex's own Saturday at the office started this week at 7:15. Last night, he had a dream about British banking baron, Oliver Dalgliesh. When Alex was still in the mergers-and-acquisitions business, he'd worked on a number of projects with Oliver. They'd made a good deal of money for each other, but it had probably been seven years since they'd spoken and at least three years since Alex had even thought about Dalgliesh.

Oliver's cell number wasn't on Alex's current Blackberry, the result of a purge of his contact list the year before, so he needed to log on to his office computer to get it. It was just after noon in London, so there was the distinct chance that Oliver wouldn't be available, but Alex remembered that the banker tended to spend the early part of Saturdays in his library catching up on the week's reading before going for the late afternoon country drives he found so restorative.

Oliver picked up his phone on the second ring. "Dalgliesh."

"Oliver, it's Alex Soberano."

"Alex," Oliver said brightly. "My goodness, this is like getting a call from a distant planet."

"Well, I hardly disappeared off the face of the Earth."

Oliver chuckled. "No, you certainly haven't. I read that piece *Inc.* did on your company a few months ago. You're a walking conglomerate these days. So what's the occasion of this out-of-the-blue Saturday afternoon call?"

"Nothing special, really. I just realized that we hadn't spoken in a long while and I decided to rectify the situation."

Alex heard Oliver shuffle around a bit on the other end before he spoke again. "It's an interesting thing that you should choose to phone today, actually. I had dinner with Lloyd Bramington last night. I assume you know about the little internet project he launched a couple of years ago."

"Of course. He certainly gets enough publicity for himself from it."

"He's getting more than that these days. It has become his top profit center. So much so that he's decided to sell his core business."

Alex threw his feet up on his desk. This was becoming interesting. "He wants to sell Bramington Communications?"

Oliver shuffled some papers around. "It's a very solid company with a good slice of market share. I think Lloyd is out of his mind, personally, but he never had the stomach for explosive growth, and so I might have predicted a move of this sort. He's afraid he won't be able to keep everything afloat."

"Are you sure that's really the issue and not that his core business is somehow hemorrhaging money?"

More papers moved on Oliver's end. "I have the financials right here. The numbers don't suggest that at all, though obviously any buyer would need to explore every nook and cranny. Lloyd brought this up for the first time last night. He wants me to help him put the deal together. Your name didn't immediately leap to mind, but perhaps we're experiencing a little serendipity here. You might want to take a serious look at this acquisition."

Assuming the numbers were as solid as Oliver suggested, Bramington would give Alex's corporation a quick and considerable leap in size. Serendipity indeed. Perhaps that was the theme for the day. Here was yet another reminder of why Alex always followed up on the messages his gut sent him, even if those messages sometimes seemed to come from nowhere.

"You might be right about this, Oliver. I'm going to be away for the next two weeks, but I could fly to London soon after that."

"No rush; something like this isn't going to come together overnight. I'll set up a meeting between you and Lloyd. This could be an interesting match. It'll be good to see you again, Alex."

"I look forward to it."

They said goodbye moments later. Alex put his phone down and reclined in his chair with his feet still up on his desk. He loved it when things like this happened.

Within a minute, though, he was back on the phone. An acquisition the size of Bramington was going to require significant funding. Alex could probably pull it together with his current creditors, but it would make any other acquisitions impossible for a while – something he didn't want to do now that he'd finally gotten his staff moving forward bullishly. An equity partner would be ideal, and none would be more ideal than Prince Aldo Springer, a man Alex had met when he worked in London and with whom he'd partnered on several acquisitions over the years.

Aldo had been second in line of succession to a small Northern European municipality when his government was overthrown by a conservative organization. Aldo desperately wanted back into power and Alex and he had had numerous conversations about accomplishing this. Alex had shown him that a dominant position in a country's economy afforded enormous influence over that economy. Alex showed Aldo a series of calculations that proved that, if you could control fifteen percent of a nation's GDP, you essentially controlled that nation. For the past several years, Alex had been helping the prince accumulate holdings. Before he'd picked up the phone, Alex had gone online to confirm what he already knew – many of Bramington's brands were registered in Aldo's municipality because of their very attractive tax laws. Therefore, a deal the size of Bramington would put the prince over the top.

When the prince answered the phone, Alex wasted no time. "Aldo, I can get you over the fifteen percent."

A few minutes later, Gene Eagleton, Alex's COO knocked on his office door. "Most of us have gathered if you want to get started."

Thinking of Chrissy, Alex pulled his feet off the desk quickly. "Yeah, let's go. I don't want this thing to run all day today," he said as he started toward the small conference room with Gene.

"You're really going to be completely incommunicado for two weeks?" Gene said as they walked.

Alex gestured casually. "In an ideal world, yes."

"That's a lot of time."

Alex tipped his head toward his second-in-command. "Are you saying I don't deserve a couple of weeks off?"

"Hell, no. I'm the one who's always telling you to get away more often. I think this is going to be great for you. The suddenness of the news kicked a few of our colleagues into hysterical mode, though."

"They're adults; they'll deal with it."

"Well, many of them are adults, anyway."

Alex opened the door to the conference room and had not even completely entered when three of the half-dozen people in the room descended upon him. Words like "budgets," "reengineering," and "recruiting" jumbled together to form a jagged mosaic of process. Alex ignored all of it as he prepared himself half of a sesame bagel with lox and capers. Then he sat calmly at the head of the conference table and indicated that the others should take their seats.

"You were saying...Meg," Alex said, turning toward his CFO and making it clear that the others would need to wait.

Meg leaned forward. "The next round of forecasting is due on Friday."

"I realize that."

"And you're not going to be here on Friday."

"I realize that as well."

This response seemed to stop the woman cold. In her late thirties and with a degree from Yale and an MBA from Northwestern, Meg normally radiated confidence. Here, though, she seemed bewildered.

"Are we on track?" Alex asked, trying to get her back into gear.

"Well, the Sandbank thing threw us off a little, but the year is looking good."

Alex tipped his bagel in her direction. "Do you think your new forecast is going to suggest that we're on the verge of bankruptcy?"

Meg chuckled nervously. "No, of course not. I mean, the economy is rough, but – no, of course not."

"Then there probably isn't going to be anything in the new numbers that you and Gene can't handle for a week."

Meg dipped her eyes. "Okay."

Alex turned toward his Director of Business Development. "Sarmistha, you wanted to say something?"

"There's the Lansing thing."

"What about it?"

Sarmistha rubbed the side of her face, as though she were dealing with something that required intense concentration. "You know; the executive training company we've been looking at?"

Alex's eyes narrowed. Like Meg, Sarmistha was exceedingly bright and competent. Yet right now, she seemed like an entry-level employee meeting the big boss for the first time. "Yes, I know. We've been discussing Lansing for six months now."

"We talked about having them in."

"Actually, if I recall, the last thing we talked about was not *talking about* it anymore and actually getting them in."

Sarmistha held up her Blackberry. "I did that. They're coming in the Monday after next; at least they were until Kathy told me that you were going to be gone."

"You like these guys, right?"

Sarmistha finally put down her phone and looked Alex squarely in the eye. "Yeah; I think we could do a lot with them."

Alex shrugged. "Then bring them in and blow them away."

Sarmistha cast her eyes upward.

"What?" Alex asked.

She looked at him again. "Blowing them away isn't as easy when you aren't around."

Alex got up to get a glass of orange juice, suddenly feeling the need to move. "You're kidding, right?"

Sarmistha seemed knocked dumb by the question. When it became clear that she wasn't planning to respond, Alex's gaze slid from her to Mark, his executive assistant.

"She's not wrong, you know," Mark said.

Alex sat down again, beginning to feel the tiredness he felt on Thursday. Less than a half-hour ago, he was brimming with excitement over the prospect of an acquisition the size of Bramington Communications, not to mention the prospect of hot chocolate with the most adorable child on the planet. Now, he was having trouble controlling his anger. "She *should* be wrong."

"Maybe she should be," Mark said, "but she isn't. You're the lead singer, the star quarterback, the captain of the ship."

Alex threw up his arms. "We aren't a ship. We're a *fleet* of ships. Entire fleets don't have captains; they have admirals – and the admirals have captains."

Alex expected a response from Mark, but he didn't get one. Nor did anyone else in the room speak. Even Gene had nothing to say.

"Look," Alex said running his eyes over everyone in the room. "We're growing quickly. Our stated agenda is to grow dramatically this year in spite of an awful economy and we have a strong plan in place to do exactly that. Just this morning, I discussed an opportunity with someone that would make this company considerably larger. If we're going to have a big organization – and we *are* going to have a big organization – the entire staff can't be waiting for direction from me every step of the way."

Again, no one spoke. Did they not comprehend what he was saying? Or did they not believe that he meant what he said. He hadn't been worried about stepping away from the corporation for a couple of weeks, but now he was beginning to wonder if he should be.

He stood up and gripped the edge of the table. "I'm not supposed to be delivering lectures during Saturday brunches." He looked down at himself. "I'm not dressed for it." He looked up and smiled. "I'm going to get myself another half of a bagel. Then we're going to start over. I'll be gone for two weeks and each of you is capable of handling anything that emerges. When I sit down again, we're going to pretend that you believe what I just said and we're going to approach the rest of this day as though it were any other Saturday."

Ultimately, the meeting ended only fifteen minutes late. Uptown traffic wasn't terrible, and Alex's driver handled the flow as masterfully as he always did. He got to Daniela's three minutes early to find Chrissy waiting for him.

When she leapt into his arms, he knew it was going to be a very good afternoon. The brilliance in her eyes when she sipped her chocolate drink a half-hour later confirmed it.

"Can I get another one?" she said with the straw still in her mouth.

Alex leaned toward his niece with a grin. "You still have most of the first one to drink. But yes. You know, this place is famous for its ice cream sundaes."

Chrissy's mouth formed into an elongated "O." For a three-year-old, she was capable of eating absurd amounts of ice cream. He took a sip from his coffee. "I just wanted to tell you before we ordered lunch. The sundaes are very big."

Chrissy's eyes rolled toward the ceiling, then she rested her head in her two tiny hands for several seconds before she said what Alex knew she was going to say. "Do I have to get lunch?"

"Well, you know that Uncle Alex has a lot of very important meetings at restaurants all the time, right?"

Chrissy shook her head – which was still in her hands – slowly.

"And at these very important meetings, it is very common for me to order nothing but ice cream."

Chrissy's eyes grew wider and she took a long sip on her frozen hot chocolate. Sundaes for lunch it was. Daniela would try to lecture him about this when she found out, but both of them would know that the lecture was pointless. If Alex could do something to delight little Chrissy, he was going to do so. Everybody – including Chrissy – knew this.

ANHELO, 1928

Vidente poured coffee into two of the aqua and burnt sienna ceramic cups Erika had given her after she'd done a series of readings for the seamstress last summer. Vidente's son Javier took enough cream to lighten the coffee to buff while Vidente always took hers adorned only with a sugar cube. She took the cups and their saucers into the parlor, and then returned to the kitchen to retrieve a plate of sugar cookies with browned edges that a neighbor had delivered this morning as thanks for a look at her colors.

Javier took the coffee to his lips, his erect posture on the couch seeming as relaxed on him as if he were lying down.

"The stores are doing well?" Vidente asked as she sat in the club chair adjacent to him.

"Yes, very well."

Vidente didn't need to ask. Javier had a soul for business. When he was in his early teens, he made money selling discarded objects that he cleaned and refurbished. By the time he'd become an adult, he'd taken the small stake his parents had provided to him and turned it into a trio of food markets. When his father died, Javier kept the family construction business alive for nearly three years before selling it for enough money to keep everyone very comfortable for decades. Now, at thirty-seven, his grocery stands dotted the entirety of Anhelo, Javier had a prominent spot on the town council, and he'd invested in a sugar refinery that he planned to make the biggest in the country or maybe in all of South America.

"And Johanna?"

"She is also very well. She's visiting her mother today."

Vidente shifted a bit in her chair. "She's a good girl."

Javier reached for a cookie, and then leaned back on the sofa. "I know you don't like her very much, Mother."

"That isn't true at all. Johanna seems like a lovely woman. She seems warm and concerned about you. I've just come to taking a casual approach to your girlfriends. It seems a waste for me to get to know them because they seem to disappear so quickly."

Javier laughed softly and took a bite of his cookie. Vidente knew he wasn't going to argue the point with her. Javier had never found a woman that pleased him for very long. Vidente had viewed her son's colors on numerous occasions and she knew that he didn't hate women. On the contrary, he seemed to like them very much. Loving them, however, was an entirely different story.

"This one might not disappear so fast," Javier said. "She has already been with me for nearly two months."

Vidente clasped her hands in mock excitement. "I'll have Erika begin working on my dress for the wedding."

Javier laughed and threw his head back. "I don't know; maybe you should."

Vidente watched her son carefully. He wasn't being his usual flippant self when talking about romance. "Are you saying that you are going to ask Johanna to marry you?"

Javier sat up straighter. "I'm saying that I'm thinking about it." He paused and gave his mother a steady gaze. "I might be even thinking about it seriously."

Given her vision, Vidente didn't find much in the world surprising. However, she'd long since stopped anticipating ever hearing such words from her older son's mouth. "This is good news. You should come to dinner with her soon. I will start getting to know her better."

"You'll like her, Madre Vidente."

Vidente leaned forward and patted her son on the knee. "As I told you, I already like her. And I'm beginning to like her more. She'll give you good babies."

Javier held up a hand. "I'm not ready to start decorating a nursery just yet."

Vidente decided not to pursue this further, though the thought of her son fawning over children tickled her. She took a cookie and bit the crusty brown edge. "Have you seen your brother lately?"

Javier shrugged. "I see Mauricio only slightly more often than you do."

Vidente frowned. "In that case, perhaps we should check to be sure he's still alive."

"Oh, he's still alive. I get reports on him from customers regularly. They seem to find it amusing that Mauricio has such a...youthful soul."

"And I thought Luisa had tamed him."

"But she has. Before, he would stay out until all hours of the night. Now he only stays out until the early morning."

Vidente shook her head in frustration. Her younger son was a man with a job, a wife, and two children. Yet he was still a boy. She'd never been able to say anything to him to convince him to take a less fanciful approach to his life. He'd even once suggested to Vidente that she was no more grounded than he was, given her "excursions into the supernatural," as he put it. Vidente didn't speak to him for a week after that. Then, it was because she was angry with him. Now, it was common for much more than a week to pass between visits even when there was no rancor between them.

Dark thoughts about her son segued into dark thoughts about her future. It was curious to her that the pleasant news about Javier's potential wedding had not led her to wonder if she would still be alive for the event, but that the mention of Mauricio could lead her to think about how she was going to leave this Earth.

"When I die, I want a procession down Calle Adorar," she said abruptly.

Javier's face showed obvious confusion over the sudden shift in conversation. "What?"

"I want a horse-drawn carriage. And flowers of every color and description."

"Mother, why are you talking about –" Javier leaned toward her, pointing a finger. "Madre Vidente, did you *see* something?"

Vidente should have known that Javier would instantly reach this conclusion. "No, no, of course not. You know I don't seek wisdom on my own future."

Javier relaxed slightly. "Then why this declaration from out of nowhere about your funeral procession."

It took Vidente a moment to devise a believable response. "We were talking about your brother. The thought came into my mind that I wouldn't want to trust him with something like my funeral plans. Since that will naturally leave things to you – whenever it happens – I thought you should know of my desire for a horse-drawn carriage and flowers."

"If talk of my brother leads you to think about such things, maybe we shouldn't talk about him any longer."

"Don't be silly," Vidente said casually. "I was just musing. I think of many things when I think of your brother."

"I think of many things as well," Javier said coarsely. "I choose not to say most of them out of respect to you."

Javier took another sip of his coffee. The cup covered much of his face, but Vidente could see enough to know that his mood had dimmed. For several minutes, neither said a word. Javier's attention seemed to be on the violet and red tapestry. Vidente looked out the window at a young girl playing with a ragged doll.

"I'm also going to give away all of my money."

Javier's gaze shot back toward her. "Are we still talking about your demise?"

"You don't need it, though I will bequeath a sum to your future babies. And Mauricio, well, who knows what he would do with it. I'll set things up so his children will have a comfortable life even if their father cannot provide it." Vidente wondered if she truly had enough left to offer her grandchildren such safety, but she pressed on anyway. "The rest will go to the church."

Javier grumbled. "I think I would like to stop having this conversation now."

"Yes, yes, of course. What am I doing musing about such morbid things, anyway? It is a beautiful day and my son is here for a visit. Would you like to go for a walk? You can tell me more about your wedding plans."

అ

JOYA DE LA COSTA, 1920

Khaled had yet to step into one of Joya de la Costa's ornate churches, but today he did so twice. The first time came in the early morning. He'd risen even earlier than he did on work days to go to the church a few minutes away from his home. There, he knelt and lit a candle for Nahla, Tarek, May, and Mona.

"Everything has been so sudden in my life lately," he said to their spirits. "That's a funny thing for a man who only knew sameness for so long. I didn't anticipate any of this. I hope you have found peace and happiness where you are. And I hope you can appreciate the happiness I've found. I never saw this coming and I certainly never went looking for it. It's a strange world, no?"

He bowed his head silently for several minutes after that. No clear thoughts came to his mind, only the sense that he needed to reach out to the lives he'd been absented from, to seek their acceptance before he started out on his new life.

Then he rose to prepare for his visit to a different, much larger church. The church where he would marry Lina.

They had only met one month and one day before, but Khaled wasn't sure that he would have been able to wait a moment longer to consummate their love. He wanted this woman with such hunger that his body physically ached for her.

The time from their meeting at the café to now had been a cascade of exotic pleasures for Khaled. Conversations that prompted his imagination. Outings that tickled his heart. Kisses that vivified his body and his spirit. Within one recent three-day period, they'd walked an expansive stretch of beach for hours, spent most of an evening translating words from Spanish to English and then to Arabic, and then Lina rooted for him boisterously while he played soccer with her very athletic brothers and some of their friends. Since his arrival in Legado, Khaled had felt as though he had been transplanted into a mysterious and heretofore unknown world. With Lina, though, that strangeness took on new levels of wonder. He felt renewed, as though at thirty-eight his life had suddenly started. He took it as a sign that he found Lina so soon after learning about the death of his first family. It was as though his life had been split into partitions with only thin lines separating one from the other.

The wedding was a raucous affair orchestrated by Lina's doting mother and her older sister who was married with four children. Khaled learned that some people in her family had begun to wonder if the twenty-two-year-old Lina would ever marry. How she had gotten to this age without doing so was inconceivable to Khaled (the only clue he'd received were a couple of her references to Legado men as "silly"). Regardless, Lina's friends and relatives saw her marriage as cause for celebration – and celebrate they did. There were roasts and stews and acres of fruit. There were flowers and bunting and candles everywhere. There was music and dancing and impromptu speeches. And there was wine; a nearly comical amount of wine.

Khaled drank very little, though. He did this not from any sense of temperance or moderation, but for one very specific reason: he did not want his senses diminished in any way when he was finally alone with his new wife. Khaled and Lina had experienced a multitude of passionate kisses together, but she had strictly forbidden anything else. Lina needn't have worried about Khaled forcing the issue. Though he hungered for her like nothing he'd ever wanted in his life, he would never have compromised her virtue. Still, when she accepted his marriage proposal and said she wanted to be married as soon as possible, Khaled felt as though he'd spotted an oasis in the desert.

As the wedding celebration began to wind down (though Khaled wondered how many revelers would continue the party into the morning), Khaled and Lina made their goodbyes and returned to his apartment, which would now be their home. He'd festooned the modest living quarters with bouquets and floral arrangements in honor of Lina's arrival. Lina gasped in surprise when she saw it.

"You've turned the living room into a garden," she said with unrestrained glee.

Khaled spread his hands around the space. "I wanted to let you know you were welcome."

She moved into his arms and he hugged her close. "I feel very welcome."

They kissed then. This was not like the chaste kiss at the end of their wedding ceremony or like those they shared when celebrants toasted them during the party. This was slow, soft, and passionate enough to send ripples of desire through every part of Khaled's body. He needed Lina with a fervor that made him wonder if someone had taken over his soul. He had no reference for the things he was feeling. He wanted to give himself up to the overwhelming sensations.

At the same time, he didn't want to lose himself to his carnal instincts. This was a singular moment, an experience that was going to redefine experience for him. He didn't want to be rushed or sloppy. He wanted to live this moment as long as possible.

And so for several minutes, they stood in the living room, kissing deeply and pressing their bodies tight against each other. Finally, Khaled swept Lina up in his arms and carried her into the bedroom.

Khaled looked into Lina's eyes as he did so and found the mirror of his desire. Her eyes told him that she wanted him as much as he wanted her, and the fervor this generated in him made it nearly impossible to walk.

He laid Lina on the bed. He'd filled this room with flowers as well. Candles also, but now he didn't want to let go of his wife to light them. As Lina's head nestled against her pillow, he moved on top of her. Again, they kissed. He was sure he could kiss Lina like this forever. He ran his finger down the silken length of her arm while she drew her fingernails across his back. Once more, the temptation to push things quickly goaded him, but he continued to take his time.

Lina still wore her wedding dress. He slid some of the fabric back to kiss her shoulder and then he continued his kisses along her already-naked arm. As he did this, Lina ran her fingers through his hair, causing his nerves to prickle. He reached her hand and laid tender kisses on her palm and each of her fingers.

Lina offered a sigh of pleasure and said, "I love you, Khaled."

He looked back up at her face and saw an expression that spoke of adoration, longing, and invitation. Suddenly, he couldn't hold himself back any longer. Returning to her lips, he gave her a fiery kiss while sliding his hand around her back to release the buttons of her gown, her long hair mingling with his fingers.

The gown slid with a hiss along the bedspread. Lina's remaining clothes soon followed. Worried that his admiring her nakedness too long might make her uncomfortable, he drank in only the briefest glance before pulling down the bedclothes for her to get under. Still, the image that he took was one he knew he'd hold in his mind for the rest of his days. Long, supple legs and smooth, flat stomach. A patch of hair as inky black as the long strands that ran down her back and the gentle, firm rises of her breasts. Khaled had imagined that Lina would be this beautiful from the moment he saw her.

He quickly removed his own clothes and slid under the covers next to her. Seconds later, they joined. The feeling nearly overtook him. He shuddered and believed that he might explode into her immediately.

"Does this give you pleasure?" Lina asked him. Her voice was a sensual instrument.

"Everything about you gives me pleasure," he answered huskily, trying to hold himself back.

"Then make it last. For both of us."

Lina's exhortation inspired him. He drew in a deep breath and moved further into her. He would not be quick with Lina. He would not love her that way. He would love her the way a man loved something precious.

Slowly, they gyrated together. At one point, Lina's breath caught and he stopped for concern that he was causing her pain. But her plea of, "More, love" set him in motion again. The quivers of pleasure he felt flowed through his body. He felt them in the back of his calves and in the pads of his feet. At last, he felt them seemingly everywhere at once: his stomach, his wrists, his neck, his arms. Lina moaned ever so softly and he thought that this might be the single most beautiful sound he'd ever heard.

Finally, he could no longer control his desire for release. Clenching his buttocks, he let himself go. The sensation rose to the point where he felt himself growing outward. A growl emerged from him at once primal and triumphant. He stayed at this peak for longer than he imagined possible before floating back onto Lina's downy body.

It took him a long, rapturous stretch before he recaptured his senses. When he did, he kissed Lina's neck and then, luxuriously, her lips.

"Was that enjoyable for you?" she said.

He gave out a full-throated laugh. "Yes, my love. That was very enjoyable for me." He hesitated for a moment and then said, "And you?" He'd never asked Nahla such a question.

"I couldn't have expected anything so wonderful," she said.

Khaled pulled his wife tight against him. He couldn't believe how happy he was to hear her say this.

For several minutes, they lay together silently. Then Lina said, "We made our child tonight."

Khaled propped up on his arm and smiled at her. "You know, that doesn't happen every time a man and woman make love."

Lina looked at him lovingly and then looked to the ceiling. "It happened tonight, though." She kissed him tenderly. "I know."

✍

WASHINGTON, DC, 1986

Dro headed back to Legado in early July to spend some time with his family and friends before starting at MIT for the fall semester. On his way, he flew to Washington to be Viviana's guest. The diplomat had surprised him a few days after they met in Cambridge by calling him at the house where he was living. He'd told Melanie and some of his other friends about having drinks with Viviana at the Ritz, but he truly suspected that Viviana's expression of interest in retaining contact was nothing more than politeness. During the call, though, she spoke to him as though they'd known each other for years and she reiterated her invitation to come down for a visit. Dro hardly needed a beautiful woman to express interest twice. The fact that this particular beautiful woman was also powerful, renowned, and surrounded by lavish things made it that much easier to accept the offer.

"So, do you think she needs to consult with you on the state of the Legado economy?" Melanie said on the phone before he left. She was back in Colorado where she was summering with her boyfriend.

"I think she has a team of advisors for that – though she probably already knows more than her advisors can tell her."

"Hmm...maybe she wants to consult with you on the thickness of your biceps."

"You know, not everyone sees me as a piece of meat the way you do."

"Just make sure you wear clean underwear, boy toy."

The Legado Embassy to the U.S. was a stately townhouse on a street dotted with the embassies of other nations. New York was the only other place Dro had been that exuded this combination of money and power. Boston couldn't send this message; no matter how wealthy or influential some of its residents might be, it was too staid and far too quaint. Nothing in Legado came close, though Dro considered the possibility that he himself might affect a change in this at some point in the future.

After Dro cleared an extensive security check at the embassy entrance, an aide led him up a marble staircase to the second-floor offices of the ambassador. Original paintings lined the wall of the staircase: the vibrant colors and overt political commentary of Debora Senteles; the earthy geometrics of Estrella Delgado. Dro had studied these artists in school, as had every student in Legado. However, the only time he'd ever seen original paintings by these artists had been on a family trip to the Museum of Fine Art in Joya de la Costa, a town in northern Legado. He was relatively certain that there were more paintings from these artists in the embassy than there were in the museum that day.

Another aide, this one a tall, slim woman with onyx-colored hair and expressive brown eyes, guided him to the anteroom of Viviana's office. She introduced him to the ambassador's secretary and got him a cup of coffee, then sat with him for a few minutes asking him with great curiosity about MIT. The aide was very obviously trying to hide her youth with her manner of dress, and she'd done this moderately successfully. However, her enthusiasm when she asked about his university belied the fact that she herself was a recent college graduate. Viviana had clearly used his association with MIT to justify his visit, and thinking of this caused Dro to grin internally. He had always known that MIT would open doors for him, but he wouldn't have anticipated that it would open doors of this type.

Business eventually took the aide away, though she apologized profusely before she left. For the next several dozen minutes, Dro watched as various carefully dressed and studiously composed people lobbied the secretary for the ambassador's time and attention. On many occasions, the secretary needed to interrupt such requests in order to answer the phone, during which she addressed other requests. From what he could hear, Dro surmised that one call came from the ambassador's publisher while another came from the BBC. Dro bided his time reading a newspaper from Colina, Legado's capital. At last, the ambassador's office door opened, a crisp-looking man exited, and Viviana stood in the frame of the doorway, calling his name, exuding professionalism.

Dro stood and approached her. Determined to appear as professional as she appeared, he extended his hand and said, "Madame Ambassador, it is so good to see you again."

She took his hand, escorted him into the room, and closed the door without letting go of him.

When the door closed, she pulled Dro toward her and kissed him on both cheeks.

"I thought I already told you to call me Viviana," she said brightly.

Dro nodded toward the door. "It didn't seem appropriate here."

Viviana followed the angle of his head and then threw her eyes upward. "Yes, you are very astute. We don't want to make my staff jealous. Convention forbids them from addressing me by my first name."

Dro offered her a wry expression, though he was sure his eyes were gleaming. "Is this your way of telling me that you won't be hiring me when I graduate?"

Viviana tilted her head, as though she didn't understand that he was joking with her. Then she smiled and shook her head slowly. "Your destiny is not as a functionary, Dro. Far, far from it."

Dro allowed himself to take a long, admiring glance at this stunning woman. "That's good," he said. "I far prefer being able to call you Viviana."

The ambassador seemed to be appraising him as well, though Dro couldn't be sure if she were examining his physique or reading his future. After a long moment, she gestured him toward a sofa. "I hope you don't mind that I asked you to meet me at my office. Are your hotel accommodations okay?"

Dro considered the place where Viviana had chosen to put him up. The hotel accommodations at the historic and newly reopened Willard were spectacular. He'd never stayed anywhere so lush and he suspected that Viviana knew that he certainly could never have afforded to stay there if he were paying for the room. "The hotel is beautiful, thank you."

Viviana smiled. "I'm glad. I thought we would have dinner in the restaurant there tonight. It has quickly become a favorite of mine and it is very quiet."

As it turned out, dinner would be the first real chance they would get to speak. Mere minutes after Viviana welcomed him into her office, her secretary entered with news of an urgent phone call. An emergency meeting took place directly after that, followed by two more calls that couldn't wait. At the end of the second, Dro suggested that he get out of her way until they could reconnect for dinner, and a car took him back to the hotel.

The Willard Room was undoubtedly the most elegant restaurant Dro had ever visited. Dozens of crystal chandeliers. Elaborate window treatments. Polished silver upon textured linen tablecloths. Viviana seemed to float through life in a bubble of luxury. He wondered if her feet ever touched the pavement of Washington's urban streets. Perhaps members of her staff simply carried her from her limo indoors. It was quite a way to live.

Two members of that staff were positioned discreetly in the dining room now. In a city as full of targets as this one, it was difficult to imagine why anyone would ever threaten the life of the ambassador from Legado, but bodyguards came with the job and Dro guessed that Viviana was just fine with that.

The waiter came to the table with their menus, but Viviana held up her hand before he could deliver them. "Could you please ask the chef what he is excited about making tonight?" she said.

The waiter tucked the menus under his arm. "Certainly. Would you like to discuss it with him?"

"That won't be necessary. We would be happy to eat whatever he would love to serve us."

Dro had never heard an exchange like this before, but it seemed to give both Viviana and the waiter a considerable amount of pleasure. Dro had always had an adventuresome palate – something he'd tested at some of Boston's seediest late-night dives – so he had no qualms about leaving his meal in the hands of the chef. Or the decision to do so in the hands of the estimable woman seated across from him.

"My second husband found it threatening when I did that sort of thing," she said as the waiter walked away. "Actually, he found it threatening when I did any sort of thing. I still wonder to this day who he thought he was marrying."

Dro had read about Viviana's two failed marriages. The first one, to an eternally furious poet, began and ended when she was in her early twenties and seemed to be about two people evolving in separate directions as they grew into their lives. The second was to a prominent businessman and happened not long after Viviana left academia for public service. It lasted four years but, by all accounts, the couple had spent virtually none of the last year and a half in the same place.

"I don't feel threatened," Dro said.

Viviana's eyes sparkled. "I didn't think you would. You're a next-generation man, aren't you?"

"I'm not sure what you mean by that."

The sommelier brought the wine. Viviana tasted and approved it.

"A man who acknowledges that gender roles have evolved. American men seem to be contending with this better than the men from our country have. But I can sense it in you. You aren't going to let convention rule you. That's especially valuable in these times."

Dro felt flattered, though he wasn't entirely sure how Viviana gauged this in him. Was it because he respected her? How could any man not respect a woman as accomplished as she was? Was it something about his manner? In their brief time together, Dro had gotten the sense that Viviana was appraising him in some metaphysical way. He'd long heard stories about how several women in his family had the ability to "read" things about people, but he'd always dismissed it. Did Viviana believe she could do this as well? Or was this something that all women thought they could do with varying degrees of success?

The meal moved through three sumptuous courses with the conversation seeming to shift with each. During the appetizer, it was politics, ranging from the tense and complicated conditions at home to the relationship between Legado and America. For the entrée, the discussion became philosophical. What defined an accomplished life? How did one set appropriately ambitious goals? For dessert and port, the conversation became decidedly personal.

"I was sixteen when a man broke my heart for the first time," Viviana said, gazing into her wineglass.

"That was one incredibly stupid man," Dro said.

Viviana looked up at him, seeming for the moment unguarded. She reached across the table for his hand. "That was very sweet of you."

The sensation generated by Viviana's touch surprised Dro. He was hardly a stranger to contact with women, but the squeeze Viviana gave his fingers set his nerves on alert.

"I'm happy that you thought what I said was sweet, but it was really just a statement of fact. Any man who broke your heart would have to be incredibly stupid or ridiculously self-absorbed."

Viviana ran the nail of her forefinger across his palm. Dro immediately felt the effect in his groin. "Ah, to be able to see things in such obvious ways again," she said.

Dro tightened. "Are you saying I'm naïve?"

Viviana strengthened her grip on his hand, which surprisingly had the effect of calming Dro down. "No, I'm not saying that at all. Actually, I'm saying that I envy your perspective."

She looked down at the table for a moment and when she raised her eyes, they held Dro as firmly as if she'd wrapped her arms around him.

"Dro, do you find me appealing?"

Dro felt his skin warm. "I think you might be the sexiest woman I've ever met in my life."

"My age and position don't repel you?"

Almost as though someone else were controlling his actions, Dro leaned forward and lifted Viviana's hand to his lips. "Your age makes you infinitely more attractive and your position mesmerizes me."

Viviana held tightly to his hand and Dro wished desperately that there were not a dining table between them.

"Dro," she said languidly, "I would very much like to be with you tonight. I would invite you back to my residence at the embassy, but there are too many eyes there. However, your rooms are just upstairs."

If there was conversation that took place after that, Dro didn't remember it. Nor was he conscious of how they moved from the dining room to his suite or where the two bodyguards went when Viviana and he went upstairs. He only acknowledged the palpable electricity Viviana's nearness generated and the pounding need he felt within him.

He'd barely closed the door to his room before they wrapped together. Backed against the wall, Dro tugged at Viviana's blouse, freeing it from her skirt and running his hand beneath the silk to caress the eminently softer skin underneath. She moaned and kissed him deeply, grinding her hip against him. The motion took him to a new level of passion. Reaching to the hem of her skirt, he raised the fabric and cupped her buttocks before running his fingers to the waist of her hose and pulling downward. Turning Viviana toward the wall, he lifted her skirt completely and then, kneeling, drew down her stockings and panties. He was barely aware of Viviana's long fingernails running through his hair as he ran his tongue along the inside of her thigh. He gave both thighs careful, luxurious attention, which Viviana seemed to adore. Then he brought his tongue up to her. He probed her gently, eliciting a soft intake of breath and then a deepening growl. He tasted her, consumed her, felt her become engorged. Then, with a series of gasps, Viviana cupped his head and pulled him against her. Her release seemed to follow a course of ever-heightening peaks.

Finally, she drew him up, kissing him hungrily while reaching for his belt. She slipped his pants and underwear down and then backed toward the arm of the couch. Pulling up her skirt, she sat and directed him inside of her. Her heat and her power overwhelmed him. Dro drove himself inside of her, wanting at once to satiate himself and to stay on the edge of satisfaction indefinitely. For several minutes, he remained in this magnificent purgatory. But when Viviana began to peak again, he lost all control. He poured himself into her and his release drove both of them tumbling onto the couch.

Eventually, they moved into the bedroom, where they took each other three more times before the night was over. Only the third time was less frantic. Never before had Dro met a woman this erotic or this capable of coaxing new levels of sexual energy from him. When he slept at last, he fell into deep, dreamless slumber.

He awoke the next morning to shimmering sunlight. The clock on the bed stand read 10:47 and Viviana was no longer there. Allowing himself several minutes to revel in the events of the previous evening, Dro took his time getting out of bed and showering. When he at last made it to the living room, he found a note from Viviana.

Dro,

I need to go back to being "Madame Ambassador" for a while, but the image of your body and your soul will be with me the entire day. You will inspire me.

I can barely wait to be with you again
tonight.

Love,
V

Suddenly ravenously hungry, Dro called room
service for breakfast. While he waited, he stood at
the window and watched the vibrant city below. He
was planning to explore it today, but he knew that
doing so would only serve as a way to bide his time
until the evening came and Viviana returned to his
bed.

He sat on the couch, thought about the evening
before, and laughed. Then he thought about Melanie
calling him "boy toy" before he made this trip, and
he laughed again. Though he confided nearly everything to Melanie, he wouldn't mention the events of
last night to her. Viviana Emisario had provided him
with a timeless memory, one he was sure he would
bask in regularly as the years went by, but one he
would keep to himself.

4.

NEW YORK, 2010

Sitting in a restaurant with Angélica always generated affectionate memories in Alex. The very first time he met her, she was sitting across from him at their middle school cafeteria in Anhelo. She'd recently moved to the school and Alex's friend Catalina had taken Angélica under her wing. Back then, Angélica had hair that barely touched her long neck, she didn't use a hint of makeup, and she was a bit on the gangly side. Still, even at that point Alex could tell that she was going to become a great beauty. Her high cheekbones, the soft contours of her face, and her glimmering eyes all bore testament to that.

More than anything, though, Angélica projected niceness on that first day. "Nice" wasn't a word that Alex had used terribly often when he thought about girls, especially at age thirteen when his body made binary decisions for his mind about all females. But that was a conclusion he reached (along with the conclusion that she was going to be beautiful one day) within minutes of their first conversation. Through the rest of his school years, Alex had numerous fits of pique with various friends, all of which involved some level of teenaged nastiness. Never with Angélica, though. It was as if she exuded some kind of pheromone that kept him at the very least pleasant with her at all times. He'd always appreciated that about her. She enriched him.

Del Posto, the restaurant where they now sat was much more than just a continent away from their original cafeteria, and the sunchoke crudo that Angélica ate was exponentially more elegant than the torta she chewed delicately on the day they met. But it still triggered memories.

"Are you going to eat that entire plate of lobster salad yourself without offering any to me?" she said archly.

Alex looked down at his plate. "I was saving the best piece of lobster for you." He pointed to a particular chunk. "I was going to give it to you at the end as a surprise."

Angélica eyed him suspiciously. "Maybe you should eat it all. Who knows when you're going to have another meal like this? Ashrams aren't much for food, are they?"

It was the first time Angélica mentioned tomorrow's trip since he met up with her after his playdate with Chrissy. She'd brought it up multiple times last night, each time with less perplexity in her voice. This was the first time she'd been playful about it, though.

"That's an extremely good and thoughtful point," he said. "You're right; I should eat all of the lobster. Don't even bother to ask me about my pasta when that comes out."

Angélica chuckled and returned to her sunchokes. Alex allowed a minute to pass and then put a generous morsel of lobster on Angélica's bread plate. She smiled at him, cut the piece in half, and ate it. Without commenting, she went back to her own food, a wistful expression on her face. Did the lobster send her off on some kind of sense memory the way the restaurant did him?

He watched Angélica eat silently. Finally, she said, "You don't know what you're missing next Saturday, do you? It's our eight-month anniversary."

She was right that he had no idea that Saturday marked this "occasion." He recalled their celebrating – and his remembering – the half-year anniversary of their first date, but they hadn't noted the seventh month in any way. Was there some significance to eight months of which he was unaware? For that matter, wasn't the anniversary of their first date especially arbitrary in their particular case? They'd known each other as teens, reconnected more than a year ago when Alex read an article Angélica wrote for *New York* magazine, and went out to multiple dinners together before the night they kissed for the first time. One could easily argue that the most important anniversary in their history was that initial day in the cafeteria, but they'd never celebrated that event in any way. He wasn't even sure of that date, though it had to have been in September. It was entirely possible that the anniversary was this very day.

"See?" he said. "Now you've ruined another surprise. I was going to fly back on Saturday just so we could be together."

A brief wash of sadness came over Angélica's face before she hid it with her water glass. She took a sip and returned the glass to the table in slow motion. "Did you ever think we'd be together for eight entire months?"

The melancholy undertone in Angélica's voice confused Alex. "To be honest, yes," he said. "I really thought we would."

This caused her to look up at him, her eyes flashing their usual brilliance briefly. This dimmed quickly, though.

"Why?" she said.

This conversation was getting increasingly slippery and Alex's comfort with it was diminishing in direct proportion. "Why? Because I love you." He arched an eyebrow. "I've decided that I like having you around."

She smiled, but looked away, obviously unwilling to play with him. "What does that mean?"

It wasn't as though Alex had never seen Angélica this contemplative before. But he'd never seen her being this contemplative about him. "It means I fully expect us to be together for our nine-month anniversary."

Her eyes stayed averted. "And then?"

"Ten months?"

Alex regretted being so flippant as soon as the words came out of his mouth. He could see that it bothered Angélica and he hated that. A long silence followed while he contemplated how much it hurt him to disappoint her.

"I need to get past this nightmare with Opal," he said when Angélica didn't make any effort to speak.

"Does that mean something for us?"

Alex glanced around the room. "I don't know if it does or not. I only know that these protracted divorce negotiations are like having some kind of chronic disease. That entire conversation about paintings yesterday had nothing to do with the Boteros, you know. She has her eyes on something else and she's trying to set me up by making an issue over something that she'll *concede* later in exchange for the thing she really wants. How sick is that?"

Angélica shook her head slowly. "It's sad that things turned out for the two of you the way they did."

"Is it?" Alex said sharply, his ire building. "Or was it just inevitable?

Angélica's expression grew wistful again. "Maybe it was. That doesn't seem sad to you?"

"I don't know. I'm too pissed off about it to be sad."

The longest silence of the night came after that, causing Alex to steam in his anger over Opal.

"I'm not her, you know," Angélica said when Alex had gotten deep into his own head.

The declaration caused him to realize that he'd been missing the point of this conversation. Angélica wanted to get some sense from him about where they were going and his response to this had been to drench the discussion with the poison of where he'd been.

He put down his fork and knife. "No, you are definitely not her."

"And yet she looms over us."

Alex considered this for several seconds before he said, "She looms over me; not us. I'm trying to get her out of my life completely."

"And then?"

"And then I'll be able to breathe. I'll be able to think much more clearly once I'm breathing again."

Angélica seemed to be tossing Alex's words over in her mind, her eyes still dimmed. Then she speared the last bit of sunchoke on her plate with her fork. She started to move the food to her mouth and then stopped.

"Did you want a taste of this?" she said. "I just realized I didn't offer you any."

"Sure, it looks good."

Alex reached for his fork in anticipation of Angélica giving him the bite. Instead, though, she put the last taste in her mouth and chewed slowly, her eyes gleaming.

"It *was* good," she said.

✑

JOYA DE LA COSTA, 1921

The latest shipment of Palestinian crafts was moving so quickly that Khaled had sent an emergency telegram to his brother this morning to tell him to get more inventory on the next boat. Once again, he thought about mentioning the fate of his wife and children – and the new marriage that had caught him utterly by surprise – and rejected it. Even though business had been very good, the cost was still far too dear, and at this point he would have to write a very long telegram to say anything that made sense. He did, however, mention that his brother should increase the amount of olivewood in the next shipment because it seemed to be a favorite of so many in the area. Even Lina loved it, keeping several vases and statuettes to display around the apartment. This depleted precious inventory and cut down on profits, but if these trinkets made Lina happy, Khaled would never deny her them.

The shop where he'd just completed an order was one of the largest in all of Joya de la Costa. Ruben, the shop owner, employed more than a dozen people and Khaled had never been there when there weren't at least a half-dozen employees scuttling about. Ruben had been skeptical of Khaled's products at first, promising only to consider them during Khaled's first two solicitations. Now, though, he'd become one of Khaled's best customers and the order he'd placed today was the single biggest ever. Even the dolls with the tahriri dresses sold here when they were nearly impossible to move elsewhere.

As Khaled repacked his sample case, Ruben and the others prepared the store for closing. Khaled watched as Ruben made one last sale and then walked the customer to the shop's door. When he was finished, he turned and caught Khaled's eye.

"Khaled," the tall, jovial man said, "you're welcome to stay here as long as you'd like, but if you do, you're going to have to help us clean up."

Khaled snapped the case shut. "Hand me a broom, then. Bring me a glass of rum, and I'll clean the windows for you as well."

Ruben laughed boisterously. "Maybe I should have you come around at closing time every night. The rum is going to have to wait, though. We can go for a drink at the café across the street when we're finished here."

Khaled had been to the café with Ruben before, though it was entirely possible the other man had forgotten about it. After all, they drank until after midnight that night. That was before Khaled had met Lina, though. Now, Khaled had no desire to stay out late into the evening.

"I have a better idea," Khaled said. "Let's go back to my home." He turned to the other employees. "All of you. We'll make a party out of it. It's Tuesday night and we've all had a busy day."

Khaled had never spontaneously invited ten people to his home before, and he wasn't entirely sure how Lina would respond. Certainly her relatives showed up at the door regularly enough, and certainly Lina and the two people Khaled had hired to help her always cooked far more for dinner than they could ever eat in an evening – though never more than *twelve* could eat in an evening. Lina seemed to like having company as long as the night wound down eventually. Khaled had expected to find her tired in the evenings now that she was six months pregnant, but if anything, she always seemed to have more energy when he came home than she had when he left in the morning.

Less than an hour later, Khaled walked into the apartment with Ruben and three of his employees.

The others would be arriving shortly. Khaled kissed Lina on the lips and then kissed her belly, saying, "How are you this evening, my child? Did you have a good day with Mommy?" Lina had become pregnant immediately after their marriage. She continued to be convinced that this had happened the first time they made love, though Khaled remained skeptical. Considering how often they lay together in the days after their wedding, when it happened would always be subject to some speculation, and entirely beside the point, really.

When he rose back up, he said, "We have guests this evening."

"I can see that," Lina said, greeting the others and eyeing Khaled curiously. "Something told me that we should make a large pot of stew today. I'll have the table set."

Khaled excused himself from the others so he could help Lina with whatever preparation she was doing. He never understood why she did so much around the house when others could do the work for her, but she seemed intent on it.

"I bought some cheese and bread on the way home," he said as they headed into the kitchen. "Ruben bought us some more rum."

"That's good, since you invited the neighborhood to dine with us tonight."

Khaled touched Lina on the shoulder. "Do you mind?"

She turned and kissed him, their bellies touching before their lips. "Of course I don't mind. I think this is a very nice turn of events."

The others had arrived by the time they came out, which caused Lina to call out for additional dishes since Khaled hadn't told her that still more people were coming – not to mention so many more people. She seemed to think the entire thing was very funny.

It appeared that there was much that those gathered found funny this night. Ruben did comical impressions of some of the shop's customers. Khaled thought this was somewhat disrespectful and that it might even invite bad luck, but he laughed nevertheless. Khaled even made several of his own jokes. He'd never considered himself particularly funny, but tonight people seemed to find him clever. Perhaps it was the rum or Lina's spirit-elevating cooking. Food this delicious tended to put everyone in good humor.

Of course, Lina's pregnancy fascinated everyone. Khaled had noticed this everywhere they went together. Strangers would ask Lina how she was feeling and whether she had any instincts about the gender of the child, not knowing that Lina's instincts about this extended to certainty that she was carrying a boy. Khaled didn't recall such fascination with babies from others when he was in Bethlehem, but perhaps he was simply not paying attention. Tonight at the dinner table, though the majority of the guests were men, they seemed endlessly fascinated with the child's movements and the sensations these evoked in Lina. This warmed Khaled's heart.

As midnight approached, Lina was telling yet another story about impending motherhood when she stopped mid-sentence to yawn. Ruben stood immediately.

"We're keeping you awake, Lina, and you need your rest," he said.

Lina began to protest, but she yawned again and admitted she was getting a bit tired. All the guests were gone within minutes.

"That was fun," she said when the last of them had left and she and Khaled were finally alone together.

"It was," Khaled said, wrapping an arm around her shoulders. "It wasn't too much for you?"

"Not at all. And it is good for you."

Khaled kissed Lina on the top of her head. "You are good for me." He placed a hand on her stomach. "You and the little one. Come; let's get both of you to bed."

❧

ANHELO, 1928

Edgar and his son placed the ornate chair on the sidewalk, forcing several people to shift their positions. "Will this view be good, Tia Vidente?" Edgar said.

Vidente sat in the chair and looked up the street. For a moment, a young man stood in her line of sight, but he turned, saw Vidente, and moved away quickly. "It is good. Thank you, Edgar."

From the time she was a little girl, Vidente's heart lightened in anticipation of the Holy Week ceremonies that were legendary in Anhelo. Tourists poured into the city, people decorated the outsides of their homes in shades of purple, and shopkeepers gave away candy. Though the week marked a time when all good Catholics reflected on the sacrifice of their savior, the citizens of Anhelo celebrated the magnificence of that sacrifice and how it allowed them to live the lives they led. By the time Vidente was old enough to comprehend how death could lead to ultimate joy, she'd already absorbed such a notion into her sensibility.

Vidente's favorite part of the entire week was the procession she now awaited. For more than a hundred years, the many churches of Anhelo had been joining to parade their religious statues from one end of Calle Adorar to the other accompanied by the sounds of sacred music played by accomplished musicians from all over Legado. The priests, dressed in their sacramental finery, led the way, followed by parishioners costumed as the apostles. Then the statues came, each enclosed in a golden trellis lit with sixteen tapers and placed upon a wooden platform. Eight of Anhelo's sturdiest young men – both Javier and Mauricio had served on multiple occasions – carried each statue, four in the front, and four in the back, dressed in long ultramarine robes. Finally came the statue of the crucifix. Each year a different church received the honor of parading its crucifix in the procession, and that fortunate church employed artisans to beautify the statue for most of the year leading up to the event. This year Iglesia de la Inmaculada Concepción would close the procession. The son of Vidente's friend Monica had been the primary artist to work on the restoration of the church's crucifix and Vidente knew that he had taken the commission very seriously.

Vidente heard the opening notes of "Adoramus Te" and turned toward the music, which came from a platform on the opposite side of the street and perhaps three hundred feet away. Though her view was unencumbered, Vidente noticed that the crowds were thicker than she had ever seen them. Of course, everyone in town was here. But there were more visitors as well, a good sign for the future of Anhelo.

Padre Antonio caught Vidente's eye as he passed. A few days earlier, she'd gone to Iglesia de la Santa Madre to pray and she saw the priest on her way out. They chatted briefly and Vidente suggested to him that he might have to face the prospect of larger opportunities at some point in the future. She counseled him that he should embrace such an opportunity when it arose. Padre Antonio looked at her in much the same way that he looked at her now, with a combination of bewilderment and appreciation.

Twenty minutes into the procession, the music changed for the fourth time, this time to "I Know That My Redeemer Liveth." With it came the three sarcophagi, representing Christ's temporary home before his ascension. This was always an emotional moment, and it was common for attendees to weep or even throw themselves on the ground keening.

The appearance of the sarcophagi had long held special meaning for Vidente beyond what it represented to the assemblage. When her husband was still alive and her children were still young, they'd come together to the procession. When the second sarcophagus passed, Vidente – who people did not call "Vidente" then – felt an intense wave of vision.

She rarely "saw" things in this way, but the image was unmistakable for her.

"My father's bones are in that sarcophagus," she said to her husband.

"That's not possible, *mi amor*. These sarcophagi are for ceremonial purposes only. They are empty."

"This one is not."

Her husband refused to discuss this further with her, but Vidente could not let it go. Back then, people knew that she had "intuitions" on occasion, but they had not come to know her yet as a seer. When she mentioned her vision to others, they reacted the same way her husband had. Until two weeks later when it was learned that her father's grave had been robbed and the bones stuffed in the ceremonial sarcophagus. It turned out to be one of a series of grave robberies committed in Anhelo during the time. Vidente's vision and her persistence led to the capture of the thieves and contributed greatly to the reputation she now had.

As she watched the third sarcophagus pass, a new sensation struck Vidente. It was not a vision, per se, but an overwhelming sensation.

Next year, this structure will carry my bones.

Vidente felt a hand clasp her arm.

"Yes, Vidente, I share your tears," Edgar said. "This part of the procession is always so sad."

∾

CAMBRIDGE, 1986

Cambridge in autumn was stunning. The colors that rose on the trees and swept over the lawn were like nothing Dro had known in Legado. Autumn didn't really exist in his home country, at least not the way people in America saw it. It rained more in October and November, but the temperatures remained consistent throughout the year. And since the temperatures didn't change, the vegetation didn't change appreciably either. Dro's first experience with the golds, ambers, and crimsons of a New England fall came last year. Still, it felt different on the MIT campus. More vivid. More real.

"I like it when the air cools down a little," Melanie said as they walked through campus after one of their three-times-a-week lunch dates. "It always feels great to put on a sweater for the first time after the summer."

Dro blew on his hands. It got chilly like this in the mountains of Legado, and sometimes at night in Anhelo, but temperatures in the low sixties (he was just beginning to think in terms of Fahrenheit rather than Centigrade) were something to which he'd never become accustomed. "I started wearing sweaters a month ago."

"Poor baby," Melanie said, patting his shoulder. "Your blood will thicken up eventually."

Dro bumped Melanie softly in response to her teasing. As he did, he heard a woman calling his name from behind him. He turned to find Susan Roemer, the associate admissions director, striding in his direction.

"Do you mind if I don't walk you out?" he said to Melanie. "I should probably talk to Susan."

"No, of course not, go. I'll see you tomorrow night."

Melanie air-kissed him and then Dro started walking toward Susan. He'd seen Susan during his orientation week at the end of August, but this was the first contact he'd had with her since then.

"How do you feel things are going so far?" Susan said.

"Great," Dro said casually. "I have a huge amount of work, but I expected that."

"And you're doing it very well, by all indications." Susan looked at him coyly. "I've been asking around."

"Do you do this with every student in this school?"

She tipped her head toward him. "No, I don't."

Dro smirked. "Only the provisional students."

Susan seemed confused for a second and then her expression softened. "Actually, only the students who leave an unusually strong impression. As you can imagine, you left a very strong impression on me, Dro."

Dro blew on his hands again. "I guess I should be flattered."

Susan smiled. "Dr. Dornbusch told me that he thinks you have an incisive mind."

"Then I guess we should take Dr. Dornbusch's word for it. Does that mean I did well on last week's test?"

"I'll let him give you your grade. Let's put it this way, though: you're on the right track. Stay on it."

Dro nodded. Under different circumstances, he might have felt self-conscious or even a little uncomfortable that Susan was watching him so carefully and had taken such a distinct interest in his academic performance. Given his situation, though, and especially given his hopes for a scholarship at the end of the school year, he was fine with it. More than fine, really. He felt as though he were on a stage playing a part he knew very, very well. "You don't need to worry about me. I'll stay on track."

"I'm not worried about you. Not at all. I'm finding this all very exciting, if you want to know the truth."

Susan watched him with a satisfied expression on her face for several seconds. She seemed to have something on her mind and Dro knew instinctively not to carry the conversation forward until she expressed what she wanted to express.

"Listen," she said at last, "I don't usually extend invitations like this to students, but I'm going to make an exception in your case. I'm going to a gathering tonight that I think would be very interesting to you."

Dro found this intriguing. "Really? I didn't know you had any personal interest in economics."

Susan glanced off in the distance. She seemed uncomfortable. "This isn't related to your area of study. It's something quite different, in fact. It's a meeting of some professors and a few students interested in metaphysics."

Dro wondered if he'd heard Susan correctly. "Metaphysics? You mean...magic?"

Susan shook her head quickly. "Definitely not magic. You aren't going to find anyone in wizard's gear here. These are very serious people with very serious questions about the limits to science's ability to explain things."

"This is a gathering of professors and students at the Massachusetts Institute of *Technology?*"

Susan's eyes glinted. "Not all of them are from MIT, but yes; many great scientific minds have questions their core disciplines can't answer."

Dro felt as though Susan were turning into a different person in front of him. Where was the woman who'd spoken to him so logically about navigating his way into this school, who'd put such a premium on numbers and quantifiable performance? "What makes you think I'd be interested in this?"

Susan hesitated again before answering. "A hunch, really. My intuition is usually good. After all, I guessed right about you as a student, didn't I?"

"But this...."

"Are you saying you've never wondered about the unknown?"

Dro took a moment to consider this. *Had* he ever wondered about the unknown? "I've always been more interested in truth than speculation."

"Those aren't mutually exclusive concepts."

This was the last possible notion Dro ever expected to face on this campus. He found himself dumbstruck by it.

"I've made you uncomfortable," Susan said. "Forget I mentioned anything about this."

Dro lifted a hand. "No, no. There are some stories in my family about...I'm not even sure how to describe it. Witches, I guess." He shrugged. "When and where?"

Susan took out a small, spiral-bound pad, wrote down an address, and handed it to him. "It's at an apartment a few blocks from here. People usually show up around nine or so."

Dro glanced down at the address and then up at the admissions director who had evolved before his eyes. "See you there, then."

For the rest of the day, Dro felt as though he'd been thrown off his axis a bit. The conversation with Susan was easily the most unusual one he'd had since moving to Boston. As the evening approached, he found himself alternating between eagerness and apprehension. The one emotion that didn't vary was skepticism. Though she couldn't possibly have known it, Susan had touched a tender nerve. Growing up, Dro had heard stories about family members with extrasensory powers. He'd always found such ideas arcane and considered it somewhat embarrassing that he was related to those who took such fanciful things seriously. Yet here, at the institution he'd coveted for so long, these ideas had found him. What was he to make of this?

The location for the gathering turned out to be the home of Dr. Jignaasu, a Professor of Cognitive Sciences at MIT. The slim man, who appeared to be in his early forties, greeted Dro at the door by name. Dro wondered how the professor knew who he was – perhaps it was the display of some kind of sixth sense – but as the evening continued, the answer became obvious. Dro was the only student here. The nearest person in age to Dro was a third-year doctoral student closing in on the defense of her dissertation on Kant at Harvard.

As the music of Purandara Dasa, a composer Dro had never heard before tonight, played in the background, Dro sat on a rust-colored velvet couch drinking Chardonnay. Dr. Jignaasu had decorated his apartment in eclectic fashion. A statue of the Hindu god Brahma sat next to an outsized statue of the Virgin Mary. A necklace of plastic beads was draped onto a stand of woven bamboo. A framed poster of Bob Dylan occupied a near wall, and Dro could see photos of Pelé, Einstein, and a stately collie tucked into the bottom of the frame. No two wineglasses held by those in the gathering were the same, but all of them bore a similar faint green hue. Even the throw pillows on the couch had the qualities of seeming at once randomly selected and carefully ordered.

Dro found that the conversation tonight alternated between silly and fascinating, between scholarly and quasi-intellectual. Because of this, he'd said very little and he found his attention wandering.

"...It makes no sense to consider time as a continuum. McTaggart shattered that illusion more than eighty years ago. Therefore, if time flows in all directions, who's to say that one can't send one's consciousness back in time or that our past can't literally catch up to us..."

Dro got up to pour himself some more wine and Susan joined him at the bar.

"Time travel doesn't interest you?" she said as she reached for a piece of ice with a pair of tongs.

"Will we get to ride in a time machine later?"

"I'm afraid ours is out for repair. I'm also afraid the group isn't at its best tonight. Professor Dodderington seems to believe we've all come here to listen to him lecture interminably. The frightening thing is that he gets even more voluble the more he drinks and I think he's just downed his fourth Scotch."

Dro poured vodka into Susan's glass, noticing that the tongs she'd used bore an intricate pattern remarkably close to the traditional kanás designs Dro regularly saw in Legado, but never before in America. "Do people really just come here to talk?"

"Not usually. Most of the time, the activities are far more *active*. Are you sorry I invited you?"

"Sorry? No. I am still *curious* about why you invited me, though."

"Take that one there, for instance. His aura is screaming yellow!"

The words seemed to impose themselves between Dro and Susan, like a commuter trying to squeeze himself between them on the T. Without looking, Dro knew that the speaker – he was relatively sure it was Dodderington – was talking about him.

Susan leaned closer. "I don't think you've been as invisible as you thought you were."

Dro turned back toward the others. Everyone was looking at him except the grad student and the middle-aged linguistics professor who was engaged in intimate conversation with her.

"I'm sorry," Dro said. "Did I do something?"

Dodderington scowled. "You broadcast your doubt. Not that you could help it, being a product of your generation."

Dro took a step back toward the group. "Excuse me?"

"Your generation is so damned committed to being rational. Little more than a dozen years ago, people your age were still trying to break down barriers. Now you want to construct cubicles."

Whether the words were meant to be insulting or not, Dro found Dodderington's tone offensive. "What makes you think you know anything about me?"

The professor grinned in a condescending way. "I know many things about you. But what I knew the moment I looked at you was that your mind is closed. Your aura screams yellow."

Susan moved up next to Dro. "Karl, maybe it's time for you to switch to soda water."

Dodderington scoffed and finished his glass of Scotch.

"What the hell is he talking about?" Dro said.

"He's talking about your aura."

"My aura? I thought you said there weren't going to be any wizards here."

Susan touched his wrist. "It isn't wizardry. It has to do with electromagnetic fields. There's plenty of research on this. Everyone has an EMF. Some people can see colors within the field. The colors say a lot about a person. Yellow is the color of defensiveness and doubt."

Dro turned toward Dodderington. "My *aura* says I'm a doubter?"

Dodderington rose up to get another drink. "You're filled with doubt."

"And you know this because you have some kind of special vision."

Dodderington laughed and poured the Scotch, sloshing a bit on the side of his glass. "Nothing special. Just using my eyes the way they were intended."

"Then that would mean that I could use my eyes the same way."

Dodderington stared at him, seeming suddenly sober. "Well, of course."

Dro glanced at Susan. She gestured to him to indicate her agreement.

"Okay, show me."

Dodderington looked at him carefully, his eyes seeming to be both on and around Dro at the same time. The corner of the right side of the professor's mouth turned upward. "Yes, I will."

While others watched, Dodderington escorted Dro toward the entry foyer. There was a bare white wall there, possibly the only bare space in the entire apartment. Susan had followed them and now Dodderington instructed her to stand against the wall and for Dro to stand approximately eight feet away from her.

"It isn't best to do this with alcohol in your system," Dodderington said.

Dro glanced at the professor sideways. "It doesn't seem to be causing you any trouble."

Dodderington's eyes narrowed. For a moment, Dro thought the man was going to walk away insulted, but then he gestured with his head for Dro to look at Susan. Dro turned toward the wall and

Dodderington explained that he was going to count from ten to one slowly and that he wanted Dro to continue to look at Susan while relaxing his gaze at the same time. He said that he wanted Dro to look at Susan and *not* look at Susan at the same time. This part wouldn't be difficult because the last thing Dro wanted to do at this point was make eye contact. He wasn't sure how he would react if he did so.

As Dodderington counted backward, Dro actually started to relax. Surprisingly so, considering how foolish this concept had seemed to him just a few minutes earlier. Regardless of how he'd gotten the information, Dodderington had read Dro correctly. He'd come to this evening as a doubter and his doubts had grown as the night passed. Now, though, he'd become intrigued.

By the time the professor counted down to one, Dro felt remarkably light on his feet, as though he might faint, though he didn't seem to be in any danger of that. He'd kept his eyes on Susan and now he'd begun to notice something like a light shadow that corresponded to the shape of her body. It wasn't a shadow, though, because it was on both her right and left sides, even though the light was coming from her right. It was also thicker in some places than it was in others. Was this the aura the professor and the admissions director had been going on about?

Dro tried to examine the image more carefully, but doing so made it disappear. He relaxed his eyes again and the image returned. His mind felt very clear, as though he hadn't had a single drop of wine all night.

"I see a shape, but I don't see any colors," Dro said.

"The colors will come if you work on it," Dodderington said.

Dro's focus shifted and he turned his head from Susan. He grinned at the professor. "Does this mean that I have magic vision?"

Dodderington didn't seem to find this funny. "It means that you're among the ninety-five percent of the population who can see as much as you just saw. If you want 'magic vision,' you're going to need to spend a lot more time with this."

Susan came up next to him and Dro looked at her. "Can you do this?"

"Not with Karl's proficiency, but yes, I can." Again she touched him on the wrist. "You have less yellow in your field now."

Dro laughed nervously, suddenly feeling naked. "Can you teach this to me?"

"I can certainly try."

"Imagine that," Dro said, taking a step back toward the living room. "I'm going to have some more wine now. Sorry for interrupting the conversation."

5.

JOYA DE LA COSTA, 1921

Ruben had been keeping Khaled waiting outside of his office for longer than usual because of some sort of problem in the back room. Since Ruben was Khaled's biggest customer, Khaled was more than willing to wait as long as necessary to take his next order.

It had been a day of waiting, for Khaled. Even lunch had taken an especially long time to arrive at his table. Fortunately, Ruben was his last call before he went back to Lina. Khaled always saved Ruben for last, especially since, these days, the shopkeeper usually gave him a glass of rum while they talked. Ever since Khaled had invited Ruben to his home, the man treated him like family, asking after Lina and asking about his pending fatherhood. Ruben was definitely Khaled's favorite customer and it wasn't only because he was also his best customer.

The wait continued and Khaled found himself getting drowsy. He hadn't wanted to get out of bed this morning. This was unusual because he'd always been ready for the workday. But when he awoke and turned toward Lina, her naked belly bulging between them, he felt the deepest urge to wrap her in his arms and stay with her until the sun was high in the sky.

"You're lingering today," Lina said, half-asleep.

He pulled her closer. "I like holding you."

She sighed dreamily. "And I like when you hold me." She kissed his neck. "This is the best place for me to be."

"Then I'll keep you here forever."

She laughed. "I would love that. But you need to get started on the day. Babies are expensive."

Khaled held her as close as he could and then kissed her tenderly. Then, before getting out of bed, he rested his head against the baby's head – so big now that he could feel it straight through Lina's skin.

As he did, Lina reached for him and pulled him back toward her. "Maybe a few more minutes," she said, and Khaled was happy to comply. When he moved to rise again, she took much longer to release him than she normally did.

Khaled touched his hand to her face. "Is everything all right, my love?"

She kissed his knuckle. "We are perfect. I always want you to know that I feel that way."

"As do I," he said, kissing her deeply one more time.

The minutes waiting for Ruben continued, and Khaled reclined further in the wooden chair outside of Ruben's office. The air grew heavy around him.

He must have fallen asleep because the hand that shook his arm briskly startled him. Khaled shook his head quickly, but he had been drowsing heavily and he didn't gather a sense of his surroundings right away.

"This is the fifth shop I've been to," said the man who shook him. "I was beginning to wonder if I would ever find you. You must come."

Still dazed, Khaled didn't recognize the man at first. Then he realized it was his neighbor, Dario.

"Oh, hello, Dario," Khaled said, still groggy. "What are you doing here?"

Dario leaned down so his perspiring face was only inches from Khaled's. "Didn't you hear me? You must come. I've been looking all over town for you. Lina is in labor. Something is wrong."

Dario's words sprung Khaled from his chair. All sense of grogginess was gone now. As was all sense of relaxation. Instantly, Khaled felt jittery, as though he'd drunk too much coffee.

"What do you mean something is wrong?"

Dario threw his hands in the air, exasperation evident on his face. "I don't understand these things. When they told me to find you, Lina was screaming and the midwife was talking to me very fast."

Swiping up his sample case, Khaled left the office area and headed for the front door as quickly as possible. Dario was trailing behind him, but Khaled had no time to wait for the older and considerably heavier man. He'd thank Dario later for finding him; right now, the only thing that mattered was that he get home very, very fast.

Something is wrong. Despite the fact that he'd fathered three children with Nahla, Khaled knew nothing about childbirth. When Nahla had gone into labor, the women took over. Khaled would come back from work or wherever he was to learn whether the child was a boy or a girl. As far as he knew, Nahla had never had any complications with childbirth. He'd heard stories of children being born dead – his sister had lost two that way – but his late wife had always managed to bring healthy babies into the world.

Khaled wondered what he would do if that didn't happen this time. This baby had seemed so real to him. They'd touched heads just this morning. He'd begun to envision Lina's nurturing the child, singing to it and holding it close. He'd even imagined playing games with this one and giving it rides on his back, something he'd only done rarely with his other children. The thought that the baby he and Lina created might never come into this world alive gave him an unfamiliar ache as he walked briskly to his home.

If there really was a problem with the baby, this would be very difficult for Lina to take. Nearly from the moment that her doctor confirmed that she was pregnant, she'd been speaking giddily about having this child. She spoke repeatedly about how, if it were a boy, he would look just like Khaled and he would be loving, smart, and strong. If it were a girl, the child would still look like Khaled but with less pronounced features, and Lina would teach her to cook, to sew, and to use her intelligence to impress those around her. Just the other night, Lina had spent most of the evening talking about how Khaled and their baby would do so many things together.

"This child will give you back what is missing in your life," she'd said, obviously referring to the children he'd lost in Palestine.

"This child will mean more to me than anything in the world," Khaled had said in response. "Except for you, my love."

Maybe things aren't as bad as I'm making them out to be, Khaled thought as he got within minutes of home. Dario tended to be excitable. And he'd admitted that he didn't know what was wrong. Maybe Lina wasn't screaming so badly – women always screamed when they were giving birth, didn't they? – and maybe the midwife wasn't nearly as frantic as Dario had made her out to be. Maybe Dario had just let his imagination get the best of him as he searched all over town for Khaled.

If that were true, it would be a very good thing. Khaled wanted this baby for Lina. She would treasure this child. And he wanted it for himself. Khaled hadn't realized how much he wanted this baby until just now – when there was a chance that he might not have it.

Khaled's street was unusually still when he turned onto it. Typically, it was so busy that it was like living at an outdoor bazaar. Even now, dozens of people milled around, but they didn't seem as lively. It was just as well. On normal evenings, Khaled would find himself stopping to talk to several neighbors before he made it to his own door. He didn't have time for that tonight.

Khaled didn't hear any screaming as he arrived home. He considered this a good sign. Maybe things had turned out fine and mother and child were resting. He took a moment to catch his breath before turning the doorknob.

That was when he heard the wailing. It started low, like a moan, but it continued to rise in both volume and tone. There was no mistaking the message of that sound. Something had definitely gone wrong. As he opened the door, Khaled tried to imagine a way he could comfort his wife. They'd shared so little heartache, but Khaled knew that he'd have to work through his own sadness to bring Lina solace because this would be devastating to her.

The foyer was dark as Khaled entered, as was the living room. Khaled put down his sample case and the wailing began again. It was only then that he realized that these sounds were not coming from Lina. While he'd never heard her cry in extreme sorrow, he was intimately aware of virtually every sound his wife made and he could imagine the rest. He was hearing someone else's pain. Was Lina so distraught that she couldn't even utter what she felt?

Khaled needed to be by Lina's side immediately. He strode into the bedroom and what he saw upon entering stopped him and made his blood run cold. There, strewn across the bed in full-throated anguish, was Lina's mother. And she had thrown her arms around her daughter – the still, lifeless form of her daughter.

"My baby," the woman keened. "Why did you take my baby?"

For a moment, Khaled couldn't move. Could he really be seeing what he thought he was seeing? Then whatever had been holding him back released him, and he went quickly to Lina's side. Ignoring his mother-in-law's arms, he laid his head against his wife's. Her hair was matted, but her brow was dry. And unnaturally cool. Khaled knew the feel of Lina's skin better than he knew his own soul. This was not Lina's skin. This was something else.

Lina wasn't here.

Khaled knelt by the bed as he finally began to understand the fullness of what had occurred. He pushed his face into the mattress and sobbed in a way that he hadn't cried since he was a little boy.

Khaled had never known sorrow to cause physical pain before. This sorrow pulled at him, as though someone were wrenching layers of his insides away from him. The agony was so intense that he thought he might collapse from it. He wasn't sure how he was going to endure the next few minutes, let alone the rest of his life.

And then suddenly, in the middle of his anguish, a memory settled on his mind. It was of the third time he'd ever seen Lina, the second time he'd come to call on her after they met in the café. Her mother – the same woman whose wailing was touching the edge of his hearing now – busied herself with outdoor chores while Khaled and Lina explored the vast garden Lina had planted.

The gardens here were lush, even for Legado. The amount and variety of the plant life in this country had made an early impression on Khaled; there were rich colors everywhere. Where Khaled and Lina walked now though seemed so dense and so alive that Khaled could imagine plants growing in front of his eyes. Lina introduced him to an expanse of lulo, with jagged, heart-shaped leaves and brilliant orange fruit. Then she walked him around the corner of the garden toward a dazzling collection of Flamingo Lilies in a rainbow of colors, each with pointed tips rising out toward him. Khaled reached out to touch one of the tips and then drew back self-consciously.

"You *made* all of this?" he said, taken with the beauty of the surroundings.

Lina giggled. "God *made* this. I just helped out."

Flowers perfumed the air. The smell, the sights around him, and the nearness of Lina – by far the most stunning thing in this garden – dizzied him. "I could never do this."

"Of course you could." Lina took his hand and pulled him into a narrow clearing that left them enveloped by color. "The plants tell you what they need. You only have to listen."

"Listen to the plants?"

Lina held a finger to her lips and closed her eyes, tilting her head upward. "Listen."

Khaled tried to listen, but he did not close his eyes. Lina's quiet form, so serene and so completely part of this heavenly garden, was the single most satisfying vision he'd ever encountered. It was a vision of a home he didn't know existed. A home he didn't know he wanted until that very moment.

Much as it did nearly a year ago, that vision embraced him now, suspended him. But it could not keep him aloft from his sorrow forever. The sound of his mother-in-law's wailing and of his own sobbing broke through the memory. The vision of Lina among the flowers faded and Khaled opened his eyes, replacing it with an image of Lina he never hoped to see. As in the garden, her eyes were closed; and she appeared at peace. But if she listened for anything now, she couldn't share what she heard with Khaled.

Khaled touched Lina's cheek, his fingers feeling coarse on her cool, smooth face. His mother-in-law seemed to notice him for the first time then. She reached for his hand and then drew it to her brow and started crying again.

"What happened?" Khaled said. The words felt dry as they came up from his throat.

The woman heaved several times and then sat up on the bed. "The baby was backward. His feet came out where the head should be." Her voice shook and she stopped to cry for several long seconds. "The midwife did what she could, but there was so much blood. My Lina tried to be strong, but the blood was too much."

Khaled couldn't see any blood. For the first time, he looked down the length of Lina's body and saw that someone had covered her in their bedspread, the very same spread he'd pulled back and then blanketed his wife and himself with on the night of their wedding.

He ran his hand down the length of the bedspread and then looked at his mother-in-law. "I'm sorry Dario could not find me sooner."

The woman stroked her daughter's hair. "She said she saw you. That was the last thing she said."

She collapsed back on her daughter again. Khaled closed his eyes, willing the vision of the garden to return. But the only vision that came to him was of Lina calling his name as her life faded.

"The boy is quiet now, Khaled. Would you like to come to meet him?"

The voice came from behind him, toward the door. Khaled turned toward the sound to find Cinthya, Dario's wife. "The boy?"

"Your son was crying very hard. I gave him some milk and he's settled now. He's sleeping in the living room."

Khaled looked toward Lina and then back at Cinthya, standing. "The baby is alive?"

"Very much alive if his screaming is any indication."

Feeling unsteady, Khaled sat on the edge of the bed. "Can you bring him to me? I don't want to leave Lina."

"Of course."

Cinthya returned moments later carrying a sleeping infant wrapped so completely in a blanket that only his tiny face showed. Cinthya extended the baby toward him and Khaled reached for it tentatively, surprised by the child's bulk. He studied the child's splotched face, searching for the ways in which Lina would appear on it as the years went by.

He looked up at Cinthya. "A boy, you said?"

"Yes, Khaled. You have a new son."

A new son. Khaled held the child to his chest, feeling the boy's placid breathing. *On a day when I've lost more than I ever thought I could lose, I have a new son.*

He hugged the child to his breast and wondered how their unimagined future would unfold.

∾

NEW YORK, 2010

Alex helped Angélica into her sweater and they stepped into the cooling pre-fall air. The food at Del Posto had been especially good tonight, as had been the '04 Conterno Barolo. The latter seemed to warm Angélica considerably, as their conversation grew relaxed and her hand on his more sensual after the somewhat tense start to the dinner.

As they hit the street, Angélica turned to him and kissed him deeply, her mouth tasting of fine Italian wine and the butterscotch of her dessert. He wrapped an arm around her as they began to walk down Tenth Avenue.

"This has been a very pleasant night," she said dreamily.

Alex tugged her a little closer. "It has. And it is still young."

"Yes, it is."

He kissed the top of her head. "Why don't we stop by SoHo House for a drink or two?"

Alex felt Angélica pull slightly away from him. "Do you really want to do that?"

"We always have a good time there."

"I'd been thinking of a different kind of good time. Especially with you leaving tomorrow morning."

Alex leaned into her. "And we will definitely have that kind of good time as well." He looked at

Angélica, but couldn't read her expression. "Come on. We love it there and I'm going to be living the life of a monk for the next two weeks. I need one more loud crowd. You can order one of those crazy drinks you like. We won't stay long, I promise."

Angélica leaned her head against his shoulder as they walked, letting out a long sigh. Their nights before his trips had always been especially passionate and he would make sure that this one was no different. He never wanted Angélica to feel neglected by him in any way.

For now, though, he wanted a little more time around people. The idea of spending an extended period in the austere environment of an ashram seemed appealing in an exotic way, but Alex still felt the need to fortify himself for the trip.

Alex had been a member of Soho House since the private club opened in 2003. The nondescript exterior of the half-block long building in the now fully emergent Meatpacking District offered an understated calling card to the careful detail and elegance contained within. The club's six floors housed a hotel where Alex had often put up corporate guests, a spa, a screening room, a library, a rooftop pool, and the restaurant and bar. Alex had spent time at all of these facilities (including the hotel during the darkest days of his marriage), but it was at the bar that he felt most at home. Members of SoHo House ranged from celebrities to corporate giants to the media elite, but at the U-shaped bar and surrounding leather sofas, they merged into a casual and cohesive whole. As Angélica and he entered the room, Alex nodded to Talia Matson, the long-legged star of the summer's surprise blockbuster comedy, Gene Borlotti, who'd just picked up his eighth Clio for advertising art direction, Nancy Sun, SVP of marketing for Luisant Cosmetics, and Mort Brown, the ancient saxophonist who made a killing in Manhattan real estate in the fifties and liked the company of men half his age and women a quarter of it.

As they prepared to sit, Parker Harding gestured them over to his table of six. Now in his mid-forties, Parker had written a novel in his early twenties that had served as the clarion call for his generation. The fact that he'd only written two coolly received novels and a lauded collection of essays since didn't prevent him from keeping his name in the press and on the city's A-lists.

"Now the evening can finally start," Parker said to his guests as Alex and Angélica sat. "We've been spending the last couple of hours telling ourselves how important we are to the culture. It'll be nice to have someone at the table who is actually doing something with his life."

Alex grinned. "You must be doing *something*, Parker. Considering how much I read about you, I'd say that you're doing quite a bit."

"That's how my publicist justifies her ludicrous monthly fees."

A waiter came to the table and Alex ordered a snifter of Delamain Cognac. Angélica, taking Alex's earlier suggestion, ordered a Honeyberry Margarita. Parker ordered a refill of his specialty martini and then introduced Alex and Angélica to the others. As was usual with Parker, his cohorts tonight were primarily literati. Alex guessed that all of them were here on Parker's tab, though it was entirely possible that at least one of them had achieved some level of commercial success. As much as Alex wanted to read more books, he rarely had time for it. His daily regimen included cover-to-cover reviews of the *Financial Times* and the *Wall Street Journal*. He also perused *The Economist* and *Barron's* every week and any number of business magazines monthly. Along with the endless reports he received from his staff, his eyes couldn't absorb much more.

"We were having a lively conversation about legacies just before you arrived," Parker said.

"Really?" Alex said. "Yours, of course, is assured."

"Assured, but not complete," a woman at the end of the table said. Though Parker had introduced Alex to her only minutes before, Alex had already forgotten her name. That only meant one thing to him. "From the portions Parker has let me read of his new novel, his legacy has only begun,"

Parker tipped his glass toward the woman and then Alex. "Thank you both. Of course, I'm paying for Emily's drinks, so her enthusiasm might be suspect. Alex, are you telling me that I need to pay for your drinks as well?"

Alex held up his hands. "My enthusiasm comes free of charge."

Parker nodded. "We've been talking about how much time one should dedicate to the task of considering one's legacy."

Alex's drink arrived and he took a sip before responding. "Does 'none' count as an acceptable amount?"

Carson Barnes, an impish magazine editor with excessive ear hair tipped his head toward Alex. "Are you seriously saying you don't think about the mark you're leaving on the world? Aren't you doing your best to become a legend on two shores?"

Alex scowled. "I'm doing my best to be a successful entrepreneur. If that makes me a legend anywhere, it's just a byproduct."

"Alex shuns publicity," Parker said. "He's the anti-me. Still, I would think that anyone who has accomplished anything wonders about and even works toward the impact those accomplishments have on the future."

Alex looked over at Angélica and laughed. "If I live to be a hundred, I'll think about such things. Until then, I have too much else on my plate."

Parker seemed baffled by this. He shifted his focus. "Angélica, you write about celebrities, don't you?"

Angélica rolled her eyes. "Never, actually."

Parker furrowed his brows. "Hmm. Well, certainly you write about people who *do things*."

"Well, yes. Readers wouldn't be particularly interested in stories about people who didn't do things."

"And don't you think those people think about their legacies?"

Angélica took Alex's hand and kissed it while keeping her attention on Parker. "I don't know. It doesn't usually come up in conversation. If you're asking if I think accomplished people *should* think about their legacies, I'd have to say yes." She squeezed Alex's hand at this point. "I think an individual's effect on future generations can be enormous. I think if you're conscious of this, you make different decisions."

Parker raised his new martini in Angélica's direction and then glanced over at Alex. "What is it like to be dating a woman who is so much smarter than you?"

Alex took Angélica's hand and raised it to his lips, pausing a moment before kissing it. "At least you know I'm not dating her because she agrees with everything I say."

The conversation thankfully slipped from this topic a few minutes later. Alex had a second cognac and, when she finished her margarita, Angélica ordered something neon-colored. Meanwhile, several other people stopped by to say hello, one member of the group left, and a number of others sat down. By the time Alex was ready for a third drink, the gathering numbered a dozen. When the waiter came by again, Alex asked that he put all of the drinks on Alex's house account and then stood. Angélica got up quickly to join him.

"Why don't we take this party over to my apartment?" he said to the assemblage, counting the number at the table one more time to be certain.

Parker agreed loudly and others started to rise.

Angélica touched him on the arm. "But Alex, your early flight tomorrow."

He kissed her brow. "Just a nightcap. Or two."

Angélica dropped her head and Alex had momentary second thoughts about the invitation. She usually had as much fun with large gatherings as he did, and he certainly wasn't concerned about getting sleep before he boarded the plane in the morning, but for some reason she didn't seem thrilled about this. Should he switch gears?

Before he could think about it more, though, he caught Parker's eye. Parker nodded to him to lead the way toward the exit.

When they got to the apartment, Alex guided everyone toward the living room while he headed into the kitchen. In the freezer, as anticipated, the housekeeper had left a dozen glasses with ice on a tray along with two bottles of Imperia Vodka. Alex pulled out the tray, dumped the ice, and filled the glasses before bringing the drinks to his guests.

"Did I mention that I am going to be embarking on a spiritual journey tomorrow?" he said to the group as they took their glasses.

Carson swigged his vodka. "Aren't you on a spiritual journey every day, bowing at the altar of capitalism?"

Alex chose to ignore the sarcasm of someone he'd just welcomed into his home. "This is a different kind of spiritual journey. An ashram in Southern California."

Parker let out an exaggerated gasp. "Are you saying that you've found God?"

Alex laughed. "I'm saying that I'm going to see if he'll accept my phone call."

Alex hadn't intended this to be as much of a conversation starter as it turned out to be. Talk of religion and spirituality carried considerably more momentum than the earlier discussion about legacies. It lasted through both bottles of Imperia and half a bottle of Grey Goose. The only thing that stilled it was Emily's wandering over to the corner of the living room, where she found Alex's rosewood Gibson SJ-200 guitar sitting on its stand.

"Hey Alex, do you play this?" she said, managing to elevate her voice above the din.

Alex grinned. "On special occasions, I do, yes."

She carried the instrument toward him. By the way she held it, it was clear that she had no idea how much the guitar cost. "This is a special occasion, isn't it?"

While several others cheered Alex on, Parker said, "When did you find the time to learn guitar?"

Alex took the guitar from Emily and strummed it. He looked at Parker. "I didn't say I played it well."

"What are you going to play for us?" came a voice from Alex's left.

Alex regarded the group. "You really want me to play a song?"

Parker pressed his palms together and bowed toward Alex. "Please do."

Alex put the strap around his shoulders and got a pick from the drawer of a lamp table. "I'll play you a classic folk song from the place of my birth. Where I come from, women sing their children to sleep at night with this song, and grown men cry when they sing it together at celebratory events."

He checked the tuning on the guitar. Then, with a smile he couldn't repress, he started to sing Boston's "More than a Feeling." *I looked out this monring and the sun was gone....*

Several people laughed when he started, obviously expecting a Latin lullaby, but many came to join him in the chorus.

Angélica had stopped drinking after her first glass. As the last few guests lingered, he noticed that she was struggling to stay awake on the couch next to him. However, Emily, on his other side, was as vibrant as ever. Since they'd gotten to the apartment, she been trying to corner him for conversation, and since they'd been sitting, she'd been touching his arm and leg repeatedly.

"I do need to get up awfully early for my trip tomorrow," Alex said to those who remained, standing and guiding them toward the door. He received an extended goodbye from Emily, who seemed bent on making an impression. She succeeded, though Alex doubted that it was the one she wanted to make.

By the time he turned back to the living room, Angélica had gone into the bedroom. He found her brushing her teeth in the bathroom, and he kissed her lightly on the cheek. "That was certainly an animated group. Parker's friends might not do much with their lives, but they certainly know how to talk about *anything*."

"Mmm," Angélica said, putting her toothbrush away and heading out of the bathroom.

Alex finished preparing for bed a few minutes later. He'd packed earlier and now he checked to make sure he hadn't forgotten anything. Then he stripped and slid under the covers toward Angélica, surprised to find that she was wearing one of his T-shirts.

"Everything is ready for tomorrow?" she said flatly.

"Everything." He pulled her against him and began to stroke her hair. "The night isn't as young as it once was, but...."

"I'm afraid the night got old for me an hour and a half ago."

The words stopped his hand in mid-motion. "Really?"

Angélica held his eyes with hers. "This wasn't exactly what I had in mind." She reached toward him and kissed him lightly on the lips. "Goodnight, Alex. Wake me before you go."

With that, she closed her eyes and turned away from him, leaving Alex feeling confused and unfulfilled. He propped himself up and watched Angélica, eyes closed, turned away from him. Her body language was unmistakable, but he couldn't read anything more than that.

Lying back on his pillow, he stared at the ceiling for a moment, trying to comprehend the abruptness with which this night had ended. If he'd known Angélica was going to be so cold to him, he wouldn't have broken up the party.

He shook his head, turned on his side away from Angélica, and closed his eyes, feeling more than ever that he needed this trip to California.

≈

ANHELO, 1928

Vidente awoke with the image of a nearby land in her head. She always dreamt vividly and often spent the early minutes of any day thinking about what her dreams meant. This particular dream was especially vivid, though; the type of vision that she usually only had when awake. She saw a sign at a train station reading DEBERES, a town whose name she'd never heard before, felt herself getting down from the train, and smelled the food that vendors were selling on the sidewalk. She even felt cobblestones under her feet as she walked from the station to a shop down the street. It was all very real.

When she got out of bed, she learned from a book that Deberes was in Mediana, the country south along the coast from Legado. Was this the trip her earlier vision had told her she was going to be making? According to the book, Deberes was about fifty miles inland from the coast, along a flat plain. She knew from the sensations she felt while trying to read Ana those many weeks ago that her fateful journey was going to take her to the mountains, so this could not be that trip. Yet her instincts told her that she needed to take it, and that she should go soon.

When Javier came to visit that afternoon, Vidente asked him to accompany her. Her son told her that this was a very busy time for the shops and that something important was happening at the sugar refinery; he wouldn't be able to go for at least a week.

"I don't want to wait a week," Vidente said. "I was thinking I would go tomorrow."

"I'm sorry, Mother, but there's no way for me to make this trip in the next few days." He threw out his hands as though to say that she was foolish for even thinking he would be available. Then he added, "When was the last time you were in Mediana?"

"I haven't been out of Legado since your father died."

"You know that you can't go there by yourself, don't you?"

Vidente was fully aware of Mediana's reputation as a nation of bandits and a place especially inhospitable to women. Now it was her turn to make a dismissive gesture. "Of course I know that. Why do you think I was asking you to come with me?"

Javier looked at her as though she were a small child. "I just don't want you thinking that you'll follow this vision even if no one else can go with you."

"I never said that I would do that," Vidente said, though she knew she was going to take this trip under any circumstance. "I'll ask your brother."

Javier scoffed. "If Mauricio is willing to go with you to Mediana, I'll run around the square in an ass's costume."

Javier had no reason to worry about embarrassing himself in this way. Mauricio was of course busy. However, Vidente's nephew Humberto agreed to accompany her. Humberto was very quiet and he wouldn't make for an entertaining traveling companion, but he was also very large and athletic, an important trait in Mediana. Vidente was certain that Humberto's heft would keep her safe, even if he said very few words during the four-hour train ride.

They left that Tuesday. As expected, Humberto spent most of the journey staring out the window, leaving Vidente to the escape of the novel she'd brought with her and another of her favorite exercises – reading her fellow passengers. The woman three rows up and to the left had strong anxieties about her romantic future. From what Vidente could glean, she guessed that the woman believed that her husband didn't love her anymore. The man sitting opposite her was worried about the pain that was building in his stomach. Vidente might have said something to him about this, but she knew that it was already too late for the man to do anything to save himself from the disease. Vidente scanned others to pass the time. One worried that someone would learn his secret; one thrilled at the prospect of seeing her grandchildren; one felt excitement about starting life over in a new town; and one simply counted backward from one hundred.

The hours passed quickly even though her only conversation with Humberto came when she bought him a torta in the dining car. It was mid-afternoon when the train pulled up to Deberes. Vidente's car stopped directly in front of the station sign, just as it had in her dream. Other moments from the dream materialized as well. A man bumped her right shoulder on the way out of the train. A baby squealed. A vendor hawked empanadas while another shouted headlines from the day's newspapers.

Without thinking much about a direction, Vidente found herself on the cobblestone street leading away from the train station.

"Do you know where we are going?" Humberto said. It was the first time he'd spoken to her all day without her saying something first.

Vidente looked up and down the bustling street, hoping for something to point her in a particular way. Her dream had only taken her to the cobblestones. Shrugging, she pointed to her right and said, "Let's go over there."

For a small town inland from the coast and far away from Mediana's bigger cities, Deberes was surprisingly busy. Dozens of people strode down the street, children played games and wove in and around other pedestrians, and shopkeepers called attention to their wares. They passed a cobbler, a butcher, and a store that sold exotic crafts. Certainly, her dream had not sent her here to repair her shoes or to buy a joint of meat. But why had it sent her here?

They came to a street corner across from which she counted eight men about her age simply standing around talking. They didn't seem to have gathered for any particular purpose and they didn't seem to be headed anywhere. They simply stood and talked quietly, with little animation. In Anhelo, men sat around at cafés. Here, it appeared they just stood. Looking beyond the men, Vidente saw an understated sign for an antiques store. For the first time since she exited the train, something called to her.

She gestured toward Humberto and then pointed to the store. "Let's go over there."

The store was dusty and cluttered. The goods seemed to have no sense of order to them. Decorative items, housewares, jewelry, books, and paintings were interspersed, as though a child had simply dropped them where he had lost interest in them.

The shop owner, or whomever it was who sat behind a counter in a far corner of the store, was definitely not a child. With unkempt white hair and a thick white beard, he looked like he might have been an elderly man when the oldest of the items he sold had first been made. Vidente caught his eye and he grinned, showing youthfulness in his eyes that he didn't express anywhere else.

"Welcome back," he said with a surprisingly strong voice.

Vidente nodded toward him. "Thank you."

"It has been a long time. So good to see you again."

Humberto leaned toward her and whispered, "Tia Vidente, you've been here before?"

Vidente shook her head quickly. She didn't want to appear rude to the shop owner, who'd obviously mistaken her for someone else. The thought of this left Vidente feeling a bit uneasy. She couldn't recall ever being confused with another person.

She thanked the man again for his hospitality and walked toward a table that held a variety of spun goods, some candlesticks, a framed map, and a brazier. She picked up a scarf of vermillion, auburn, and cerulean, the threads woven together in spirals. It was in perfect condition except for a fray along one side. She thought that Humberto's sister might like this very much. Vidente put it back on the table, but reminded herself to look at it again before leaving the store. The map was of the Legado city of Joya de la Costa, an odd thing to find in a small town in Mediana. It had been a long time since Vidente had been to that coastal city. She'd gone with her sister and brother-in-law and they stayed on the ocean and visited the most remarkable garden. Perhaps she'd get this for Fernanda as a reminder of that time. It had been a truly lovely few days.

The longer she stayed in the store, the more Vidente had the feeling that she'd come here for a reason. But surely, that reason couldn't be to purchase trinkets for her loved ones. Anhelo had no shortage of antiques shops. She frequented them often, collecting items that she subsequently displayed all throughout her house. If she wanted presents for her family, she didn't need to go to another country to acquire them. For that matter, she didn't even need to leave her home, as she already had so much she had to give away before her time ran out.

Humberto had left her side to examine some wooden carvings. Vidente glanced over at him and then turned in the opposite direction to go toward another table. The shop owner had come up beside her, surprising her with his sudden presence.

"We have gotten so many new things since you were here last," he said brightly. "Did you notice the crystal? It came from a wealthy man in Bahia de Puesta del Sol after his wife died."

Vidente followed the man's pointed finger toward four beautifully cut glasses. Perhaps the woman he'd mistaken her for had an interest in these, but crystal had never appealed much to Vidente.

The man waved the pointed hand. "Not for you, of course. I just thought I'd point them out." He took her arm and tugged her gently toward a case in the front of the store. "You might find these interesting, though."

Vidente's eyes fell on a display of rings. Several sported oversized garishly colored stones. They immediately brought to mind local women in Anhelo who wore such things ostentatiously, somehow believing that others found this kind of showiness impressive. Not all of the rings in the display were like that, though. Vidente leaned to examine the collection more closely. The shop owner opened the case, removed the display, and set it on a table next to her. Now that she was this close to the rings, Vidente could see how cheaply made they were. Together, the display represented a collection of common items pretending to be something more. Vidente wondered briefly if she should find it offensive that the shop owner picked these out for her, but then she accepted the gesture.

She examined the case again and found that one ring called to her, even though it might have been the humblest of all. Vidente couldn't be positive, but she guessed it was made of tin. Yet it had a level of dignity the other rings lacked. Someone had taken time to make this ring carefully, weaving strands of metal together to form a complex design. She took the ring from its holder and held it between her thumb and forefinger. The dull finish seemed to absorb light, yet it also compelled her to keep looking. Vidente had no need for a ring. Nor could she think of anyone she would give it to. As modest as the materials were that made it, the artistry of the ring demanded that one bestow it upon its recipient with much more ceremony than a mother, a sister, an aunt, or a neighbor could provide.

"I'll take this," she said, extending the ring to the shop owner.

"Yes, of course."

He took the ring and walked Vidente to the counter, where she paid him for it.

"Do you want to wear it now?"

Vidente looked at the shop owner with curiosity. Wear it? She hadn't considered the idea of putting it on her finger at all. In fact, she had no idea if it would even fit.

"No, it's not for me."

"Oh, I see. My mistake."

He put the ring in a small bag and handed it to her. What *was* she going to do with it? Vidente had endless pieces of jewelry stored in boxes waiting for a turn for her to wear them around town. She didn't want to put this in one of those boxes, though. Rings became anonymous there. At the same time, she couldn't put it on display somewhere in the house. It was too small and it would blend too easily into the background. Another puzzle to ponder. She walked over to Humberto, who was running his fingers along the side of a carved bookend.

"Do you have books to hold up?" she said lightly, knowing that Humberto was not a reader at all.

Humberto's eyes stayed fixed on the dark wood. "The use of the fishtail tool is magnificent here. So many tiny curves."

Vidente examined the bookend more closely. "I didn't know you cared so much about crafts."

Humberto finally looked at her. "Only this type of craft. This artist loved his work. I love how an artist can bring things alive in wood. "

"Really? You've never told me about this before." Vidente nearly laughed to herself when she said this, realizing as the words left her mouth that Humberto didn't tell her about *anything*.

He put down the bookend and turned away from the table. "Father thinks I don't have the talent."

Vidente didn't find this surprising. Her severe brother-in-law was especially judgmental; never more so than with his son. She'd often considered Humberto disinterested in nearly everything. The passion he expressed when he held the wood in his hands, though, made her wonder if his father had belittled him into indifference. She would discuss this with her sister the next time she saw her.

"Would you like me to buy those bookends for you?"

Humberto seemed embarrassed by the question. "No, no. My father will only ask me why I wasted your money since I don't have anything to do with books."

Vidente felt anger reaching under her, but she pushed it back. "You've come with me on a long trip. This would hardly be payment enough."

Without waiting for a response, she picked up the bookends and took them to the shop owner. Humberto followed her closely.

"By the way," Vidente said, "this was a fortuitous time for me to learn about your interest in woodworking. I need a new decorative shelf in my dining room. I was going to hire one of the local artisans, but I'd far rather hire my nephew. Do you think you could do that for me?"

Humberto's eyes brightened. "I'd like that, Tia Vidente."

They left the store with their bags, Humberto's much larger than Vidente's, and spent the next few hours visiting the other shops of Deberes. They looked at many things and Vidente exchanged pleasantries with several other shop owners, but she didn't purchase anything else. Vidente kept waiting for the sensation that she felt when she first saw the sign for the antique shop – actually, she was looking for a sensation considerably stronger than that – but one never came. When the late afternoon train heading toward Anhelo arrived, she and Humberto boarded it.

"Thank you for coming with me today," Vidente said to her nephew as they settled in their seats.

"You're welcome, Tia Vidente." He hesitated, and then asked timidly, "Did you find what you hoped to find?"

Vidente's brow creased. Then she smiled at Humberto. "Of course I did. We found your wooden carvings, didn't we?"

Humberto hefted his bag. "So your vision was about buying this?"

"That and hiring you to beautify my dining room."

Humberto nodded slowly. "I didn't realize your vision was all about me."

This seemed to make her nephew happy, though Vidente had made the comment flippantly. *Maybe Humberto was the reason for this trip,* Vidente thought, confused by the vagueness of this experience after the vividness of the dream. *That explanation is as good as any other.*

She looked down at the bag she held in her hands. "I never showed you the ring I bought," she said, pulling it out of the bag and holding it up for Humberto. "Beautiful, isn't it?"

6.

PALESTINE, 1921

The baby awoke as the ship entered port. Khaled held three-month-old Leandro to his chest and thought about whether to feed him before they disembarked. His son had been remarkably good during the long trip, taking lengthy naps, smiling readily for fellow passengers, and allowing the many women who asked to hold him to do so without complaint. It would easily be another hour before they could get off the ship; there was no reason to make Leandro wait to eat. Holding the baby with one arm, Khaled reached into his bag and retrieved the bottle he'd filled with milk at the ship's galley an hour earlier. Leandro started to fuss as he did so, but immediately settled when the nipple reached his mouth.

"Drink your fill, little boy," Khaled said to the sucking child. "You deserve it. You've been a very good traveling companion, you know? This is good.

I promise you that we will go on long trips together in the future since you are such a fine traveler. We will see things, you and I."

While Khaled was speaking, Leandro locked onto his eyes. He'd seemed so attentive from the moment Khaled first held him. Cinthya tried to tell him that a baby's eyes don't see much for the first few weeks, but Khaled didn't believe it. His son knew who his father was and he held his gaze with great intensity. It was as though he understood that he'd already lost the most important thing in his life and he wanted to make sure he didn't lose sight of his only remaining parent. Khaled tried to assure him in every way he could think of that the baby had no reason to worry that such a thing might happen.

As every day passed, Leandro seemed to take on more of Lina's characteristics. His hair had started to come in and it already showed some of his mother's dark waviness. His mouth had Lina's shape and Khaled could swear he heard some of Lina's intonation in the nonsense syllables that came from that mouth.

"Will your words sound like songs the way your mother's did?" Khaled said. "That would be a very good thing, even for a boy. The girls will love that." He adjusted the bottle to make sure the milk kept flowing. "At least the girls in Legado would. Here, I'm not so sure."

Leandro had drunk half of the bottle rapidly. With effort, Khaled pried the bottle from the baby's mouth and put him up on his shoulder, patting the boy's back until he issued a belch that sounded like it came from a sixty-year-old man instead of a little child.

Khaled held Leandro out in front of him and smiled at him. "The girls won't like that so much, though. Let's just keep the burping between you and me, okay? It'll be one of those father-son things."

The boy smiled back and his entire body wiggled. Khaled hugged him tightly and kissed the top of his head before returning him to the rest of his meal. Leandro was finished and bouncing on Khaled's knee when the ship came to a halt. A short while later, they had their luggage and they set foot on shore. A shore that only a few months ago Khaled believed he'd never see again.

The decision to leave Joya de la Costa and to return to Bethlehem had not been an easy one for Khaled to make. Khaled had his thriving business. He had the friends and neighbors he'd grown so fond of and the lush, colorful land that had enchanted him at first sight. Most of all, he had the reminders of Lina. She was everywhere for him in Joya de la Costa. In their home, of course, everything bore her touch – the tiles she'd painted in the kitchen, the dolls she'd arranged on the side table in the living room, the sheets and pillows she'd enchanted with her presence, and her unmistakable scent in the bedroom.

The streets echoed her as well. A flowerpot set off memories of Lina's magnificent garden. A café sent him back to the moment when they first met. A giggle from a passerby brought Lina's laughter to his ears, and two lovers walking hand-in-hand reminded him of Lina's thigh against his.

For two months, Khaled tried to remain convinced that he could maintain a life for Leandro and himself in Joya de la Costa. Cinthya and the other neighbors would help while Khaled sold his wares. While the butler would be no help, the maid he'd hired to assist Lina could be useful. Then, at night, he would take care of the boy, feeding him, rocking him to sleep, and waking up with him in the middle of the night to offer him the food and the soothing the baby needed. They would be a family together.

But two months was enough time for Khaled to realize that he couldn't take care of a child by himself. Cinthya had a sick adult daughter and many grandchildren. The other neighbors had lives of their own. The maid was far more adept at cleaning the kitchen than she was at nurturing a child. These were good people and they genuinely seemed to want to help. Asking them to aid him in raising Leandro was asking too much, though, more of an imposition than you could make upon those who did not share your blood.

After these two months, Khaled sent a letter to his sister, Leila, telling her that he would be returning to Palestine and letting her know about everything that had happened to him when he was in Legado. Khaled did not like writing letters and his only communication to the country of his birth had been the occasional telegram to his brother asking for more supplies. His brother never wrote back, though the deliveries always came in a timely fashion. Leila didn't write back either – no one in the family ever had any need for letter-writing because no one had ever gone away as Khaled had – but he knew that she wouldn't refuse his request to help him raise Leandro. She had four children of her own and she knew all of the things that women instinctively knew about child rearing that Khaled could never hope to learn. Adding Leandro to her brood would be entirely natural to her.

Two things struck Khaled immediately as he carried his son down the pier. One was that the aromas were headier here than they were in Legado. For the first time since he'd been on this pier to go in the other direction, Khaled longed for some of the foods of his native land.

The other was the color, or more specifically the relative lack of color. The landscape here wasn't necessarily dull, but it paled in comparison to Legado's vibrancy and the incomparable hues of Joya de la Costa. This was a beige world; Legado was a rainbow.

Khaled received the first confirmation that Leila had received his letter when he saw her husband Ali waving to him from the end of the pier. Since his hands were full with Leandro and luggage, Khaled could not wave back, but he smiled and tipped his head in greeting.

Just then, the boy standing next to Ali turned around and the sight caused Khaled's knees to buckle. It was the image of Khaled's son Tarek. But Tarek was dead, killed with Nahla and their daughters. Why had his ghost come to haunt him upon his return to Palestine?

For a long moment, Khaled could not keep moving forward. He could only stare at the boy. Tarek would have been fifteen now. His face showed greater definition and his shoulders were broader. Did ghosts continue to age? "Why have you stopped walking, Khaled?" Ali said from perhaps twenty meters away. "Tarek and I have been waiting a long time. We want to get home and we still have a very long trip."

Ali could see Tarek as well. Confusion petrified Khaled. He wasn't sure he could have moved his legs even if he tried to do so with all of his will. Time passed and people walked around him, several times cutting off Khaled's vision of his son and his brother-in-law. The third time this happened, Khaled looked to his right as a caravan of men passed. When he turned back, Tarek was no more than a few steps from him.

The boy reached for one of Khaled's bags and Khaled let go of it involuntarily.

"You're alive," Khaled said haltingly.

Tarek stood up straight, his eyes accusatory. "Of course I'm alive. I didn't realize I was supposed to be dead until your letter came."

"But they told me you were dead."

"Who told you this?"

Khaled's legs still felt unsteady and he still hadn't moved from where he stood when he first saw his "dead" son. "Samih. His father has the mules. I saw him in Joya de la Costa."

Tarek's stance slackened and his eyes clouded. "And you didn't think to confirm this?" There was insolence in the boy's tone. Tarek had never spoken to Khaled with the reverent tone that one should use with one's father, but now he was being flatly disrespectful.

"Why should I doubt Samih? He told it to me as a fact."

"Mother wrote you three times," the boy said sharply. "You never responded to any of our letters. It was we who were beginning to wonder if you were dead – except that we knew Uncle Rashid kept sending things to you."

Khaled had never received any of the letters. He'd heard from others that the mails between Palestine and Legado were unreliable, even though a ship arrived every two weeks. But none of the three letters?

"Your mother is also still alive?"

"Yes, even though you left her completely without money."

"And your sisters?"

"*Everyone* is alive. The old woman down the road died. Did Samih fail to mention that?"

Khaled couldn't find any words. Tarek was alive in front of him. Nahla was alive. May and Mona as well. He had been certain that all of them were dead. He'd been sure of it from the moment Samih brought him the news. He'd even held a service to honor them.

Leandro began to fuss and wriggle. Khaled hefted and rocked the baby to quiet him.

"So this is your new son," Tarek said.

Tending to his baby gave Khaled something to do with his body. "His name is Leandro."

"A foreign name." Tarek said with disgust. "Have you become a foreigner, Father?"

At that moment, Ali came up next to Tarek. Had Nahla moved in with Ali and Leila when the money ran out? Khaled had returned to Palestine in the hopes that Leila would help him raise his son. It now appeared that she had already been doing that.

"Let's go home," Ali said. "We've been waiting a long time and I'm sure your trip was taxing on you."

Ali took Khaled's other piece of luggage, leaving him holding only Leandro. Tarek stared at him – it seemed as though he'd been staring at him the entire time – and Khaled glanced at him quickly before he finally found a way to get his legs moving again.

The journey back was still not finished. It was more than two hours later when they entered Ali's modest home. Leandro had fallen asleep in Khaled's arms. Khaled wished he could have also arrived in such a casual manner. Ali's three sons wrapped themselves around their father's legs when he opened the door. Behind them stood Leila who only bowed her head at her brother.

At which point Nahla stepped into the foyer, flanked by the two girls. The children didn't move toward him in any way, as though he were a stranger or an unwelcome guest in their home. Tarek walked around Khaled and led each of his sisters by the hand out of the hallway. Ali also left with his children. Khaled, Nahla, and Leila stood silently for several seconds.

"Welcome back, brother," Leila said before turning and walking away.

For an eternal moment, husband and wife stood absolutely still. Then Nahla took a number of steps in Khaled's direction. At first, it seemed to Khaled that she was planning to hug him. But when she reached out her arms, she directed them toward Leandro instead. Khaled released his slumbering child to his wife who wasn't dead, and tried unsuccessfully to imagine a more uncomfortable homecoming.

Nahla held the infant to her chest and the boy cooed in his sleep, adjusting his head to snuggle. Nahla patted him on the back.

"Leila tells me his name is Leandro. Is that right?"

"Yes, it is."

She tucked her chin against Leandro's hair. "It is very sad about his mother."

Khaled knew that he would never be able to express to Nahla the sadness he felt at losing Lina or the grief he felt that his child would never know his mother. "That is kind of you to say."

She made eye contact with Khaled for the first time then, before quickly glancing away. She hugged the baby closer. "This child needs to sleep. I will take him to the crib we have set up for him."

Nahla left the foyer, leaving Khaled standing there, his luggage by his side.

"Samih told me," he said to her retreating back. Again, he felt disinclined to move.

He had returned to his homeland. But he didn't feel at all at home.

✑

WASHINGTON, DC, 1987

"**M**adame Ambassador, I have sensational news," Dro said into the phone through a broad grin.

"Really, Professor? And what would that be?"

Viviana had taken to calling him "Professor" in the last few months, since he reported his grades from his first semester at MIT. He wondered what she was going to nickname him when he told her the reason for this call. "I'm no longer a provisional student at MIT."

"Well, that *is* good news."

"It is, but it isn't *the* good news. That would be that they've offered me a full scholarship for my last two years."

Viviana squealed, which made her sound much more like one of the coeds on campus than an important dignitary. "How fantastic for you. I knew something like this would happen, of course. You've been so dedicated to your work. At least when I haven't been *distracting* you."

Dro thought about the "distractions" Viviana had been providing on occasion during their dalliances over the past year. The memory of her last trip to Boston set off rifle shots of erotic memories. Cambridge held an abundance of sexual pleasures for Dro and he'd quickly learned to use his "exotic" heritage to his advantage there, but none of the women he slept with on campus could come close to electrifying him physically the way Viviana did.

"Come down here," Viviana said, shaking him from his ruminations. "We need to celebrate. I've been feeling the desperate need for a 'celebration' with you for the past few weeks anyway. When can you make it to DC?"

"I'm starting a summer internship with an investment bank on Monday."

"Then come down this weekend. I'm supposed to be receiving the head of the Chamber of Commerce from Cima Saturday afternoon, but I'll make it short. Señor Fonseca is a very dull man. And you, Professor, are most definitely not dull."

Viviana chuckled, this time sounding not the least bit girlish. This took Dro back to a similar chuckle she offered after he'd brought her to ecstasy in the back of a cab on his last trip to Washington. It was just another of the many sexual highlights their trysts had provided. If Dro were in fact Viviana's "boy toy," he was a toy with which she certainly seemed to enjoy playing.

"I'll come down Friday night."

"I'll book your suite at the Willard. Unless you'd like to stay somewhere else this time."

Dro laughed. "No, the Willard will be perfectly satisfactory."

As it turned out, the Willard was exceedingly satisfactory. They didn't even make it out of Dro's hotel room on Friday. Viviana joined him a little more than an hour after he arrived and they were naked only minutes later. It had been two months since the ambassador's last trip to Boston and she consumed Dro with a hunger that might have been overwhelming if it weren't so physically thrilling. Despite the difference in their ages, Dro felt like the one who needed to catch his breath during their sexual gymnastics. Viviana's stamina and energy made him consider the possibility that he needed to get in better shape, even though he'd maintained an athletic trim since he'd been a teenager and he worked out on campus four days a week.

As Viviana crested for the third time, Dro released himself, feeling as though he levitated from the bed for several seconds before a rush of pleasure threw his head back against his pillow. When he finished, Viviana finally slowed her bucking, grinning down at his spent body.

For the first time since she arrived, Dro took a moment to read the air around Viviana. Her aura was a radiant red. She was clearly enjoying herself. Dro had never had the discipline to read Viviana in the middle of their sexual exploits. If she were this red now, he could only imagine how hot she glowed as she approached orgasm. He told himself to try to check this the next time they made love, though he knew there was an excellent chance that his mind would be elsewhere.

Viviana disengaged and settled against him, pulling a sheet up with her, and kissing his neck. "It's good to see you again, Professor."

"Not as good as it is for me to see you, Madame Ambassador."

Viviana offered him a sultry smile and then nuzzled his neck again. She rested her head against his shoulder and played with the hair on his chest. "I'm very impressed with you, you know."

"Really? I would think that any man could bring you to three orgasms if given the right incentive."

She slapped his chest. "That's not what I'm talking about – though you are very impressive in that regard as well. I'm talking about your scholarship. Do you realize what you've accomplished in the past two years?"

"Ah, it was simple. These American universities are nothing compared to Legado high schools. Now getting out of *there* was a challenge."

She laid three kisses on his shoulder. "Don't be modest. What you've done is a tremendous thing. I'm proud of you."

Dro pulled her toward him and kissed her deeply on the lips. Surprisingly, he found himself stirring again. "Thank you."

"This scholarship is going to look very good on your resume."

He stroked the length of her arm. "As will the letter of recommendation from the world-famous ambassador from Legado."

She lay on her back and put her hands behind her head, allowing Dro to run his fingernails along her taut stomach. "So you think all of this bedroom pleasure is going to make me say nice things about you to a prospective employer?"

Dro propped himself up on one arm, his resurgent penis resting upon Viviana's hip. "You've seen right through my ploy."

Viviana shifted her leg to stroke him. "I don't write letters of recommendation for simply anyone, you know."

Dro climbed on top of her, entering her in one movement. "Then I'll just have to make sure I prove my worthiness."

Viviana threw her head back, arched her hips, and their conversation ended.

Breakfast the next morning was room service followed by a lengthy shower for two and then another tussle on the loveseat in the living room. In the early afternoon, Viviana donned oversized sunglasses and a fedora, and they took a cab to an outdoor café in Georgetown.

"I'm so glad you could come down this weekend," Viviana said after they ordered. "I'm leaving on Tuesday to go back to Legado and I'll be there for at least ten days." She shook her head slowly and, even though he couldn't see her eyes, Dro knew that something was troubling her. "As I'm sure you've heard on the news, the guerilla situation is boiling up to crisis level again."

Dro had been reading about the situation just a few days earlier. La Justicia, the guerilla organization founded more than forty years earlier and kept under some level of control by Legado's previous president, had been performing increasingly larger acts of terror over the past year. Only six months ago, they struck their largest nonmilitary target, blowing up a bus and killing all sixty-four passengers, including several children. In the period that ensued, the organization had kidnapped three wealthy executives, murdered a journalist, and set fire to a large flower farm.

"I'd heard that the violence had escalated," Dro said.

"And that is only what has been released to the media. I've implored the president to be transparent about everything because it will increase public support for action, but he fears the impact on tourism."

"I would guess that the impact on tourism would be much worse if La Justicia ever harmed an American or a European and the media found out that the president had been suppressing details of the guerillas' acts."

"None of us wants to consider such a possibility but, as we've discussed in the past, I have counseled the president about being more forthcoming and he has expressed very little interest in this counsel."

Dro recalled some of their earlier conversations about the topic. Interestingly, Viviana was never willing to discuss it over the phone. "Is that why you're going back to Legado now?"

"No. That subject is not open for discussion at the moment. However the guerillas are making noise about being considered a legitimate political party in Legado."

"Do you think they're serious about this?"

"It's doubtful. But we can't ignore it, either. They're sending several members of their leadership to Quesada and the president has asked me to be there."

"Are you nervous?"

Viviana tossed up her hands. "Only about wasting my time. I've known Guillermo Gordillo since I was in high school."

Dro leaned forward in his seat. "You're friends with the leader of La Justicia?"

Viviana shook her head quickly. "I wouldn't say that we're friends. No, no, I wouldn't say that at all.

But we know of each other and, more importantly, we both know where we came from. Gordillo is a radical and his methods have grown increasingly destructive, but he understands that we are both icons in our country. However, while he is an icon of fear, I am an icon of something else entirely. Attempting to take down an icon of my sort would have devastating implications for his cause. He will not give me trouble."

Lunch came a moment later and the conversation shifted to less daunting topics. Viviana discussed a recent state dinner and Dro contrasted this with details of his latest meeting with Susan, Professor Dodderington, and the other members of the metaphysical group he now met with weekly. Dro didn't mention how adept he'd become at reading auras, though he talked at length about his growing fascination with the science behind electromagnetic fields.

As always, the food was remarkable. Viviana had the ability to track down great cooking even when they went somewhere casual. She'd introduced him to places in Boston he'd never known existed, even though several of them fit within Dro's meager budget. Though they'd only been together a handful of times, Viviana had been responsible for nearly every great meal he'd eaten in America – and the few he'd eaten on a surprise weekend of erotic adventures in Paris.

Viviana huddled close to him on the cab ride back, stroking his arm. Dro briefly wondered if she were looking for a reprise of the taxi trip from his last visit, but when he moved to reposition himself, she simply pulled his hand to her lips and then snuggled closer.

Dro got out of the cab first when they arrived at the Willard. He'd just crossed the three-columned entrance and was nodding to the doorman when he heard a male voice call, "Ambassador Emisario?"

He turned toward the voice and saw a slim, graying man approaching from a limousine. Viviana was no more than three steps from Dro – close enough that he could hear her whisper to him, "I'll meet you upstairs." Then she extended her hand toward the man and greeted him cordially. Dro continued into the lobby, and then turned to watch Viviana at work for a minute. The gray man was easily a foot taller, yet somehow the ambassador seemed to gaze down upon him. *I need to learn how to do that*, Dro thought. At just over six feet, he was rarely at a height disadvantage, but the way Viviana positioned herself when she engaged another was about something else entirely, something that required special skill. He observed the two for another moment and then turned toward the elevators.

Viviana didn't come upstairs for nearly fifteen minutes. Dro had begun to wonder if she'd gone off with the gray man or if she'd forgotten that Dro was there. He could hardly have complained either way. He was well aware that Viviana's time was precious and that many clamored for a piece of it. As nothing more than one of Viviana's pleasurable diversions, he was low on the priority list. If she needed to do something other than shacking up with him, he would certainly understand.

When she opened the door to the suite, Viviana seemed rattled. It was the first time that Dro had ever seen any signs of stress on her face. Even when officials and aides had besieged her at her office on the first day he visited her, she seemed to become calmer as the demands on her grew.

"That man was the CEO of the largest telephone florist in America," she said. "He does a great deal of business with our country."

"Was he lobbying you for a better deal?"

Viviana took off her sunglasses and hat – had she been wearing them the entire time she spoke with the gray man? – and shrugged off the thin coat she had on, dropping it unceremoniously on a chair. "Not today. No, today he only seemed to want to make small talk."

Viviana said this stiffly, which confused Dro. "Why are you so upset, then?"

She sat on the sofa and put her feet up on the coffee table. "He wanted to know where my car and driver were. He knows that I tend not to go anywhere in Washington without my cortege. I think he might have seen us getting out of the cab together."

Dro tried a sly smile to cut the tension. "I'm surprised he could even tell who you were considering how you covered yourself up."

"Mr. Cain is very perceptive."

"Is that a problem?"

Viviana rolled her neck and then sat forward. "His brother is the publisher of *Icon* magazine."

Dro had seen the celebrity magazine at supermarket checkouts, but he'd never opened a copy.

From the covers, he assumed it focused on gossip. "Do you think he'll write about this?"

Viviana patted the seat next to her on the sofa and Dro joined her. "Probably not. They haven't written much about me since my divorce. They don't do book reviews and they certainly don't cover foreign policy. But this little episode has called attention to how I've been letting my guard down when we're together."

"I'm not sure you can disguise yourself better than you already have. To be honest, I thought the fedora was a little on the comical side."

"Then I'll need to find other ways to be circumspect." She took Dro's hand in both of hers. "It would not be good for our country for people to think their American ambassador was involved in a salacious affair with a boy less than half her age."

It was ironic, considering how steamy their encounters had been, but Dro had not considered what they were doing to be "salacious" until that moment. "Viviana, if this is going to cause a problem for you –"

"– No. That's not what I'm saying. No, not at all." As she did in the cab, she kissed his hand tenderly. "We just need to take special care in the future."

She moved into his arms again at that point. Not long after, she seemed to have set the incident aside. But Dro couldn't help wonder if their days together were approaching their end. For someone like Viviana Emisario, erotic adventures were one thing; careers were something else entirely.

❧

NEW YORK, 2010

At 5:45 a.m., fifty-three minutes after he started casting glances at his alarm clock, Alex decided to get out of bed. The alarm was set to go off in another fifteen minutes anyway, and he just didn't feel he could stay prone any longer.

He put the covers back in place and then, standing naked on his side of the bed, he watched Angélica's still form. She was curled away from him on the far edge of the king-size bed. From this perspective, it seemed as though she were yards away. She hadn't stirred while he had been tossing for most of the past hour, and she didn't budge now.

He stepped toward the bathroom, turning one more time to glance at Angélica. She'd never refused him sex before. She hadn't technically done so last night – only a few hours ago, actually – but he was certain of what would have happened if he'd tried to seduce her. It didn't require second sight to understand the signals she was sending out when he slipped in next to her after the party had ended.

Exhaling slowly, he went into the bathroom and started the shower. He took a little longer than he normally did under the water this morning. Lathering his hair with Sisley Botanical shampoo, he massaged his scalp for several minutes. He rarely allowed himself a luxury like this, but he had extra time before his driver arrived, and he imagined that the showers at the ashram were likely to be designed for function rather than comfort.

When he was finished, he wrapped himself in his cashmere micro cotton bath sheet without either toweling himself off or getting out of the shower. He felt water dribbling down his ankles and pooling around his feet. For several minutes, he held this pose, the inaction feeling both like a rare pleasure and like the only appropriate option. Then he finished getting ready to leave the apartment.

The mirror in the bathroom had steamed from the excessive run of hot water in the shower. While he brushed his teeth, he opened the door dividing the bathroom from the bedroom to let the humidity drop. He wouldn't normally do such a thing with Angélica still asleep for concerns about waking her, but he was uncomfortable. He needn't have worried in this case, though. When he came out of the bathroom fully dressed, she was still huddled on her edge of the bed.

He watched her intently for a long minute. A lock of her ebony hair had fallen over her eye, both underlining the peacefulness of her repose and sending subtle reminders of her allure. Angélica was a different kind of beautiful from any other woman he'd known. Her beauty pulled at him. Even now, when she was keeping her distance from him.

Drawing his eyes away from the woman he loved, he looked at the alarm clock on his night stand. He'd allowed himself considerably more time than he usually took to get ready. The excess minutes his early awakening afforded had evaporated, and now it was time to get going.

Angélica had told him to wake her up before he left. Considering the way things had ended last night, he never really considered it. And now he needed to leave. He thought about kissing her forehead, maybe brushing back that lock of hair, but he didn't want her to open her eyes now. It would not be good for him to stir her only to tell her that he needed to run. Instead, he touched her blanketed foot lightly on his way into the living room.

As he got to the foyer, he ran down his travel checklist one more time, finding that he'd covered everything. He picked up his luggage and then remembered that he hadn't packed anything to read. He'd already read the weekend editions of the *Financial Times* and *Wall Street Journal,* and his weekly magazines were already a week old. He could pick up a book or some magazines at the airport, but he didn't want something that would simply pass the time. He walked over to his bookshelf to see if anything seemed appealing among the books he'd collected but never had a chance to read. While browsing the shelves, he came upon a space left by a recently vacated volume. The missing book was on Angélica's night table. It was an ancient history of his family published in the mid-1930s by a small South American publisher. Alex hadn't read it himself since before he went to college, though he'd flipped through the pages every time he re-shelved the book after moving apartments. Angélica had taken the book into the bedroom a few days ago. To the best of his knowledge, though, she hadn't actually started reading it.

Realizing that he might make her angrier doing so, but also realizing that he felt a sudden need to dip into the distant past of his ancestors, Alex walked softly into the bedroom and took the book from the table, noticing that Angélica had turned in the other direction since he was last there. The book smelled musty and the jacket art had faded, but the pages seemed remarkably sturdy. He riffled the pages quickly, as though checking to determine that they were all still there, and then went to the foyer to put the book in his carryon.

Taking one more glance toward the bedroom, he picked up his luggage and headed down to the car he knew would be waiting for him.

7.
ANHELO, 1928

T his is so wonderfully generous of you, Tia Vidente," Sonia said. "Thank you very much."
The woman was admiring the ceramic plates that Vidente had bequeathed to her. Vidente touched her on the arm. "I just wanted you to have something special from me."

Sonia picked up one plate and turned it carefully. "The border is really eighteen-carat gold?"

Vidente nodded. "Artisans used such extravagances a hundred and fifty years ago."

The girl carefully put the plate on top of the others. "These must be so special to you. I don't know how you can part with them."

Vidente smiled. "I want them to be special to you. I want them to be an important heirloom to you and that man of yours."

Sonia's cinnamon eyes misted. "Is Camilo my special man, Tia Vidente?"

Vidente rested her fingertips softly on Sonia's cheek. "I see you eating very many meals on these plates with Camilo. You might want to use other plates for your children until they are old enough to avoid breaking them, though."

Sonia started crying at that point, and she threw her arms around Vidente. "You've brought me many presents today. You will sit at a table of honor at our wedding."

"That would be a pleasure," Vidente said, knowing she would not be around for the occasion. She hugged the girl close again. "I need to go now. I have other stops to make."

"Stay for some coffee. It's the least I can do after you've given me such an exorbitant present."

Vidente kissed the woman's cheek. "Some other time, Sonia. Use the plates well."

Vidente stepped outside to rejoin Humberto, who was waiting for her with a cart of goods. Since their trip to Deberes, Humberto had been spending more time with his aunt, doing jobs for her around the house and eating several evening meals with her.

"Did she like her present?" Humberto said.

"Sonia was very happy."

The girl certainly seemed very glad and Vidente knew that she would always consider the plates precious. Even if she someday learned that the gold around the borders was nothing more than paint. Like so many of the items in her home, Vidente had found the plates while rummaging through an antiques shop. She had no idea of the true provenance of the plates, but she doubted they were actually one hundred and fifty years old. Still, the plates had spirit; spirit that spoke to Vidente enough to cause her to buy them for a few pesos and to give them a place of honor in her house. In her mind, this was more valuable than gold. If she embellished the story about the plates and about the other things in her home and in this cart, it was only because it was easier than attempting to describe their value in any other way.

Humberto looked toward Sonia's doorway. "She is a very attractive woman."

Vidente smiled at her nephew. "She is very attractive. She is also spoken for, Humberto. Do not worry, though. You will find your own wonderful woman."

"Did you see this in my future?"

"I didn't need to. I know that a fine man like you will draw many worthy women."

Humberto tipped his chin higher. Vidente was so glad she'd been able to spend this time with him before her mysterious journey – the real one, not the small excursion to Deberes – began. She hoped he would remember it with fondness.

Humberto began to pull the cart. "Where are we going next?"

"Santa Madre. I have something to bring Padre Antonio."

Humberto glanced down at the cart, obviously trying to determine which item Vidente intended for the priest. Vidente couldn't be sure if he ventured a guess and he didn't mention if he had. They walked quietly for the next several minutes, the only words being Vidente's returned greetings to passersby. Vidente noticed that Humberto rarely made eye contact with others along the way. She would try to get him to change this; he was never going to show people who he truly was if he always looked away from them.

When they arrived at the church, Vidente told Humberto that he should once again wait outside, and then she pulled a pristine, lacquered guitar from the cart. This seemed to puzzle Humberto, but Vidente turned to scale the steps of Santa Madre without explanation.

She found Padre Antonio in his office in the hallway behind the altar. Though the church was rich with color from the stained glass windows to the mosaic ceilings to the deeply hued ceramic clothing dressing the statues of the saints and the blessed mother, the priest's office was spare and monochromatic. Padre Antonio looked out of place here, his crimson vestments making him seem all the more so.

"Tia Vidente, what a surprise and a pleasure to see you," the priest said standing and moving to the doorway to kiss her on the cheek. "Come, sit."

Vidente settled into the chair as the priest returned to his. She held the guitar out toward him. "I've come with a present for you."

Padre Antonio reached for the guitar, his face bright. "This magnificent instrument is for me?"

"I know you like to play. I've never played this guitar myself – I don't have that talent – but I had new strings put on it for you."

The priest rubbed the polished wood and then plucked a few notes. He adjusted the tuning and then played again. "It has a lovely sound." He held the guitar in front of him. "I'm not familiar with this manufacturer."

"Really? I assumed that someone who loved the guitar would know about the artist who created this, even though there are only a few hundred in the world and far, far fewer in South America."

Padre Antonio studied the name on the neck more closely, as though doing so would spur his memory. "I somehow missed this. And where did you find such a magnificent instrument?"

Vidente tipped her head. "You know my fascination with fine things, Padre."

He positioned the guitar on his lap again. "Indeed I do." He played several bars of a song that Vidente recognized as "Gloria in Excelsis Deo," then laid the guitar gently against the wall behind his chair. "This is quite a present. What is the occasion?"

"I just wanted to give you a little something." Vidente leaned toward the priest and spoke in a conspiratorial whisper. "Before you embark upon your journey."

Some of the exuberance left Padre Antonio's face. "You know about the offer from Dios Misericordioso?"

She moved her head closer to him. "I didn't know the name of the church until just now."

"Can I assume that you learned of this through your own special methods and not because word has somehow gotten out? I wouldn't want my superiors here to discover this from anyone other than me."

Vidente waved a hand in front of her. "No one has spoken about this. I've been seeing this for you for some time. When do you plan to leave?"

The priest examined his fingertips. "I haven't actually decided that I'm going to do it yet."

"Don't be silly," Vidente said briskly. "You must do it. Anhelo is too provincial for a great orator such as yourself. You owe it to the churchgoers of Legado to spread your inspiration to a larger congregation."

Padre Antonio's shoulders relaxed. "You're a pretty great orator yourself," he said with a smile.

"I only speak from my heart." Vidente stood. "I must go, Padre. I have others to visit today. My nephew is waiting outside with a cart."

The priest's brows dropped. "You are bringing presents to others as well?"

Vidente wondered if she'd said more than she should have. "Just a few things I'm divesting myself of."

"Special things like this guitar?"

Vidente chuckled. "Well, nothing is special *like* that guitar. After all, it is very rare."

Padre Antonio watched Vidente wordlessly for several very long seconds. Thinking that perhaps their conversation was over, Vidente began to turn toward the door.

"Are you sure you aren't planning to embark upon a journey of your own?" the priest said.

"Don't worry about me, Padre," Vidente said as casually as she could. "I just received a vision telling me to share some of my treasure. Please enjoy the guitar. Maybe you can sing to your new congregation from the pulpit on occasion."

Feeling more uncomfortable than she'd ever felt in this church before, Vidente left at that point before the priest could question her any further.

᷈

BETHLEHEM, PALESTINE, 1921

After losing Lina, Khaled thought he'd experienced all of the grief his heart could absorb. Now, two months after returning to the land of his birth, he realized that his sense of loss had not reached its peak at all. Every time he awakened to Leandro's cries in the middle of the night, he would arise from a dream of being with the first woman he'd ever understood love with. And as Nahla went to tend to the baby who was not hers but who she treated with care regardless of how the boy announced her husband's passion for another, the sense memories would return. They extended not only to Lina's musical voice and delicate perfume, but also to brilliant flowers, salty air, grilled meats, and boisterous neighbors. He had come to realize slowly that he pined not only for Lina, but for Joya de la Costa as well.

Midday was only marginally better. His brother Rashid had convinced him to start a new business venture, the latest among the many they'd attempted in their lives together. It was physical work; much more taxing than the selling he had done in Legado. Also unlike his enterprise in his adopted home, this business generated very little income. Rashid kept telling him that the money would improve as they developed more customers and as they hired others to work with them, but Khaled was not convinced that he would ever make more than a small fraction of what he was making before he came home to find his wife's still, forever-gone form. The only advantage to this work was that the intensity of the labor sometimes drove him to a state of mindlessness. During these hours, he didn't grieve Lina or Joya de la Costa nearly as much.

The only thing that gave his life color at this point was Leandro. Nahla had provided the mothering the boy needed and Khaled was grateful to her for this. But his favorite moments of the day came in the hour or so after dinner when the boy would bounce on his lap, or attempt to climb on his shoulders, or turn himself upside down in an effort to reach the floor. Leandro spouted nonsense sounds endlessly during this time, as though narrating his exploits. Khaled would babble back at him, leading to lengthy "conversations" before Nahla took the boy for bath and bedtime. May and Mona would often stand by the chair, attempting to join in. Leandro found Mona's hair fascinating and often reached for it, which made Mona giggle. Khaled was glad that Leandro found his half-sister entertaining, but he also found himself jealous of this time with the boy. Mona had other times during the day to play with Leandro. Khaled only had now.

"Father, will Leandro be handsome like Tarek when he grows up?" May said from the side of the chair that night.

"Leandro will be extremely handsome," Khaled said. It was difficult for him to think of Tarek as handsome these days – though he knew the boy was very good looking – because Tarek seemed to be scowling at all times. He'd always had a sullen disposition, but in the time Khaled had been gone, that sullenness had soured. Tonight at dinner, Tarek had refused to answer a question about where he had been that afternoon, ignoring his father in the most disrespectful manner. Khaled had nearly risen from his seat to slap the surly boy in the face, but he held his temper. With any luck, Tarek would soon be out of the home. Hopefully, Leandro would not learn any ugly tendencies from him before that time.

Leandro giggled as Mona tickled his belly. The sound was like the tinkling of the wind chimes that hung in Lina's garden and it immediately erased any thought that Leandro could ever have as much bitterness in his heart as Tarek did. Nahla took the baby for the evening a few minutes later. May immediately tried to occupy the vacant place on Khaled's lap, entreating him to play a game with her and her sister.

"I am too tired for games," Khaled said sternly. "I have been working all day. Go play with your sister for a little while. Your bedtime will be coming soon."

May moved down from the chair and disappeared from the living room. Khaled leaned his head back and closed his eyes. As he had done many times in the past few months, he imagined what this very moment would have been like if Lina hadn't died. For one, he wouldn't have been nearly as tired as he felt. While he dedicated himself to his sales back in Legado, such work did not tax him physically as the labor he was doing now did. For another, he wouldn't be considering the evening nearly over. Once Lina had put Leandro to bed, they would have their time together. Maybe he would have brought home one of the guava pastries that Ruben's sister made in the back of her husband's shop and they would share it with some rich, bitter coffee. Maybe she would have sat wrapped in his arms telling him of the new things Leandro learned that day while he informed her of something funny that one of his customers said. Maybe they would have softly made love, offering each other quiet pleasure, determined not to awaken the baby. Maybe they would have simply opened their windows to take in the fragrances and listen to the sounds of the streets of Joya de la Costa. Hernan singing tango to impress his latest girlfriend. Valeria loudly scolding her sons for being too noisy. The men boasting to one another while they played cards. The soft and melancholy guitar that Khaled so often heard but had never identified.

Eventually, Khaled opened his eyes and returned to the reality of his life. They'd moved out of Ali's house a month ago and taken up residence in this colorless place. Nahla must have put the two girls to bed because he heard nothing but some faint rustling. No sounds from the street. No music of any kind.

A few minutes later, Nahla came into the room, seating herself on the couch at the end furthest from his chair. She folded her hands in her lap and regarded him. She had done this nearly every night for several minutes before picking up her tatreez and concentrating on her cross-stitching. Tonight she seemed to be watching him longer than usual. Nahla had never openly challenged Khaled and he knew that she never would, but her stare felt especially burdensome now. It seemed as though she was waiting for him to say something, though he had no idea what she wanted to hear from him. And as much as he wanted to justify his actions in Legado, to help this woman he'd been arranged to marry understand how he could have let his passions guide him in South America, he couldn't begin to do so.

As the silence lengthened, almost without will, words formed at his mouth. "I want us to move to Joya de la Costa."

Nahla's expression rarely changed, but he saw her eyes open and the corner of her mouth wrinkle before her face reset itself. "I thought you left Joya de la Costa for a reason."

"I left because I couldn't take care of Leandro by myself." He paused and looked away, needing to loose himself from the burden of Nahla's eyes. "Mostly that, anyway. But that would no longer be a problem if we all went together. We talked about this possibility when I left Bethlehem the first time. You knew that I would send for you if my business went well."

"And I didn't die."

It took a moment for the insolence of Nahla's comment to register on Khaled. She'd never before spoken so sharply to him. At the same time, he'd grown so accustomed to the women of Legado speaking their minds that such a comment actually seemed natural.

He'd let the statement pass. "I can start my business there again instantly. In fact, now that I know how much of a market exists, we can ship supplies ahead."

Nahla took up her cross-stitching and remained silent.

"And you have become very good at tatreez. We can sell some of what you create. Maybe you can even provide special orders for customers who are willing to pay more."

Nahla continued to say nothing. What would Khaled do if she refused to move? He could force her to come, of course. Or he could go by himself, though that would leave him once again without help for Leandro. He wouldn't let that be an issue. He would find someone to care for the boy if necessary. He realized now that he probably hadn't explored that as completely as he should have before boarding the boat back to Palestine.

"When do you want to leave?" Nahla said without lifting her head from her work.

Khaled felt lighter instantly and he was certain he could smell flowers.

"The next ship leaves in eleven days. We will be on it."

8.
CAMBRIDGE, 1989

Even though they'd been sleeping together on occasion for nearly three years now, Viviana was still capable of taking Dro to sexual destinations that he simply couldn't reach with anyone else. In the fall of his junior year, he'd actually started a semi-serious relationship with Karen, a management major. Karen was great, and she didn't feel threatened by his having a female best friend in Melanie, as so many other women had. He thought he might even be falling in love with her, but during the one weekend he had with Viviana that fall, he realized what was missing with his steady girlfriend, even though she was a soulful, earnest lover. He split with Karen a couple of weeks later. Since then, his MIT relationships – and the Boston College women Melanie attempted to fix him up with – were either intensely physical or entirely platonic.

Meanwhile, his erotic exploits with Viviana were increasingly adventurous and acrobatic. They'd screwed underwater, standing, and with the use of a variety of fabrics, accouterments, and even foodstuffs. Nearly all of this came from Viviana's creative mind. Dro was perfectly happy to have some variety, but considering they only saw each other a half-dozen times a year and considering how exciting things could be between them simply facing each other on a bed, he didn't necessarily need it.

Dro had begun to let go after Viviana's third orgasm, but when she started to peak again immediately thereafter, he found a way to hold back until she finished. His subsequent release made him feel as though he would shoot right through Viviana, right through the ceiling of her suite at the Ritz, right through the penthouse, and out into the Boston springtime.

It took him several minutes to gather his senses afterward. When his eyes refocused, they landed on the briefcase on the floor a few feet away. He'd been carrying it when he entered the suite and he'd still been holding it when Viviana pulled him onto the bed. The briefcase had nothing more in it than the draft of an essay he'd been working on and a copy of Modigliani's *Collected Papers*, but Viviana had implored him to use the prop ever since their close call in DC. If someone saw Dro entering her room, she wanted to be able to say that he'd come there on business.

After Viviana's run-in with the flower executive, Dro was convinced that she would stop inviting him for rendezvous. She didn't need the risk given her position and her place on the international stage. Dro would miss her body and he would miss their conversations, but he'd always understood that what they were doing would end whenever Viviana deemed it would end. Surprisingly, though, she called him as soon as she got back from Legado, asking him to meet her on "neutral ground" in New York in August, where she would be addressing the U.N. She'd been especially inventive with him during that stay. He assumed her speech went well also.

Viviana rose up from the bed, kissing his penis as she did. She walked into the living room of the suite and returned with a wrapped box. The aura around her naked body was a rich red, which Dro interpreted to mean that their sexual gymnastics would resume sometime soon.

"What's this?" Dro said, taking the package.

"It's a pre-graduation present."

Dro tore the paper to reveal a polished wooden box. Inside was a Montegrappa tortoise shell fountain pen. Dro only knew about the expensive Italian pen company because Viviana had shown him the pen that her father had given her when she became ambassador. He looked up at her, speechless.

"I want you to sign your senior thesis with it, Professor."

Dro took the pen out of the box and felt its weight between his fingers. "You know, they would let me graduate even if I signed the thesis with a crayon."

Viviana crawled back into bed and kissed him on the neck. "Do you like it?"

Dro kissed her deeply on the mouth and then watched the pen in his hand again. "I've never had anything this extravagant."

"Just imagine what I'll get for you when you actually graduate."

She laughed boisterously then and Dro laughed along with her. A moment later, she took the pen from his hand, replaced it in the box, and put the box on the night stand next to Dro. Then she covered his chest with kisses and the pen receded to the back of his thoughts.

Around midnight, they remembered that they hadn't had dinner. Viviana ordered lobster cocktails and champagne and they ate in the living room while wearing the hotel's plush robes.

"I read in the *Boston Globe* that there were two La Justicia attacks in Colina last week," Dro said. "Does this mean that the reality is considerably worse than those reports?"

Viviana's face stiffened and she closed her eyes. "Even if I could tell you, you wouldn't want to know."

Dro put down his champagne glass. "I guess that answers my question. Ordinary people are starting to get nervous, you know. The violence seems less and less strategic and more and more random. Even my mother feels threatened, and she is not a woman who feels threatened easily."

"I wish I could tell you something that would help ease her mind. Gordillo's statements to the media are becoming increasingly incendiary. The president fears he has lost touch with the rebel agenda. He...." Viviana stopped as though she were searching for a word. But then she put up her hand. "I've said too much already. Suffice it to say that the *Boston Globe* doesn't know everything. And neither does your mother."

That last sentence chilled him. "Should I be telling my family to get out of Legado?"

Viviana reached across the food for his hand. "No, no, of course not. The guerillas are a danger and the danger is escalating, but your family shouldn't leave Legado over this. Not at all."

Dro leaned toward her. "Am I speaking to Viviana or Madame Ambassador now?"

She squeezed his hand. "Both of us would tell you the same thing."

Dro didn't feel mollified. Until this conversation, he'd thought that his mother was being overly dramatic. However Viviana's faint assurances made him begin to wonder otherwise.

Still holding his hand, she rose up and moved onto his lap. She kissed him on the cheek and stroked the side of his face. "Gordillo has been pushing for a summit in the jungle. He has told the president that he only wants to meet with me. I've been avoiding it because I don't feel that I have a fix on him any longer."

"Is this supposed to make me feel better?"

Viviana kissed his nose. "It's supposed to make you feel that I'm being honest with you. Gordillo and La Justicia have the government worried. Still, the chances of this affecting your family are tiny. I might feel differently if they lived in Colina. Where your mother lives, though, she stands a better chance of being hit by a car."

Dro chuckled, relaxing a little. "Is *that* supposed to make me feel better? The drivers are crazy around there."

She wrapped her arms around him. "Dro, I'm never 'Madame Ambassador' with you."

She straddled him and worked at his robe. It took Dro a few minutes to stop thinking about his family being in danger, but Viviana managed to coax the fear from him.

The next morning, the sun was as brilliant as it ever was in Boston in mid-April. Though they were sealed in their climate-controlled cocoon, Dro could tell that the temperatures were in the low eighties simply by watching the number of bare-armed women in shorts who passed on the street twenty stories below. He felt a strong desire to be out there amongst them, but he knew that Viviana would never agree to go for a walk with him. They rarely hit the streets together at all anymore, and if they did, it was only at night. They had a vampiric romance.

Viviana came behind him at the window and ran her hands through his robe to rub his chest. "Pretty day," she said.

"We don't get a lot of these up here this time of year."

Viviana kissed his terry-covered back. "We get many more of them in Washington. The cherry blossoms are out. You should come see them before they go away."

Dro turned toward her and she kept her arms around him. He brought her closer. "Are you inviting me down so soon after our current encounter? Aren't you concerned you'll become bored of me as a plaything?"

She kissed his chest through the space she'd opened in the robe. "You've never bored me yet. I don't think you could ever bore me."

Dro chuckled and kissed Viviana's hair. He felt himself stirring. Truth be told, he never had enough of her, either. If he went down to DC in a couple of weeks, would his desire for her still be this strong?

Viviana took his hand and drew him toward the loveseat in the living room. He began to undo her robe, but she moved him toward the seat next to her. "Tell me what is happening with your job offers."

It took Dro a moment to switch gears. "I'm still juggling the offer here and the two offers in New York. I obviously need to make a decision soon. They won't keep these on the table for me forever. I've definitively decided against San Francisco, though. I don't think I'm a San Francisco person."

Viviana shifted slightly so that her right knee was touching his left. "Why haven't you considered any positions in Washington?"

The question baffled Dro a bit. "I never really thought about Washington. I spoke to a couple of recruiters from Washington firms, but DC isn't really the center of my universe."

Viviana's eyes dropped. "But if you were in DC, we could be together much more. Don't you think it's time for that?"

"Time for us to be together?"

"In a real way, Dro. Away from hotel rooms."

Dro couldn't get a clear fix on Viviana's aura from this angle, but he could still see hints of red. For the first time, though, he also noticed a bit of deep orange there as well. Deep orange indicated humility, an emotion he'd never seen Viviana express.

"I thought that DC would be the last place in the world where we could be away from hotel rooms."

Viviana pivoted to face him a bit more. "I know that we need to be discreet. But at some point, it becomes time to flout discretion, no? I've been thinking about ways that we could slowly introduce you into my circle. This would be so much easier if you were actually employed in Washington. No one would ever need to know about the last three years."

Dro felt unsteady. He had no idea that Viviana had any interest in taking things further with him. He'd always considered himself an excellent judge of people and their motivations. How could he have misread the intentions of someone with whom he'd been so intimate? "Do you really think your circle would accept your involvement with someone more than twenty years your junior?"

Viviana smiled softly, though her eyes maintained their intensity. "Are you forgetting that I am a master politician? I have been extremely successful over the years at making people adopt my position on things."

Dro studied the joining of their bare knees. "I'm a little nervous about how this would play back home," he said, though the thought had only occurred to him when he spoke those words.

Viviana placed a hand on his thigh. "Don't be. We could have a great story for everyone. It needs to start with your working in Washington, though. All you'd have to do is make a phone call to a few of those recruiters. They'd be climbing over each other to get to you."

This conversation was so unexpected that Dro had no easy way to make sense of it. He loved his time with Viviana. How could he possibly not love being with a wise, brilliant, important, and beautiful woman who regularly brought him to new sexual peaks? But when he'd thought of the future with her, he'd only wondered about when their time together would end. What they were doing together was a fantasy. All fantasies ended at some point, didn't they? He'd never allowed himself to think of a deeper relationship with Viviana because the idea of his having that level of involvement at this point in his life with someone of her station seemed absurd.

But now that she was asking him to think about it, he needed to face the conditions under which that relationship could take place. And as he flashed on a future on the arm of "Madame Ambassador" in DC society, with photographs in newspapers all across Legado, he realized that this didn't connect with the vision he'd imagined from the day he set foot on the M.I.T. campus.

Viviana was offering an "arrangement." As tempting as it was to consider moving beyond "boy toy" status with her to something slightly more elevated, he was still going to be a plaything – and this time a plaything with a public profile that labeled him as such. He hadn't studied as hard as he had, and he hadn't worked so diligently on his dream to be trivialized by Washington society and his own country's leaders.

Yes, spending more time with Viviana would be heady and rewarding on multiple levels. But it came with too high a price.

"Viviana, I don't think working in Washington is the best way for me to begin my career. In fact, I think I've just now decided that I need to be in New York."

Viviana took her hand from his thigh and sat back. Her eyes were cloudy. "I didn't know that New York meant so much to you."

"If I'm going to be who I want to be, I need to do it there."

She tipped her head and offered a glimmer of a smile. "And us?"

Dro felt a rush of affection for this remarkable woman at that moment. He wrapped her in his arms. "I love what we have. It's a dream for me. And New York is much closer to DC than Boston is. I can come down whenever you want me."

Viviana said nothing in response. She simply huddled closer. She stayed that way for several minutes. Then, abruptly, she stood.

"I'm going to take a shower," she said.

"Do you want me to join you?"

She gave him that same smile again. "Why don't you order us some breakfast instead?"

❧

JOYA DE LA COSTA, 1921

It had taken less than a month for Khaled to reactivate all the accounts he had before he returned to Palestine. Most of the shop owners had welcomed him warmly and more than a few were curious about the wife and children that had turned out not to be dead. He hadn't been able to rent a place in the same building where he and Lina lived, but he managed to find somewhere large enough for everyone only a ten-minute walk away. As a result, he could renew his friendships with his old neighbors. Nahla had been reluctant to join him on most evenings, unaccustomed to the conventions of a culture that was more dramatically different for her than it had been for him, but Khaled went anyway; he'd missed this even more than he realized.

"You're going to stay with us this time, yes Khaled?" said Sergio, the owner of one of the stores where sales had been growing the most before Khaled left. Sergio had just placed an order twice as large as any he'd ever placed before. "My customers like to buy these things. I need to know that you will continue to bring them to me. I was even beginning to search for a new Palestinian vendor."

Khaled finished packing up his sample case. "You can count on me to be here from now on, Sergio. Business is too good for me to ever go away again."

Khaled stepped out onto the street, suddenly feeling very hungry. He'd been in the shop with Sergio for a long time. The man was a good customer, but he liked to talk, often going on by himself for three or four minutes. It made every sales call a lengthy event. Of course, if Sergio were going to continue to place orders as large as he had today, he could talk until midnight as far as Khaled was concerned.

Khaled tried to remember which cafes he liked in this area. He realized, though, that his call route today had left him only a brisk twenty-minute walk from home. He'd left the house extra early this morning and he'd barely had a moment to spend with Leandro. Since sales had been so good so far, he could afford to treat himself to some playtime with his boy before he made the afternoon's calls.

Nahla was feeding Leandro some mashed fruit when Khaled arrived. The boy literally gushed when he saw his father, throwing out his arms and spitting a mouthful of mango at the same time. Nahla wiped Leandro's face with a cloth as Khaled picked him up and threw him in the air.

"Is everything all right?" Nahla said. "It is early for you to be home."

Khaled tossed his son up high again, reveling in the baby's happy squeals. "Everything is fine. It has been a very profitable day, in fact. Profitable enough for me to take a little time with this flying boy before I go out again."

Khaled moved as though he was going to throw the baby up in the air again, but stopped in mid motion. Leandro laughed excitedly. Khaled repeated this and the boy giggled. Finally, Khaled let Leandro fly before catching him and hugging his child to his chest. Only upon pulling the boy back did he notice that Nahla had not cleaned the mango completely from Leandro's clothes. Khaled was going to have to change shirts before he left on the afternoon's business.

Khaled took Leandro into the living room while Nahla stayed behind. He heard cooking sounds and he wondered if Nahla would attempt to make something other than the Palestinian staples she'd prepared every night since they'd arrived in Joya de la Costa. Khaled had implored her to use the vast array of produce available in the local markets and to try some of the flavor combinations that were distinctive to Legado, but he'd been unsuccessful so far. Nahla seemed intent on turning their home into Little Bethlehem, something Khaled was certain she'd ultimately find frustrating.

The house was quiet otherwise. Tarek and the girls were in school. May and Mona seemed to enjoy their new classes and they seemed to have made friends, even as they struggled to learn the language Khaled had been force-feeding them since the decision to return here. Khaled had no idea how Tarek was doing. The boy said virtually nothing to him, even answering direct questions as vaguely and blandly as he could.

Khaled sat on his chair with Leandro and extended his index fingers for the boy to hold onto. Immediately, Leandro tugged on the fingers to pull himself to a standing position, smiling brightly as his unsteady legs rocked. No more than ten seconds after he rose, he sat back down.

"You'll be running in no time, little one. You have very strong legs. You inherited that from your mama. Her legs were very strong." He looked at the baby's thighs, rolled with baby fat, and laughed. "Hers were much more shapely, though."

He tried to think of a story that involved Lina's legs, but he couldn't think of any that would be appropriate to tell a little boy, even one who wouldn't understand a word he said. Khaled knew quite a bit about his wife's trim thighs, but what he knew had nothing to do with standing or running. He'd have to come up with another story. He tried to tell Leandro something about his mother every day and he promised to continue to do so even as the boy grew into a man.

"Did you know that your mama was the tallest woman I've ever met? She was nearly as tall as me – and I am not a small man. You'll be looking up to me for a long time, little one. But your mama came up to my eyebrows. When we would go out for walks and women would come up to talk to her, she would be a head taller than any of them. I think God did that because he wanted her beautiful face to stick out in a crowd. But do you want to know something? She never acted taller than the other women. She knew how to make everyone feel –"

A knock on the door interrupted Khaled's story. He turned in that direction and bounced Leandro on his knee while he waited for Nahla to see who was there. When Nahla opened the door, she threw a hand up to her mouth and let out a little whimper. Khaled stopped his bouncing when he saw a police officer bring Tarek through the door with his hands bound. He immediately wished he'd stayed out for lunch.

"Is this your son?" the officer said to Nahla.

Khaled stood and walked with Leandro toward the door. "What has he done?"

The officer turned toward Khaled, wrenching Tarek with him in that direction.

"I didn't do anything wrong," Tarek said in Arabic as he resisted the officer's tug. He'd steadfastly refused to speak Spanish in the house, even though he had to speak it in school. "Ask him what the other boys were doing."

"Silence," Khaled said sharply. He half-expected Tarek to continue protesting, but the boy stayed quiet.

The officer tugged a little harder on Tarek. "Your son got into a fight on the street outside of his school. There were two other boys involved. Your son beat one of them pretty badly."

Khaled glared at Tarek. As he did, Leandro reached out for his half-brother. Khaled moved the baby to his other arm.

"I am very sorry you had to deal with this, officer," Khaled said as he continued to stare at Tarek.

"I could have brought him to the detention center. But as far as I know, he has never been in trouble before. You haven't been in the country long, have you? Anyway, I thought it was best to keep this a family matter. The boy is going to have enough trouble on his hands if the boy he beat has big friends."

Feeling a sense of frustration different from anything he'd ever felt in Legado, Khaled apologized again for the actions of his son. The officer left minutes later. As soon as Nahla closed the door, Khaled twirled on Tarek and, still holding Leandro in his arms, slapped the boy across the head so hard that Tarek stumbled to one knee. Nahla was at Tarek's side immediately, wrapping an arm around him while staring up at Khaled with a combination of fury and confusion.

Khaled ignored her and pointed a finger at his wayward son. "How could you have done anything so stupid? Don't you realize that we need to make a place for ourselves here?"

The boy rose up, glowering at him. "So you've told me – every single day since you decided against our will to bring us to this place."

"And yet still you shame me."

Tarek's eyes flew open. "Shame you? Is that what bothers you, Father? That what I've done will make it harder for you to live here with your beloved little son?"

"I'm trying to give all of us a good life here."

"Really? If you wanted us to have a good life, you wouldn't have torn us from our friends and our family. Can't you be honest for one minute? You were only concerned about yourself." He raised a finger toward Leandro, "And him."

The baby started whimpering. He was obviously unaccustomed to hearing two people exchange such heated words. Khaled drew Leandro closer to his chest. "Leave the child out of this."

Tarek's posture slumped. "He's all you really care about, isn't he?"

Nahla put a hand on Tarek's shoulder and he reached his hand up to hers.

The boy raised cold eyes on his father. "You really do wish we'd been dead, don't you?"

Khaled looked down at his son's feet. "Don't say such ridiculous things."

"It isn't ridiculous. It's true. Well, Father, I'm not dead, but you've ruined my life. I hate the people here." Tarek's lips curled into a sneer. "And I hate you."

The words seemed to shock Nahla more than they did Khaled. "Tarek, you mustn't –"

"I'm sorry, Mother," the boy said before pivoting and walking out of the house, slamming the door behind him.

At the noise, Leandro started wailing. Khaled moved to the chair and held the boy close, whispering to him to calm down, all the while considering the larger consequences of Lina's death.

9.

COLINA, LEGADO, 1989

Viviana ducked under the whirring rotors of the helicopter, finding it ironic that she'd once considered such swiftly beating blades frightening. She strapped into the seat behind the pilot while the man told her how honored and proud he was to be a part of this mission. She thanked him politely and then turned her head to look out the window. If the pilot glanced back at her, he would think that she was deep in thought. She didn't feel she could engage in small talk right now. And she didn't want any part of the man's patriotism.

The president had feted her on her arrival yesterday. Two days earlier, when she'd called to tell him that she was willing to go into the jungle to meet with La Justicia leader Guillermo Gordillo, he'd been overwhelming in his appreciation. The president knew that Gordillo was becoming increasingly dangerous and he knew that he wasn't equipped with the diplomatic acumen required to reach any level of accord with Gordillo. The rebel leader only wanted to speak with Viviana. Why he insisted on these terms was a mystery, though it likely had more to do with Viviana's international fame than their shared history. Surely, Gordillo understood that Viviana would require the government's approval for any concessions or recognition, so the man therefore had to understand that any meeting between them was only slightly more than ceremonial. But if Viviana could accomplish anything with this gesture, she would accommodate Gordillo's irrational demands.

The banquet in Viviana's honor last night had been embarrassing and uncomfortable. Members of the senate, business leaders, heads of citizens' groups, and the president himself offered praise to her. It seemed so far beyond what Viviana deemed appropriate or what she felt in her heart that she nearly ran to the podium to put a stop to it. She never would have actually done that, though. Her fellow citizens were watching. CNN International and the BBC were watching.

The helicopter rose into the sky and Viviana looked down to see the retinue that had joined her on the helipad waving to her. The copter banked to the left and soon the group of well-wishers was gone from sight. Now it was just she and the pilot. The president had offered a convoy, but Viviana refused it. Even if others had followed her in stealth, they could have confounded the mission. She needed to do this alone.

As she watched the landscape, Viviana thought of her flight from Boston to Washington just three days earlier. The weekend with Dro had been unful-filling in so many ways. She had been certain that he loved her. She couldn't believe she'd misread the look in his eyes or the tenderness in his touch. She was also certain that he knew she loved him. She'd surrendered to him absolutely, revealing herself as nakedly as she ever had with any man. She'd never talked with him about the future because she wanted him to focus exclusively on his studies. He had a formidable future ahead of him and she didn't want to compromise that in any way. But with his gradu-ation imminent, he could begin to think about other things. About the life that they would share. To hear that he was content with – insistent upon, really – maintaining the occasional nature of their affair dis-appointed her profoundly. She needed and expected so much more.

On the flight back on Sunday, she'd made two definitive decisions. As an attendant brought her a drink, she pulled out some paper and the pen her fa-ther had given her, the replica of which she had giv-en Dro. With it, she wrote Dro the letter she needed to write him. Then, when she landed, she phoned the president.

The density of trees grew thicker as the helicop-ter flew onward. Gordillo's compound was proba-bly about a half-hour away. She needed to prepare herself.

Her professional life had been as much of a success as her personal life had been a failure. She was one of the two or three most recognized South American women in the world. She'd promoted her message of compassion all over the globe, from the

White House to the villages of rural Ethiopia. Hundreds of thousands had seen her speak in person, millions had read her books, and tens of millions had watched her passionate speeches on television. And yet a succession of men had found her deniable. The collapse of her second marriage had been a very public thing. But numerous less public failures had preceded it. And now one very discreet failure had followed in its wake. Her friends, if she had any that saw her as something other than a world-recognized diplomat, might have told her that she was still young, that it was still possible to experience satisfaction in her soul. But Viviana Emisario was nothing if not self-aware. She knew that what had happened with Dro was the final statement on her potential for happiness. What was left was service to her country. And she would perform that service emphatically and in a way that would resonate throughout Legado and throughout generations.

"We're about fifteen minutes away, Madame Ambassador."

"Thank you."

Viviana felt her heart quicken. This journey was unlike any she'd undertaken before. She'd flown into war zones. She'd walked gang-infested streets. She'd been apprehensive then, but nothing prepared her for the ripples that now ran through her skin. For the briefest instant, she thought about instructing the pilot to turn around the helicopter. But that was never really an option; not since she'd made the decision to do this.

She pulled her briefcase onto her lap and opened it. The hilt of the knife stuck out from one of the case's pockets. Not allowing herself to consider her actions, she released her seat belt, threw down her bag, and drove the blade into the pilot's neck. He never had any idea what hit him.

Viviana gasped at the thought of what she'd just done. Shock nearly paralyzed her. But she had to complete the mission. This had to mean something. She attacked the underside of the dashboard of the helicopter with the knife and sparks ignited. Smelling smoke, she knew that she'd just insured that the copter would go up in flames upon impact. The fire would destroy all evidence of what she'd done here. Only one person would ever know, and he wouldn't ever tell that story to the world. To everyone else, she would be a martyr. The international community would finally have a face to put on Legado's guerilla nightmare. The outcry to solve the problem would overcome the president's impotence. At the very least, public outrage would drive Gordillo and his followers much further underground while leaders with real fortitude made plans to prevent their return.

The helicopter began to careen downward. It spun spasmodically, throwing Viviana against a wall.

As she hurtled toward her death, she reached out for memories of Dro's embrace.

✍

CAMBRIDGE, 1989

D ro was having lunch on campus when Melanie approached his table out of breath.
"Hey, what are you doing here?" he said.
"I didn't screw up one of our lunch dates, did I?"
Melanie reached out for his shoulder and squeezed it tightly. This instantly sent chills down his spine. The only other time she'd done this was when she had to tell him that his beloved uncle had suffered a heart attack.

"Your ambassador friend," Melanie said, seemingly incapable of saying more.

"Viviana? What?"

Melanie gripped his shoulder tighter, looked down at the ground, and then locked eyes with him. "She's dead. It's all over CNN."

Dro rushed to the nearest television and switched to the coverage. CNN was reporting that a helicopter carrying Legado's ambassador to Washington had crashed. By the time rescuers arrived, fire had consumed the craft and incinerated the bodies.

The network showed footage of the ambassador's most recent UN speech and a montage of her with important international figures. Finally, they showed an image of the smoldering crash site and Dro felt his legs weaken. Viviana had said she wasn't going to accept Gordillo's invitation for a meeting. And now La Justicia had shot her down.

Viviana was dead. He didn't even know she'd gone back to Legado. They'd talked about so little during their last few hours together. The stiffness and distance that came after he turned down her suggestion to move to Washington had been the first he'd ever experienced with her. Now it would forever be the way they ended the time in each other's lives.

Dro felt cool beads of perspiration on his forehead. He wanted a glass of water, but he wasn't entirely sure he'd be able to keep standing if he tried to walk.

"You guys had gotten to be pretty good friends, huh?" Melanie said, though as he'd been watching the television, he'd forgotten that she was standing next to him.

"She was amazing."

"I'm so sorry, Dro. This is an awful day for your country."

Dro had never told Melanie about the extent of the relationship he had with Viviana. He'd discussed every romance, every tryst, even every casual friendship with Mel, and he'd certainly told her about several of the visits he'd made to see the ambassador (fending off Mel's allegations that he was a "closet gigolo"), but he'd never been able to tell her how close to the truth those allegations were. Therefore, he couldn't let Melanie see him react the way he needed to react.

"Mel, I think I need to go back to my place for a while."

"I'll come with you."

Dro shook his head slowly. "Not this time. Thanks."

Slowly, barely keeping his legs under him, he made his way back to his apartment. The superintendent stopped him on his way up the stairs, telling him that a courier had delivered a package for him that morning. Inside was a letter from Viviana.

My love,

This weekend I realized that we had never been as intimate as I thought we were. I believed that you were feeling the things that I had been feeling. We never spoke about them because it wasn't time to speak about them, but I was sure that you were experiencing the same intensity of emotion as I was – something that went beyond pure passion to a truer and more eternal connection. I never would have expected to feel this about someone so much younger than me, but I blossomed in your presence. I felt free and uninhibited. Even though our encounters needed to be clandestine, I felt unburdened when we were together. I couldn't wait to be with you again and I waited with growing impatience for you to be out of school so we could explore a richer phase of our shared lives.

To discover that you didn't have this same desire devastated me. I believed I knew you so well and that the look in your eyes and the tenderness of your touch revealed how much you wanted us to be together. I assumed you were too shy to speak these things aloud. Instead, it turned out that you simply didn't feel them.

This is a repeating pattern in my life. How ironic is it that someone who has gained fame for touching the souls of the masses has such an impossible time understanding the heart of any individual? You know of the previous men in my life. What you don't know is that in every case I misread their emotions entirely. There is only so much heartbreak any person can endure. I know now that I have come to my limit.

As I've contemplated the implications of our last day together, my thoughts have gone to the people of Legado. Maybe I can do more for them in a single act than I could ever hope to do through years of diplomacy. I hope so, because they and only they have returned my love.

I did love you, Dro. Perhaps I cannot identify love in others, but I am certain I can identify it in myself. I could not have been as unabashed with you if I didn't love you. The thought of losing that unabashedness yet again, of living without it for untold time and then attempting to recapture it with another, has led me to realize that I can no longer summon the effort.

Please keep this secret between us. Allow this gesture to mean something. I wish you the best in New York. Always try to be extraordinary. I know you want that. And I know the world wants it from you.

Love,
Viviana

Dro read the letter three times, his mouth dry, the tips of his fingers numb. The image of the smoldering crash site returned to his mind. For a moment, he felt as though he could share Viviana's thoughts as the helicopter plummeted. *She was lying in my arms and kissing my shoulder.* And then the connection snapped. It was as though the vision had been yanked out of him. It was such a violent action that he thought he might stumble.

Feeling cooler and frustratingly clearer, he tried to imagine himself with Viviana again. Thoughts came, but nothing deeper. He tried rereading the letter, but Viviana's voice was no longer in it. He tried to recapture the shock and dismay he felt when Melanie brought him the news.

But all he felt was half-empty.

10.
ANHELO, 1928

Vidente twirled the ring on her left finger while she read Ximena. Her old friend was so easy to read these days. Carlos' health had returned, her children were married, and the biggest thing on Ximena's mind was whether she would have as much time as she wanted with her grandchildren. Ximena's colors were honey and plum: she was at peace and she was ready to be there for her family as often as they wanted her. The colors of her future were equally warm and satisfying.

Still, as easy as Ximena had always been for Vidente to read, Vidente found that the colors came to her faster when she twirled the silly tin ring she'd picked up at the antiques shop in Deberes. Something about the ring had tickled her from the moment she saw it. She kept it under glass for a few days after her return from Mediana, but then impulsively decided to wear it, slipping it onto her left hand next to the wedding ring she never took off, though her husband died so long ago. The new ring was the tiniest bit loose, but not so much so that she had to worry about it falling off. The day she wore it for the first time, she did a reading for a lovestruck boy down the street that afternoon and she had the toughest time finding his colors. She folded her hands, found the tin ring, and impulsively began twirling it. Suddenly the boy's colors bloomed. Vidente thought it was a coincidence that day, but subsequent readings made it clear that the ring did something to amplify Vidente's vision. Maybe it was just that the ring helped her concentrate better. Or maybe it was something else, a certain power in the ring that had drawn her to it by sending her to Deberes to retrieve it. Regardless, Vidente wore the ring every day now and it had become nearly as much of a favorite of hers as the ring that resided on the finger next to it.

She gave the tin circle another spin and a mix of colors emerged that made Vidente smile. "You are going to have a very long visit with your grandsons soon, Ximena. I believe your son wants to take his wife away for a vacation."

Ximena wriggled excitedly. "And he should. They have had so little time alone since the boys arrived. It will be good for them." She giggled. "And it will be very good for me. Can you tell me when?"

The only difficulty with reading Ximena was that she always wanted more detail. This often required taking the reading deeper than Vidente liked to go. Still, if knowing an approximate date would make her beloved friend happier, Vidente would do it for her. With her fingers still on the ring, Vidente closed her eyes and Ximena's colors danced liquidly in front of her. She prepared to take herself past the colors when she felt a tug in the other direction. It was as though a child were pulling on her arm while she was trying to have a conversation with another person. Vidente attempted to ignore this and the tug became more insistent. Was something telling her to avoid looking further into Ximena's future? That made no sense; not with the colors she'd already seen. Gradually, the colors dissipated, leaving Vidente only with the image of the back of her eyelids. And still the tug was there.

Vidente opened her eyes.

"This Sunday?" Ximena said excitedly. "Are they coming this Sunday?"

Vidente smiled at her friend's excitement, hoping the confusion she felt didn't show on her face. "I'm not sure yet. Sometimes the images are more reluctant to come to me."

Ximena threw her hands to her face. "He's decided not to go on the vacation, hasn't he? Just now he decided not to go."

Vidente drew down Ximena's hands and held them tightly. "I truly haven't seen anything yet. This happens sometimes; you know that." She rose up from her chair. "I think I'm going to get myself a glass of water and then we'll try again."

She patted Ximena's hand to assure her, and then walked into the kitchen. The serving girl was there and Vidente asked her to leave the room for a few minutes. Vidente could of course have called for the girl to bring the water to her, but she felt the need to walk around a bit. And if she were alone, she could try to concentrate on the tugging feeling that she still sensed, even though she was no longer trying to get past Ximena's colors.

She poured herself some water and sipped slowly. She closed her eyes again and the tug became more insistent. It was no longer a little child pulling at her sleeve; it was someone perhaps the size of Humberto taking her by both shoulders. She opened her eyes and put down the glass, afraid she might drop it, which would have brought both Ximena and the serving girl into the kitchen.

Was this an indication of the disease that was planning to take her? Though she believed in the vividness of the vision of her death, she'd never learned how that death would happen. Would she waste away? Would it be something much more violent? And if she were getting sick now, what of the journey she was supposed to make before she died?

The tugging sensation stopped suddenly. It was immediate enough to cause her to lurch in the other direction. Vidente straightened, feeling peaceful and light. And then she began to feel like something was lifting her. She tried to look down at her feet, but her vision swam with robin's egg blue. The color engulfed her and filled her until her world was blue on the outside and blue on the inside.

And she rose.

ری

Ximena tried to be patient. How could Vidente present her with such wonderful news about an upcoming vacation with her little grandsons and then not tell her when this was going to happen? She loved her friend dearly, but sometimes Vidente could be so erratic. If a glass of water would clear up her vision, though, then Ximena thought that Vidente should drink her fill.

But it did seem as though she were taking a terribly long time to refresh herself. Easily, ten minutes had passed. Was Vidente trying to brace herself to deliver bad news? Ximena knew it! Her son wasn't going to go away. Her babies wouldn't come to be with her.

Finally, Ximena could not bear it any longer. She got out of her chair and went to the kitchen to find Vidente. There was a water glass on the counter, but her friend was nowhere in sight. Ximena checked the other rooms of the house. She asked the serving girl if she'd seen Vidente and the girl told her that Vidente had sent her out of the kitchen and she hadn't seen the woman since.

Ximena checked both doors to the house, though Vidente would have had to have walked past her to get to the front door and the back door always creaked when someone opened it.

Vidente hadn't left. But she wasn't here. What could possibly have happened to her?

❧

JOYA DE LA COSTA, 1921

S ipping a coffee before his next appointment, Khaled thought back on leaving the house that morning. He'd touched Leandro lightly on the back before going off to work, just as he always did. The baby was deeply asleep and didn't shift at all, as he would on occasion. He stopped at the girls' room next to watch them sleep, something he'd started doing a few weeks earlier. Their faces were so beautiful in repose, something he hadn't bothered to notice for far too long. They had another twenty minutes or so before they had to get up for school, so he tiptoed away from them and out of the house as quietly as possible.

Of course, he hadn't bothered to check on Tarek, not that noise would have been an issue. He could have kicked down Tarek's door and the boy still wouldn't have said anything to him. They hadn't exchanged a single word since the uproar after the policeman brought Tarek home. Last night, at dinner, Khaled thought he saw Tarek glancing in his direction with some openness in his eyes. But when Khaled tried to say something to him as they got up, Tarek turned away brusquely. It was difficult to know where this was headed. Tarek was certainly headstrong enough to shut Khaled out forever – even though the boy himself was the one who had committed the offense. *Maybe that wouldn't be the worst thing*, Khaled thought, though the thought brought surprising regret with it. Had there been a time when his heart surged for Tarek the way it now surged for Leandro?

Khaled drank his last sip of coffee and picked up his sample bag. His next stop was a new potential customer. Khaled had passed this store on a number of occasions, but he'd never thought about going in. A sign in the store's window claimed that the shop sold "magical talismans." This hardly seemed to be a match for the crafts Khaled sold, but the sister of the owner, someone who worked at another one of Khaled's accounts, told him that her brother had shown particular interest in the tahriri dolls. Khaled figured he could never put his goods in enough places, so he set up an appointment.

Brayan, the owner, was a short man with an unkempt beard. Brayan waved as Khaled entered, saying he would be with him as soon as he finished taking care of some matter in the back of the store. Khaled used the time to look at several displays, trying to imagine how his Palestinian crafts fit in. He always tried to make suggestions along these lines as part of his sales presentation, trusting that his imagination would help result in an order. Various tables held shimmering stones, strings of polished, brightly colored beads, animal sculptures made from cut paper, and a variety of objects made from tin. From the ceiling hung feathered creations and a luminous glass globe.

Lina would have liked this place. Perhaps she'd even visited it from time to time, even though she never did so with Khaled. Lina always told him that she believed she had magical powers. She certainly performed all kinds of enchantment on him. What she did with flowers was nothing less than sorcery in Khaled's mind. And she surely seemed to know things with great certainty that she shouldn't have known at all.

Khaled had always found Lina's "magic" amusing. If it made her happy to use it to know what he wanted for dinner or who they would encounter on one of their walks, he'd always been pleased to accept such frivolities. And if she truly believed that she knew the exact moment when she became pregnant with Leandro or the precise time to visit her sister when the woman was alone and choking on a chicken bone, who was he to argue with her?

Maybe I did in fact marry a witch, he thought with a smile. Still, Lina's magic hadn't helped her in the end. Had she tried to summon it as the life seeped out of her? He thought of Lina the way he saw her on that terrible afternoon. Needing to avoid the emotion the vision always brought, he cast his eyes elsewhere in the shop, hoping to find a quick distraction.

On a far side table sat some knitted dolls that seemed to Khaled far more primitive than the dolls he sold. As he examined them, Brayan approached him, extending his hand.

"These dolls bring happiness," Brayan said. "Women often put one in their kitchens and one in their living rooms."

Khaled picked up one doll and examined it. The knitting was not refined in any way. It was something someone could do with the bare minimum of experience. He put the doll back on the table. "Were you thinking you might want to put my dolls with these?"

"Actually, no." Brayan pointed toward the front of the store. "I had a different idea. Let me show you."

Khaled took two steps to follow the owner when he felt his knees wobble. He grabbed hold of a table nearby.

Brayan took several steps further before turning back to Khaled. "Are you all right?"

Khaled's wooziness intensified. "I'm suddenly feeling a little faint." He continued to hold onto the table. "I'm sure it will pass in a moment."

"Would you like a glass of water?"

"Yes, please."

Brayan started toward the back of the store. "I'll be right back. While I'm gone, you can look at those grounding charms right in front of you. Might be useful right now."

Khaled looked down at the table, noticing chunks of hard and darkly lacquered wood. He picked up one and the motion of raising it toward his eyes made him feel even more lightheaded than he had felt before. He was certain now that he was going to pass out. What a terrible way to introduce himself to a new customer! Still holding the piece of wood, Khaled clutched at the table. But he must have missed the edge, because he felt nothing. And he continued to feel nothing long after he should have hit the floor.

❧

The salesman's face looked so white that Brayan was certain the man was going to faint. He probably should have helped him to sit on the floor before he went to get the glass of water, but he didn't think of that until he was already in the back. Moving quickly, Brayan got the water and took a chair with him when he headed to aid the salesman. When he returned to where the salesman had been, though, he saw that the man was missing, as was one of his grounding charms. Had the salesman stolen it? Why would anyone go to such elaborate measures in order to rob a little piece of wood?

But then Brayan noticed the man's sample case. Surely, the salesman wouldn't have left the store with the charm but without his samples. Brayan looked around the store, but no one was there.

He retrieved the sample case and brought it to his office, assuming the salesman would eventually come back to claim it – and hopefully pay for the charm he took at the same time.

❧

Mother was busying herself in the kitchen, but Tarek could tell that she was still upset. Pans rattled and clanged. Mother had always been a neat and orderly cook.

Just then, a pot filled with lentils crashed to the floor, splattering their contents everywhere, including Tarek's shoes. Mother cried out and grabbed a towel, kneeling down and trying to clean him off.

Tarek knelt with her. "It's okay, Mother."

Mother had a distant look in her eyes, as though she couldn't actually see him. "It isn't okay. It has been three days. Your father is gone and we are alone in this unimaginable country."

Tarek took away the towel and squeezed her hand. "We have made do without Father before."

"But now we are so far from home. We don't have the money to go back, and we can't ask your aunt and uncle to help us any more than they already have. What will we do?"

She started crying then, dropping her head toward the floor. Tarek drew his mother into his arms and held her as she had held him when he was much younger. "Don't worry, Mother," he said softly. "I will be the man of the family now. I will take care of all of us."

He heard Leandro calling out from his crib. Soon he too would be wailing.

"Even my father's bastard child."

NEW YORK, 1993

I completely lost track of time," Dro said into the telephone. "I need to get going. I have an appointment in Brooklyn."

"You do business in Brooklyn?" Melanie said into her end of the phone. "Is there any business *in* Brooklyn?"

"More all the time, actually, but I'm not going there on business."

"Girlfriend?"

"Not a girlfriend, either."

Melanie chuckled. "I love when you're mysterious."

"I'm not being mysterious. I just don't have time to explain what I do with Tamara – and telling you that I don't have time is making me later!"

"Tamara sounds like a masseuse. Is she going to give you a happy ending?"

"I'm getting off the phone now."

"Wait! I want you to come to our anniversary party. It's a big deal and I'd love to have you there."

"Let's make that a definite maybe. Boulder's not exactly around the corner. I'm really hanging up now."

Dro put the phone on the cradle before Melanie could say anything else. He loved their near-daily conversations, but he would have loved them even more if she occasionally got the hint that he didn't have time for a long talk.

He headed for the subway station out of habit. Then he remembered the size of his latest paycheck – the first since his promotion – and turned to hail a cab instead. The cab driver grunted when Dro gave him the address in Caroll Gardens, Brooklyn. Screw him. Both of them knew that the driver had to take him anywhere in the five boroughs, even if it were a bitch to get a return fare. If the driver didn't try to punish him by taking some stupid route to Brooklyn, Dro would give him a nice tip for his trouble.

The ride would take twenty minutes if traffic weren't bad, which meant he would probably still make it to Tamara's on time. It also meant that he had enough time to review the top-line summary the research team had composed for the BioPrime/ Whole Health merger. Dro put his Coach briefcase on his lap and pulled out the report. It was obvious within a few sentences that the research people were going to conclude that the numbers made sense. Of course they did. In this industry at this moment, the numbers always made sense unless a moron or a thief was running the company. Dro knew that his boss was willing to commit a considerable amount of money to fund this merger, but he wasn't convinced that it made sense to do so. Dro had sat in a room with management from both organizations. He'd studied them carefully, and he didn't see how the two cultures would blend. The BioPrime people were far more predatory; a simple reading of their auras showed him that much. But the bulk of the talent was on the Whole Health side. If the predators drove out the talent, the stock was going to take a freefall. The firm had listened to his warnings about this sort of thing in the past, but they didn't seem interested in listening this time. It wasn't like Dro to shut up and do his job, but they'd essentially told him to do just that in a meeting this afternoon.

It was becoming increasingly difficult for Dro to rent his skills to someone else. Not when his instincts were so often right and yet they acknowledged them only half the time. That half had earned

him multiple promotions – he certainly never needed to see the inside of a subway car again – but he'd
been keeping score. If the firm had followed his rec-
ommendations, it would be even richer. And if he'd
been making those deals for himself, the driver would
never grunt when Dro sent him to Brooklyn because
the driver would be working for Dro full time. For
the past six months, Dro had begun to think cogent-
ly about the kind of company he would put together
on his own. He knew he needed further experience
before he could start it and he'd been thinking more
and more about going to Europe for this. London
was again becoming a significant financial capital
with US banks opening major branches there. He'd
read the other day about the development of the Ca-
nary Wharf section, and about Morgan Stanley's
presence and Citigroup's coming entry. A new Wall
Street was emerging in London. Maybe it was the
right moment to jump across the ocean.

The cab arrived at the brownstone without any
hassles. Dro gave the driver an extra ten, which did
nothing to improve the driver's demeanor. Some
people just didn't appreciate conciliatory gestures.

He walked up the stairs to the front door, and Tamara buzzed him in. As always, a Tangerine Dream
album was playing in the apartment. Tamara was
great, but she really needed to broaden her musical
horizons. There was inspired meditative music available from all over the globe, not just from a group of
Germans with synthesizers.

Tamara hugged him and kissed him on the cheek,
then directed him toward the worn green couch where
she did her work. Dro had met Tamara at a retreat in

upstate New York a little less than two years ago. She invited him to join a group that met in SoHo, and they started seeing each other weekly there. Eventually, he felt comfortable enough with her to share his concerns. Tamara thought she might be able to help him and he'd been doing solo sessions with her since.

Dro's problem was that he had ceased to be able to see auras around personal acquaintances – let alone anything deeper – since he graduated from MIT. He'd gone up to Cambridge several times to try to solicit the help of Susan, Professor Dodder-ington, and the others in their metaphysical group. No one had an answer for him, though plenty of them had theories that got him nowhere. The con-founding thing was that Dro hadn't lost his ability to read auras entirely. In fact, his vision when dealing with business associates had become increasingly stronger. But friends, lovers, people he knew casual-ly, clerks at his neighborhood shops…nothing. Dro found this intensely frustrating. He didn't like hav-ing half a talent at anything.

"How has your week been?" Tamara said as she sat in a plush chair across from him.

"Not great, actually. There's this big deal that I'm not comfortable with, but my boss –"

"– Dro, relax with the business talk. I've told you over and over that I don't like what it does to this room."

Dro held up his hands. "Sorry. It's been on my mind."

Tamara dimmed the lights with a remote con-trol. "Then let's get it off of your mind. You know how much I think you need to do that."

She turned down the music with another remote. Dro could still hear the synthesizers, but they were a hum in the background. "You're okay with doing the regression work we talked about last week?" she said.

"Let's give it a try."

"It can bring up some traumatic things."

"I'm okay with it." Dro hadn't mentioned to Tamara that he'd done hypnotic regression before and that it had never offered him any insight. He was far more likely to fall asleep (especially since he'd been out so late the night before) than he was to re-experience something traumatic. Still, he was willing to keep an open mind. Tamara had taught him more about passive receptiveness than he'd ever known before. Maybe she could bring him back to his past as well.

Dro put his feet up on the ottoman in front of him, leaned back, took a deep breath, and closed his eyes. Tamara started to count him down. She was a very good hypnotist. By the time she'd gone from ten to six, Dro felt fully relaxed and open. By the time she reached three, he felt himself to be in what he recognized to be a deep hypnotic state.

Dro lost track of Tamara's voice at that point. It wouldn't be the first time that he'd fallen asleep under hypnosis. It had been a strenuous week and he really hadn't gotten enough sleep last night. If he fell asleep now, though, Tamara wouldn't be able to proceed with the regression. She'd probably just let him nap until another client arrived.

But this didn't feel like sleeping. He was too aware of his thoughts to be asleep. If he weren't sleeping, though, where was Tamara's voice?

Dro began to feel as though he were rising. He tried to hold on to something, but there was nothing to hold on to. He'd never had this sensation of floating upward before and he found it both disquieting and comforting. It wouldn't have been a bad feeling at all, if things weren't so eerily silent.

Suddenly, the feeling of floating stopped. This was as close to nothingness as he'd ever experienced before – entirely different from anything he'd been through while meditating. He didn't like this. Whatever Tamara was doing, it had taken him more out of control than he wanted. He'd let her know that this wouldn't be acceptable in the future.

He wanted out of this immediately, yet when he tried to open his eyes, he found that he couldn't.

He would have needed a body to do that.

11.

LOS ANGELES, CALIFORNIA, UNITED STATES OF AMERICA, 2010

The pilot's announcement of the flight's final descent into Los Angeles registered dimly on Alex's consciousness. He was too focused on the last page of his family history for the words from the cockpit to represent much more than background chatter.

It would not have surprised Alejandra Soberano that the entire town turned out for her funeral. She was, after all, one of the wealthiest and most prominent people in all of Anhelo. Nor would it have surprised her that so many of the mourners, both men and women, wept openly as they approached her casket. Of course there was music, and of course people stood in line to praise her rhapsodically from the pulpit. This much she would have expected. Some of it she even arranged. Alejandra Soberano always loved a good party – she had a dozen revelers in her home every

257

Sunday – and she would have anticipated such a gathering in her honor.

However, what she could not have expected was the commitment made to her memory. She could not have anticipated that the people of Anhelo would speak of the great clairvoyant in tones of reverence for years after her death. That they would tell their children and their children's children that an irreplaceable spirit had once touched them. That the tears they shed were not only because they'd lost a beloved member of their community but because Anhelo would forever be dimmer in her absence.

Go with God, Tia Vidente, the people of Anhelo said collectively on this day. *Our loss is forever heaven's gain.*

Alex closed the book and held it to his forehead. He closed his eyes and hoped that he could hold back the tears that threatened to fall. His reaction to these last paragraphs of the book had surprised him. He'd read the book when he was a teenager; it was required in his household. He'd long known the legend of his great grandmother Alejandra Soberano, the woman known as Tia Vidente. But somehow he'd never before grasped the emotional impact she'd had on the city of his birth. Alex had built a hospital in his hometown in honor of his mother. He'd made a name for himself in the world that few of his fellows could approximate. But would anyone tell their children's children about him?

How strange was it that he'd taken this book with him on a trip designed to be a spiritual journey? According to the book, there had been "seers" in the family before Alejandra, but she'd turned this into an art form and her own distinctive version of community service. Her reputation for envisioning the future remained intact even though so many of the treasures she bestowed on others before she died turned out to be fraudulent. She'd given her local pastor – a man who went on to become a bishop – a modest guitar that she claimed was a handmade masterpiece, and she'd even once convinced her nephew that she'd given him the rarest of Stradivarius violins that turned out to be an item mass produced in Europe. Even Alex's own mother, who would have been Alejandra's granddaughter-in-law, had several pieces of rustic pottery – not five-hundred-year-old antiques – that she'd inherited indirectly from Alejandra. When Alex had married Opal, his mother asked him if he wanted one of them for their home and he'd turned it down, perhaps a sign that he was worried that someday Opal might try to steal the family heirloom when they divorced.

The amazing thing was that no one ever cast away these objects when they learned the truth about them. When Alex once asked his mother about this, she answered simply, "They have the spirit of Vidente in them." The concept seemed frivolous to Alex at the time, but the nuance made more sense now. For Alejandra, the material was illusion and the incorporeal was real.

Which meant that she could not be more different from him. Alex had honed his professional instincts to the point where he trusted them implicitly. But he never believed he was seeing into the future when he "read" an associate. What he was doing was picking up signs about a person's makeup, signs that he could process through a business mind that anticipated every eventuality, could play out any scenario. At college, Alex had come to appreciate that science had frontiers still to be crossed. But he would never accept the kind of hocus-pocus that was the stock in trade of "Tia Vidente." He couldn't.

And yet, here he was, touching down at LAX, ready to make a two-week retreat to an ashram. Alex only vaguely understood the reasons that drove him to make the sudden decision to come here. He knew the meditation, yoga, and hiking would help clear his mind of the toxic clutter that was taking up too much space there. But he'd read enough about this place to know that people sought something else there. They sought transcendence. Was he looking for that as well? And what would he do if he found it? Could he handle transcendence?

His luggage was one of the first to come off the conveyor belt at the baggage claim, which pleased Alex since he considered waiting for luggage to be one of the most pointless things imaginable. He'd nearly gotten away with traveling only with a carryon. According to the ashram's website, one didn't need much in the way of clothing. He certainly wouldn't be dressing for dinner while he was here. Ultimately, though, the carryon was simply too small to accommodate two-weeks' worth of his things, no matter how stripped down. Now all he needed to do was find his ride. The ashram was particularly insistent on providing this service even though Alex had made it clear to his travel concierge Marina that he would have preferred to take a limo. It seemed the ashram felt very strongly about not letting other cars on its property, something that struck Alex as something a little more appropriate for a militia compound than a Zen retreat.

Shouldering his carryon and rolling his suitcase, Alex moved toward the exit, finding his name on a placard held by a sandy-haired man in his early twenties. The man introduced himself as Rick, took Alex's luggage, and guided him toward a van waiting at the curb.

"Your first time?" Rick said brightly as they hit the highway.

"My very first."

"You're gonna love it. I sure hope you like physical activity."

Alex reached into his carryon for his Blackberry. "Yes, I've heard that they put you through the wringer. I'm looking forward to it."

He thumbed the phone's power switch. Should he call Angélica to let her know he had arrived? Would the conversation be awkward after last night? The ashram made it clear that there was no cell service available there, so this would be his last chance to communicate with her until he left the site. He held the phone in his hand for several minutes and then finally put it back in his bag.

As the driver continued to wax poetic about the wonders of the ashram, Alex pulled out his family history. He wanted to go back to a few passages about Alejandra Soberano.

✑

The ashram only allowed guests to check in on Sunday – yet another of its rules – and it appeared to Alex as though everyone had arrived at the same time. The facility only catered to a dozen guests a week and yet there were still three people ahead of him for the explanation of the facilities and the medical test required of all who attended. While he waited for his turn by the fireplace in the simply appointed dining room, a man sat down next to him. The man was young – Alex guessed that he was under thirty – and he had the general appearance of an international backpacker. Given the ashram's rates and exclusivity, though, Alex was relatively certain that the man didn't spend a great deal of time on the dole. He wasn't a movie star, at least not one who Alex recognized. Social networking billionaire, maybe?

"First time?" the man said when Alex turned toward him and made brief eye contact.

"It is, yes. How about you?"

"Third. First time since '08, though. A sudden impulse. I'm still trying to figure out why I got it in my head on the spur of the moment that I needed to be here this fast. The middle of last week, I just decided that I *needed* the retreat." The man leaned toward Alex and lowered his voice. "You wouldn't believe what they charge to shoehorn you in at the last minute."

Alex rolled his eyes. "I have some idea, actually." So this guy decided to come here only a few days ago as well? According to Marina, guests usually had to book a year in advance. Yet there was space for both him and the itinerant tycoon. Alex wondered if the place had taken a recent turn for the worse. Maybe Marina wasn't staying on top of things as well as she once did.

The man stuck out his hand. "Sloan Wel. One L."

The last name and the unusual spelling struck Alex as familiar, but he couldn't place it. If Wel were a newly minted mogul, the name would have struck Alex instantly. Who knew? There were so many ways to make money quickly if one tried. Alex took the man's hand and introduced himself.

"How have you been?" Sloan said. The question struck Alex as odd. It suggested that they were people who'd known each other for a long time and were now catching up rather than those who had met only two minutes before.

A member of the ashram staff called the next guest, which meant that Alex's turn would come directly after that. He recognized the guest that just got up as a bestselling novelist. "I've been well. Not that I don't have some room for improvement."

"You'll get no argument from me about that. I guess that's why we're here, after all."

Alex smirked. "I don't know how much improvement I'm going to get from this. I'd be happy enough with a little peace."

Sloan looked at him carefully, as though what Alex had just said surprised him. Then his eyes softened. "They have a lot of that here. Just as long as your definition of peace doesn't involve thirty-two ounce porterhouses."

Alex laughed and thought back to the way he'd gorged himself at dinner last night, arguing that his diet was about to shift suddenly toward the ascetic. The vision of Angélica that accompanied this memory brought him a brush of melancholy. "I think I can get by without a feast for a couple of weeks."

Sloan reacted as though Alex had said something profound. Then he pointed to the ground. "Did you bring a good set of hiking shoes?"

"Two pairs."

"Then you're all set."

"So what do you do when you're not starving yourself and going on ten-mile walks every day?"

"You mean in the real world? I'm a college professor."

Alex couldn't help being surprised by the answer. "College professors obviously make more than I thought they did."

Alex realized the reference to money might have struck Sloan as crass. The man didn't seem to mind, though. "No, they make what you probably think they make. It helps if you invent a new financial analysis tool and sell it to Merrill Lynch before you enter the field."

Alex's eyes brightened. "I suppose it would. You know, I thought about teaching once."

"It's better than you imagined if you have any inclination toward this type of thing at all. And the coeds are much more beautiful than I remember in college – and that's saying something. My office hours go by very quickly."

Alex laughed again, liking Sloan immediately. He was a type Alex didn't get to meet very often, and he found it refreshing. By this point, a staff member had come to retrieve Alex to administer a blood pressure test, take his weight, and put him through a rudimentary review of his medical history. This all went quickly, after which Alex waited for Sloan to complete his so they could walk to their rooms together.

"I'm here," Sloan said, pointing to a tan bungalow on the left. Alex's lodging was a bit further up the hill. Sloan tipped his chin toward Alex. "Are you ready to find your center?"

"I guess we'll find out."

"I'll catch up with you at dinner."

Sloan headed toward his door and Alex continued walking, glancing back down the hill and waving to Sloan before the young professor headed into his room. The man disappeared behind the door and Alex continued to walk toward his accommodations. As he did, though, a memory struck him, surprising in that it had been so long since he'd had this one. A woman; someone he never could have forgotten. Yet when was the last time he'd seen her face in his mind? How strange that she should visit him now. Was this a preview of the kind of sight the ashram offered? If so, this might turn out to be more of an adventure than he'd signed up for.

The conversation with Sloan had been refreshing, like a dip in a pool after a long day's work. But now, as Alex put his keycard into the door of his room, a wave of melancholy washed over him.

๛

Unpacking was ridiculously easy. His clothes went from his luggage to the dresser in his room in a heap. There was no Ascot Chang or Saville Row in his suitcase, and Polo and Diesel didn't require special handling. He took more care with his toiletries, lining them up on the single shelf in the bathroom. The room was easily the most modest he'd stayed in since the Kenyan safari he'd gone on with Opal, though it was not the most modestly priced. The dresser and night table were covered in laminate, the rug was a coarse weave, and a simple quilted throw topped a slim mattress. Marina had warned him that the accommodations weren't luxe. None of this concerned him, except for the bed. Even sleeping on his double-thick memory foam mattress at home was sometimes a problem. He dreaded the possibility of facing a great deal of tossing and turning in the coming days.

Alex pulled out his Blackberry and put it on the night stand, though the phone would be little more than a music player here. The ashram proudly announced that it was entirely out of cell range. Alex could have gotten a satellite phone for the trip, but that seemed contrary to the spirit of this endeavor. His office knew how to get him, just as they knew not to employ the extreme measures necessary to do so unless the company was about to go under.

The blinking light on the phone alerted him to the fact that he had forgotten to power it off when he was in the van. He thumbed the power button, but as he did, he noticed that he had a message. Someone had tried to contact him before he took his break from the technological world. Hoping it was Angélica, he called up the e-mail, frustrated when he realized that it was not.

Alex,

I hope this catches you before radio silence. I also hope that catching you means I still have a job when you get back because you expressly told us not to bother you. The problem is that I just learned that Lansing has another suitor. You don't want to know how I found out about this. If we're going to move, we need to move now. I've attached the financials. What do you want us to do?

Sarmistha

Alex nearly crushed the Blackberry in his fist. He thought that the pep talk he'd given at the last brunch was enough to keep his staff motivated and on track in his absence. He'd actually convinced himself that his senior staff was more capable of operating independently of him within his established guidelines. Obviously Sarmistha, maybe the best of all of them, was not.

Alex read the message again and thought about a response. Maybe the best response was none at all. What would his Director of Business Development do if he simply acted as though the message didn't get to him in time? Would she do what he wanted her to do – make a move on Lansing without his help – or would she do nothing and let some other corporation whisk them away? Lansing was a good fit, but he was tempted to risk losing it for what he would learn about Sarmistha's mettle.

Alex powered down the Blackberry and sat on the futon in his room reading a brochure about the ashram. Within three minutes, though, he was looking at the phone again. Throwing Sarmistha into the deep end wasn't the right move here. He tried to read the financials on the phone's tiny screen, but found it entirely unworkable. If he were going to do anything with this data, he needed a computer with Internet access. And that meant prostrating himself before the ashram's management.

Alex made his way back down the hill, passing a casually dressed but far from unrecognizable talk-show host along the way. Considering how she conducted herself with her guests, it was hard to imagine that this woman had ever been in the same time zone as transcendence, but Alex assumed anyone could get there if he or she tried hard enough.

The main office off from the dining room was quiet when he arrived. The registration rush was over. Perhaps the talk-show host had been the last person to sign in this week. The man who'd dealt with Alex earlier wasn't there now. In fact, no one was around at all. He noticed a door to the left of the desk that was three-quarters closed. He tried to gauge any sense of activity from the space in the door, found none, and decided to knock.

"Yeah," came a male voice on the other side.

Alex opened the door further. He found a man who looked to be in his late forties sitting at a desk full of papers. The man's jet-black curls mixed with the occasional strand of gray, and thick hair lined his arms and, from what Alex could see through the unbuttoned portion of his shirt, his chest.

"I'm a guest here," Alex said, still holding the doorknob.

"Mr. Soberano, yes. My name is Yusuf. I'm the general manager. How may I help you?"

"I need to get online."

Yusuf put down the pen he'd been holding. "You're the first of the day."

"Does that make me the most pathetic?"

The man smiled softly. "Not pathetic, no."

Alex finally let go of the doorknob and took two steps into the room. "I do realize that we're supposed to check all of our electronic toys at the entrance."

"It really is better for you."

Alex nodded aggressively. "And I was planning on doing so – and *will* do so after this particular time. I'm trying to wean my staff, and at least one of them is resisting."

"Yes, getting people to do what would be best for them is sometimes difficult."

Alex caught Yusuf's irony. Ordinarily, such sarcasm would raise his hackles, but he could see that the man wasn't being malicious. "I really need that computer." He looked around the room and didn't see a single monitor. "You do *have* computers, right?"

The man stood. "How would we do business otherwise? We just keep them sequestered. They offer less temptation to our guests that way."

Yusuf gestured toward a door in the back of the room, leading Alex in that direction. When Alex approached, he stuck out his hand. "It's nice to meet you, Mr. Soberano."

Alex took the man's hand. "Alex, please."

"You have a very big business from what I hear."

"Maybe getting bigger, depending on what your computer tells me."

Yusuf opened the door and ushered Alex in. "That's putting a lot of pressure on my computer. I hope it tells you what you want it to."

Yusuf sat at the machine and typed in a password. "It's a dial-up modem, the best we could do given our location. A satellite dish didn't seem appropriate." He stared at the computer and Alex did the same, waiting for the interminable booting process.

"People have told me I have the soul of an entrepreneur," Yusuf said while typing in another password. "As it turns out, though, I don't have the stomach of one."

"That's hardly an indictment. Sometimes I wish that I had less of an entrepreneur's stomach."

Yusuf looked up from the monitor, holding Alex's gaze for an unusually long time. "No you don't."

Alex smiled softly. "No, I guess I don't. I've come to this ashram, though, so I guess I'm willing to consider alternatives. At least temporary ones."

Yusuf typed in something else. It had been a long time since Alex had seen a computer this slow. Would he even be able to view the file Sarmistha had sent? "I read the piece about your company in *Inc.*," Yusuf said as he coaxed the machine's web connection with more keystrokes.

"That's not what I would have expected from the general manager of an ashram."

"As I said, soul of an entrepreneur. I found what you had to say interesting. My son –" Yusuf paused and his face dropped. He bore up quickly, though. "My son used to say similar things."

The thought of his son obviously brought Yusuf some pain. Did Alex really want to get into this with him? All he really wanted to do was view the Lansing financials, but he couldn't help himself from saying, "Your son doesn't say those things any longer?"

Yusuf again held Alex with an unusually long gaze. Alex was beginning to find this a bit uncomfortable. The general manager's eyes misted as he said, "He doesn't say anything to me now. It's been a while since we've spoken. I'm not –" Again, he pulled up short. This time Alex thought the man might begin crying and he wasn't at all sure what he would do if that happened.

Yusuf shook his head quickly. "I'm sorry. I don't know why I'm doing this. I haven't been myself all day. I see some of him in you and…I don't know, maybe I need a week or two as a guest at this place myself."

He chuckled joylessly, then looked at the monitor. "Ah, here we go. You're on, finally. Once we get a connection, we're usually okay." Yusuf stood and waved Alex toward the chair in which he'd just been sitting. "It's all yours. I'll leave you alone. Good luck."

Alex sat. Surprisingly, he didn't move toward the computer right away, watching the general manager leave instead. If this were a different kind of hotel, he'd think about asking the man if he wanted to have a drink later. Maybe they could grab some wheatgrass together instead.

Once Yusuf closed the door behind him, Alex logged on to his e-mail and opened the document with the Lansing financials. They weren't far from what he guessed they would be. Lansing had a bit more cash than he would have expected them to have and their other assets were a little shy of what he anticipated, but everything was within a workable range. He'd checked into their management well enough to know that they looked clean. Of course, he would have preferred to look the executive staff in the eyes, but if he really wanted people like Sarmistha to take an active role in expanding the corporation, he was going to have to trust their instincts more often – and get them to do the same.

Alex hit the "reply" button on his e-mail and typed a response.

Sarmistha,

You're not fired this time. No promises if you try to reach me again, though. Make your move with this. I'm okay up to $30M. If it takes more than that, work it out with Gene.

Have a good couple of weeks.

Alex

Alex sent the message, then hit the "check mail" button one more time before logging off. He promised himself that he wouldn't be tempted to check again.

Opening the door, he found Yusuf had gone back to working on his papers.

"Do you want me to turn off the computer?"

Yusuf looked up at him. "I'll take care of it. Thanks."

Alex walked past Yusuf's desk on his way out. "I appreciate your help. Listen, if you ever want your son to talk to me about business, have him give me a call."

Yusuf's face clouded over again. "Thank you. As I said, though, we haven't been talking."

"Maybe this will give you an excuse."

Yusuf's eyes caught Alex's, and Alex thought he saw something deeper in them than he'd seen before.

"Maybe it will," the general manager said.

12.

SOUTHERN CALIFORNIA, 2010

Alex had been up since six in the morning, breakfasting, doing yoga, and hiking with the others. Now an hour of free time remained until lunch, and Alex decided to spend it in a private meditation session with Valerie Sears. He'd been looking forward to this since he first perused the ashram's website. Sears had been with the ashram since its founding nearly three decades earlier. In that time, she'd authored a number of books on meditation, mind-body healing, and Omega Point theory and gained a reputation for seeing the world from a particularly off-kilter perspective. Alex had never heard of her before last week, but he'd scheduled as many sessions with her as he could during his stay because her credentials impressed him more than anyone on the ashram's staff.

Alex's mind already felt clearer since he'd arrived at the ashram. The light diet and the rigorous physical activity – combined with an absence of any further contact with the office – left him with a briskness he hadn't experienced in a while. The thin mattress was no impediment last night and, considering the workout he'd already enjoyed today, he was sure it wouldn't be during the entirety of his stay. Physical exhaustion made nearly all sleeping conditions acceptable. He awoke especially keen this morning and the sense of vividness increased during the long walk into the mountains. He'd taken most of his strides next to Sloan, his instant friend from check-in, but the group essentially moved as a unit. At first, the talk show host sequestered herself with a screen-writer, but by the second mile, they'd slipped into the pack, seemingly losing and gaining identity at once. A few of them seemed haggard by hike's end, but Alex felt charged by the experience. He almost wondered if he'd become too wired for meditation.

Sears had not yet arrived in the austere room when Alex got there. The windows were drawn with bamboo shades, though light crept around the sides. A small table holding incense occupied one corner and the floor held only a woven rug and two cushions. Alex estimated the entire space to be less than a hundred square feet, though the spare furnishings might have made it seem even larger than it actually was.

Alex had gone to the table to sniff a stick of incense when the instructor opened the door.

"Hello, Alex, I'm Valerie."

Alex walked toward the slight, grey-haired woman with aquamarine eyes, who he guessed to be in her mid-to-late sixties. He reached out his hand in greeting. Valerie took his in both of hers and regarded him with a placid expression. When their eyes met, though, her hands tightened and her eyes widened. Valerie's gaze was unusually strong and Alex felt taken in, suctioned. He didn't think it would have been possible for him to look away, though it didn't seem as though Valerie was trying to lock him here against his will.

Then she slid her glance sideways and canted her head to the right. She nodded once slowly and said, "Now I understand."

The eccentricity left Alex a little confused. "Excuse me?"

Valerie fluttered a hand across her face. "Nothing, sorry. That must have seemed a little odd to you. I promise I don't usually do things like that. The last day or so...." She gestured toward a cushion. "Let's sit. We have much to do. I noticed that you scheduled several sessions with me."

"I did. Is it okay for me to be monopolizing you like that?"

"It's fine. It's good. We'll accomplish quite a bit, I think."

Valerie seemed to have a sense that they were on a mission of some sort. Alex had only scheduled the sessions because he thought meditation would be the most portable tool for de-stressing he could carry with him from the ashram. Had Valerie gleaned some larger purpose from the stare session they'd just shared? He certainly hoped she didn't plan to "fix" him. Such a task was not on his agenda in any way.

Valerie moved into a lotus position and Alex followed suit. "Have you had much experience with meditation?" she said.

"A little bit a long time ago. And you could say it's in the family. My aunt actually had a fling with Maharishi Mahesh Yogi once."

Valerie looked up at him with an expression of surprise.

"We can get into that some other time," Alex said. "As far as my experience with meditation is concerned, I think it's safe to assume that I'm starting from scratch."

"That's good to know. It gives me an idea of how to proceed. The goal is to focus on your mantra and let everything else drop away. We'll use 'om' unless you prefer to use your own mantra."

"Om is fine with me."

"Is this position comfortable for you?"

Alex had never particularly liked sitting cross-legged, and the pose struck him as something out of a New Age book, but he felt rather comfortable on the cushion, almost as though a plush, invisible chair supported him. "It's good, yes."

"Very well. Now, the first time I work with someone, I usually employ hypnosis to help that person drop into a meditative state. Will that be all right with you?"

"Hypnosis?" Alex said haltingly.

"I'm not talking about stage magic, if that's what you're thinking." She smiled sheepishly. "I won't have you quacking like a duck in the middle of dinner tonight, or anything along those lines."

"No, no, of course. I've had some strange…you know what? Let's go with the hypnosis. I could use a little help getting back there."

"Okay, then. I'll simply count you down and then take you through a relaxation exercise. After that, I'll instruct you to say 'om' to yourself on the out-breath, letting everything else slip back. Does that sound all right to you?"

Alex adjusted himself on the cushion. "Fine, yes. I guess I'll meet you back here at the end of the session."

Valerie smiled softly. "Yes. Now take a deep breath, hold that breath, and then close your eyes as you release it."

Alex did as Valerie instructed, then listened as she counted from ten to one, and took him through the process of releasing tension from every part of his body. Any qualms he had about allowing Valerie to hypnotize him receded quickly, replaced by welcome peacefulness and a feeling of molding into the cushion. When Valerie instructed him to begin meditating, his perception of the cushion and his surroundings diminished. As welcome as that was, though, he couldn't seem to attach all of his thoughts to his mantra. Stray images – something Sloan had said at breakfast, a line from the Lansing financials, a fawn he'd seen during the hike, Angélica's face – introduced themselves and drew his attention. He succeeded in casting most of them away, though some proved harder than others, and his mind rarely stayed clear for long. He wondered how long he was going to have to practice this before he made any progress, suddenly feeling justified in scheduling as many of these sessions as he had.

Yet when Valerie counted him back out, he realized that a space of some size separated her words from his last remembered thought. Clearly, he'd gotten beyond his consciousness at some point, though it might have been for no longer than a few seconds. When he opened his eyes, Valerie seemed to be studying him. Was she trying to read him for something? She stopped whatever she'd been doing and offered him a placid smile. "Did that go well for you?" she said.

Alex got onto his knees and started to rise, feeling languid. "I think it did. Thank you."

"You might want to give yourself a minute or so before you start moving around."

Alex sat, drawing his arms around his knees. "I had a fair amount of trouble battling random thoughts."

Valerie nodded. "Monkey mind."

"Excuse me?"

"That's what we call it when your mind bounces from thought to thought while you're trying to meditate. You'll have less trouble, with practice."

Alex started to move again, the tautness returning to his muscles. "Maybe by the time I'm ready to go home."

"That might be ambitious, but we'll set it as one of our goals."

Alex got to his feet and took a deep, cleansing breath. He offered a hand to help Valerie up, but she demurred, saying she was going to spend some time meditating on her own. Alex thanked her again and headed out the door.

The noon sun was strong, having finally burned through the morning's haze. It felt warmer now and

Alex decided to head back to his room to change into a lighter shirt before going to lunch.

He'd taken no more than three steps away from the cottage when the monkeys started clamoring for attention in his mind again. It was almost as though they'd politely waited outside for him after he sent them away and were once again ready to besiege him. He wondered if he'd given Sarmistha a clear enough action plan. He wondered what Angélica was thinking now that a day-and-a-half had passed since they'd last spoken.

And then that woman came into his head again, surprising him as much as she had the night before. She'd flirted with him last evening, challenging him with a few memories. But then he let her go. Would her stay be longer this time?

Alex wasn't at all sure he was ready for the answer.

❧

They had gotten near the peak of the highest incline and Alex's breathing was firmly under control. This third ten-mile hike in as many days was going far more smoothly than the first two had gone. Alex had always prided himself on his conditioning – something that few others at his level in the business world were able to maintain – but the rigorous exercise regimen at the ashram had challenged that pride. He was well on his way to overcoming this, though, as his steady breathing and confident strides attested. He had no trouble keeping up with Sloan, though the man was easily a decade younger, maybe more. "What happens when this gets too easy?" he said to the tech-wizard-turned-professor. Sloan tossed his head toward the distance. "Well, there's always another mountain to climb." "I suppose there is. What's your next mountain?" "I assume we're speaking metaphorically at this point since, you know, we aren't near another mountain right now." The incline reached its sharpest angle and Alex felt some tightening in his hamstrings. "Metaphorically, yes." Sloan squinted toward the sun. "I'd like to believe that the mountain I'm on is high enough for me." "But you know that isn't the case." "Yeah, I do. I'd been doing a good job of kidding myself about it, though, so thanks for setting me straight." Sloan threw Alex a smirk that Alex assumed was sarcastic. Then he looked out toward the distance again. "Whatever it turns out to be, it won't have anything to do with finance; I know that much." "Really?" Sloan chuckled. "I'm a little surprised that I just said that myself. I think I mean it, though." "You're not talking about becoming a missionary or something like that, are you?" "Missionary? No, I can honestly say I've never given that a second's thought. The last few days, I've had these thoughts in my head about creating a company, though. I've never had one of those."

"I didn't realize you had any interest in that sort of thing."

Sloan gestured with his open palms. "Neither did I. You know how things sometimes just pop into your head? Last week, I was talking to one of my students – model gorgeous, by the way – and something she said about corporations got me thinking that I could see myself building an enterprise. A few days later, I find myself talking to you. There are no accidents, you know."

Alex considered this. Ironically, his conversations with Sloan over the past few days had led him to think about the days when teaching had been a serious consideration for him. Not that he had any desire to return to those days.

"Are you planning on conquering a new frontier anytime soon?" Sloan said as the path leveled. Alex noticed that they'd left most of the group behind. Only one of the instructors and a woman with the body of a marathoner were visible at this point.

"Nah, me? I'm doing exactly what I should be doing."

"Wow, you win."

"Okay, maybe I overstated that a little. Let me put it this way: I have no doubts about my profession. At the same time, I'm here."

"And on the spur of the moment, no less."

The path grew narrow and rocky at this point. For the next quarter mile, Alex needed to concentrate on his footing. He'd allowed Sloan to walk in front of him, so conversation wasn't viable. At the end of this part of the path, they emerged on an outcropping that afforded them a panoramic view and made the effort required to get here worth it. A glance to the south showed him, in miniature fashion, the hut where he'd been working with Valerie Sears. To the north the path snaked in two directions. The instructors had always taken them on the western path. Did they think the eastern path was too much of a challenge?

Alex walked next to Sloan and scanned as much of the view as he could see from this spot. "I think we're supposed to be thinking of God here."

"Does that mean I'm not supposed to be thinking about the coed that came on to me last Monday?"

"What do you think God would say?"

"He'd probably say, 'Take a pass for once, will ya, Wel?'"

"She's not *illegal*, is she?"

"Technically? No. Probably should be, though. Like fast food."

"Yeah, I hear you."

Sloan bent to tie one of his hiking shoes, though the laces appeared to be perfectly tight to Alex. Interestingly, rather than standing up immediately after, Sloan sat, pulled his knees toward his chest, and looked into the distance for an oddly long time. What could he be seeing from down there that Alex couldn't see from his vantage?

Eventually, Sloan studied the ground for a moment and then rose up, gesturing with his head that he was ready to continue the hike.

"Are you seriously involved with someone right now?" he said as Alex strode next to him.

"Up to six hours before I left to come here, I would have said yes."

"That must have been a bad six hours."

The vision of Angélica's body turned away from him slipped into his mind. "Something went wrong. I'm not sure I can say what. I'm hoping it was just a blip or that I at least get a clue as to how I screwed up. What about you? Are you serious with someone?"

"Nah. The world seems to be a better place when I'm just playing the field. It turns out that I'm not particularly resilient to heartbreak."

Alex considered the comment, unsure if he could draw a comparison to his own life. He hadn't been heartbroken when Opal and he had split. By the time he realized they were done, he had already become so furious with her that he didn't have any room in his soul for sadness. Before her, he tended to be the one who ended relationships, usually prior to any emotional attachment from either party. What if things ended with Angélica, though? Interestingly, he found it difficult to imagine this. But if it happened, would it break his heart? Certainly, he would feel awful about it. He would almost surely mourn it, maybe even for a long time. Did that constitute heartbreak?

Once again, he thought of the woman who had been haunting him since he arrived at the ashram. For so long, he'd done such a good job of expunging her from his consciousness. Was that because she'd broken his heart? Or was the damage done by her loss more severe? After all, broken hearts, by all reports, mended.

"It amazes me to talk to people who regularly bounce back from disastrous relationships," Sloan said, clearly oblivious to Alex's ruminations. "How do you go through that experience and then come back for more?"

"I don't know. I mean, I had to deal with a true disaster once. A real soul crusher. It was a very long time ago, though. Long before my marriage. Long before the woman I'm with now."

Several people in the group had moved past them, the first indication to Alex that their pace had slowed dramatically. Sloan didn't seem to notice. "So explain it to me. What made you want to go through it again?"

"I don't think I have. Not that way. Not anything remotely like it. It was a singular event and I was an entirely different person. I guess in that way you could say that it happened to someone else."

This comment seemed to astound Sloan, literally stopping him in his tracks. That seemed to be an overreaction; Alex didn't think he'd said anything particularly profound. More like bad pop psychology, actually. While Sloan stood there unmoving, a few more people passed them, glancing over as though they were wondering what the hell was going on. Alex could sympathize with that. Finally, Sloan bent down again to tie his already-tied shoelaces. When he stood, he shook his head briskly.

"I don't know what's gotten into me."

The man seemed frazzled, borderline unhinged. If thinking about a woman could do this to him, Alex was very glad he didn't have that experience in his background.

"Do you want some water or something?"

"No, I'm okay. I've just had a few unanticipated revelations this time around. I expect to do some serious thinking when I'm here, but stuff has been hitting me from all angles since I arrived."

"Maybe you should lay off the yoga."

Sloan smiled, seeming to regain his composure. "Yeah, maybe."

Alex gestured upward on the path. "Do you want to start walking again? The ice cream king just passed us. I don't know about you, but I consider that an affront to my manhood."

"Yeah, let's do that."

∝

"You haven't been able to use your vision talents for how long?"

Alex was in the hut with Valerie. She'd just counted him out of a meditation session after which he'd mentioned something that had been dancing through his thoughts the entire time.

"Since the end of college. But it isn't that I can't use them *at all*. I use them in my office all the time. I have no trouble there whatsoever, or anywhere that I'm doing business. I once was able to use them for everything, though, and now I can't."

Valerie studied him deeply. She'd done some version of this intense gazing into his eyes every time he'd been with her and it still made him squirm inside. This time was especially long. It seemed as though minutes passed while she appraised him.

"I can help you explore this."

"You can?"

Valerie nodded slowly. "It isn't a method I teach here. I'm not even sure I can show you how to use it effectively. You'd have to consider this the equivalent of using an experimental drug on a serious illness."

Alex found Valerie's words alarming. Did this issue mean enough to him to warrant the use of "experimental drugs?" He'd been getting by perfectly well all these years. He had success and a robust social life. What more could he gain from the return of his lost vision? Was it possible that getting them back might even prove to be an impediment of some sort?

At the same time, he knew he was here for a reason. In the past few days, he'd dismissed the notion that he'd come out to the ashram seeking only rest or new tools to help him manage stress. He still wasn't clear on what the reason was, but as each day passed he grew more convinced that it had something to do with the point at which a part of his vision had become inaccessible.

"What kind of methods are you talking about?"

Valerie's eyes brightened, suggesting that his interest pleased her. "You see in colors, right?"

"Yes."

"I use colors often, though my method is probably different from yours. However, sometimes the colors become occluded for me. I found this very frustrating until I taught myself an approach that allowed me to see beyond the colors. I can try to show you how to do this. If we're successful, you might also get the entirety of your color vision back."

Alex felt a trill of excitement play through his body. He'd been managing without this vision, compensating for its loss, somewhat like a person adjusts to minor chronic pain. But he'd never stopped missing it, never stopped thinking about the comfort and security the vision had afforded him. He realized immediately that his concerns about the consequences of its return were foolish. Having it back would be a welcome reunion.

"Can we do this now?"

"If you're willing to miss lunch."

"I suppose I can survive without those two hundred and fifty calories."

Valerie's eyes glittered at his little joke. Then she rose and moved to the table in the room, bowing her head toward it. Alex thought she intended to light some incense, but a minute or so later, she turned back and came to sit across from him again with nothing in her hands.

"I'm going to hypnotize you again. Then I'm going to enter the deep meditative mind I use for this method. Once I'm there, I'll try to guide you to go where I'm going. As I said, I don't teach this method here. I haven't developed the process for use with others. My feeling is that I can teach this to you, but I have no evidence to back this feeling."

"I'm a guinea pig. I get it."

Valerie looked at him closely again, and he wondered if he were in for another of her stare sessions. But then she said, "I'm glad you understand," and directed him to close his eyes.

As she had less than an hour earlier, she counted him down and then guided him through the relaxation exercises that moved him toward a hypnotic state, an experience that had proven to be more pleasurable with Valerie than with anyone who'd hypnotized him in the past; her mastery of technique was decidedly superior to the others. Once he was under, Valerie went silent for a long time. Alex wasn't sure what to do with this time. He'd already meditated for an hour, and while he certainly had plenty of areas on which he could have placed his concentration, he found that he wasn't interested in doing so with any of them. And so he did something he did so rarely that he wondered if he possessed the capacity to do it any longer: he waited.

When she finally spoke, Valerie's voice seemed to come from underneath his mind. "I want you to use the process that you use to see colors in your professional life, but I want you to do it with your eyes closed."

This seemed like a contradiction to Alex. He'd always used his eyes to see the colors, perfecting the method of looking at and around someone at the same time without their ever noticing that he'd divided his attention. He tried relaxing his vision with his eyes shut, but no colors appeared. How could they? He didn't even have a figure to think about while he was doing this, let alone someone to look at, and imagining Valerie sitting across from him generated nothing.

"I'm not getting any color," he said after several minutes.

"I would have been surprised if you were. I just wanted you to make yourself receptive in the same way that you do when you are looking for colors."

"Oh, I didn't realize."

"I understand that. Accept that we are doing something new here. Now I want you to work your way under this. I want you to move through the haze and attach your vision to an image rather than a color. Push through the veil that separates you from the pictures."

"I don't know what I'm supposed to be looking for."

"Of course you do. Look for the thing that shows you what you need to see."

Valerie's teaching had been remarkably free of "New Age-y" phrases of that sort in their work together. He'd appreciated how she made the esoteric and the spiritual seem plain. He wished she could have done that here, though she did warn him that she wasn't sure how or even if she could teach what she was trying to teach him.

He set his mind in search of the thing that "showed him what he needed to see." He realized now that, while he couldn't perceive any colors, he actually noticed waves in the darkness. It seemed like a particularly dense and dark fog rolling in front of him. Was this the veil about which Valerie spoke? Could he push through this to find the pictures she wanted him to see? He willed himself to draw closer to the fog, to walk his mind into it. He felt motion, felt himself in the midst of the fog.

Then he was through to the other side. He attempted to sharpen his vision, but he couldn't fix it on anything. In the foreground, he noticed a subtle differentiation in the darkness. A dirt path, perhaps, or a road. But as he looked upward from this, he found the darkness growing in a jagged line, as though the picture had fractured, with the rest falling into the abyss.

"I'm getting...something. It's vague. Barely visible."

"Good. That's a beginning for us. Hold on to that."

"I'll do what I can," Alex said, trying to give all of his concentration over to the image. The only thing that became clearer, though, was the jagged darkness.

"Now release the vision," Valerie said. "Try to shut your eyes completely. Allow yourself to feel all of your senses but sight."

The image he struggled so hard to attain did not go away easily. It was a bit like telling Alex to avoid the elephant in the room. Once the thought was in his head, he could not ignore it. However, he understood that Valerie was teaching him a discipline. Just as he struggled through the daily bouts of "monkey mind" to reach a more productive method of meditation, he had to will himself to ignore the things he needed to avoid.

What seemed like several minutes passed. Then, without preamble, his sight dropped away completely. No vaguely sketched path. No jagged line leading to nothingness. No fog. Instead, simple darkness.

Valerie had told him to feel all of his senses but sight. He drew his attention to these, expecting to be transported somewhere. He relaxed into this, feeling confident that Valerie's process was leading him somewhere.

As the minutes passed, though, frustration crept in. All he could feel was the cushion upon which he sat. All he could smell was the remnants of the last incense that had burned in this room. All he could hear was the occasional sound of nature that crept into the hut. All he could taste was the hunger he'd tamped down to participate in this additional session with Valerie.

All he could sense was here. Now. If there was a message in this, he was incapable of interpreting it.

He gave himself several additional minutes. Then, though Valerie had advised him against doing so until she'd counted him out, he opened his eyes. Valerie seemed to feel him doing so, as she opened hers immediately thereafter.

"I let go of my sight as you suggested and I wound up here."

He expected Valerie to offer some words of encouragement, to tell him that this kind of work took time, or to blame the experimental nature of the exercise. All she said, though, was, "You didn't sense anything."

Thinking it was a question, he said, "No, nothing."

"I know; I was there with you."

Alex wasn't at all sure what she meant by this, but he didn't want to pursue this right now. "Let's try this again tomorrow, okay?"

Valerie shook her head. "That's not going to help."

"How do you know? You said yourself that you didn't teach this method."

Valerie got up on her knees. "Alex, this isn't going to happen. Not now. That jagged darkness you saw? You need to find a way to fill in that picture. If you don't, this plane will always elude you."

With that, she stood. Valerie never got up before he did. This time, though, she seemed ready to vacate the hut as quickly as possible. Feeling disoriented and a little abandoned, Alex stood, glanced confusedly at Valerie, and then turned to leave.

13.

SOUTHERN CALIFORNIA, 2010

As the sun rose on the fourth day of his trip, Alex felt a lightness to his movements he hadn't felt in many years. The physical impact of his stay at the ashram had been dramatic and immediate. The reduced diet and the intense level of physical activity had left him freshened.

He couldn't say as much for the psychic impact of his stay, at least not so far. Until yesterday, his sessions with Valerie Sears had been illuminating and relaxing. The last session, however, had left him uneasy and unsure of what to think. Valerie had been unusually cryptic in discussing the jagged darkness Alex saw, and she'd been entirely unhelpful regarding methods to address that darkness. While before she'd been open to showing him new techniques, including the one that had led to such disturbing results, she now seemed to be suggesting that he needed to solve this problem alone.

Compounding this was the vision of the woman he'd been involved with so long ago. During his first few days at the ashram, she'd made the occasional surprise appearance in his thoughts. Now she'd taken up residence there. This was unsettling in so many ways.

He'd come back from the hike with a half hour to go before his next session with Valerie. Feeling energized and not feeling the need to go back to his room, Alex walked toward the main building. Some staff members were working there, but he was the only guest in the vicinity.

"Looking to sneak some more Internet time, Alex?"

Alex turned toward the voice, finding the general manager Yusuf standing about twenty feet away. "I've kicked the habit. I've been e-mail free for three days now."

Yusuf bowed jokingly. "Congratulations. You must be very proud of yourself."

"My guess is that several of my employees are considering jumping off a bridge at this point, but I'm pleased that I've resisted the urge to contact them."

Yusuf slowly closed the space between them. "Alex," he said in a softer voice, "I've been wanting to approach you for the past few days now. I wanted to apologize for my behavior the other night. I fear that it might have come across as less than professional to you."

"What do you mean?"

"When you came to the back office the other day. I got rather emotional. I didn't want you to think that I made a habit of burdening guests with my dramas. I take too much pride in what I do to act in such a fashion."

The man's contriteness surprised Alex. He didn't think Yusuf had unburdened himself at all. Alex had been in situations where people decided to unload their personal demons on him and he always found the most graceful way possible to go running for the hills. He didn't recall his conversation with Yusuf that way at all. In fact, he found the man's reflections on his son disarming and his immediate instinct was to want to reach out to Yusuf, though admittedly he hadn't acted on those instincts.

"To tell you the truth," Alex said, "I'd been thinking about seeking you out for a chat. It seemed that you had more to say."

Yusuf turned his palms upward. "Well, we always have more to say, don't we? Anyway, I appreciate your understanding."

This would have been an easy place to back out of the conversation, but Alex found that he didn't want to do so. He wasn't sure what made him feel this way, but he felt a sense of camaraderie with the general manager. Maybe the air around the ashram made him feel particularly open, but he had the sense that he would have wanted to get to know Yusuf better wherever they'd met.

"I have about a half hour before my next session. That's how I wound up wandering over here. Do you want to grab a...glass of water somewhere?"

Yusuf's eyes glittered. "I agree; a glass of rum would be better. I suppose a glass of water will have to do, though. I have an even better suggestion. Have you been through the gardens?"

"No, I haven't."

"Perhaps we could take a walk there now."

The gardens turned out to be a half-acre of plantings just down the hill from the main building. Yusuf told Alex that the staff took turns tending to the native flowers, which ranged from poppies to buttercups to something Yusuf called coffeeberry. Also here were the vegetables the ashram served to their guests and staff daily.

"I don't spend as much time here as I should," Yusuf said. "Just the last few days, though, I've been trying to be out here more. To spend more time listening to the plants."

"Listening to the plants?"

Yusuf's face showed a hint of embarrassment. "Just one of my things."

He guided Alex to the center of the garden where, invisible from the outside, there was a small meditation space. They sat on a bench and neither spoke for a minute. Alex adored Manhattan, but he wondered if his life wouldn't somehow be amplified if he had the opportunity to sit somewhere like this for at least a few minutes every morning before entering the fray.

"So tell me about your son," Alex said.

Yusuf watched a butterfly as it alighted on a nearby flower. "He's very strong. Very, very strong. From the time he was a baby, he had opinions and ways of doing things and he wasn't much interested in advice. That can be tough on a father."

"It can also be a very good thing in the real world."

"It can, I suppose. And he seems to be handling the real world well. The last I heard, his employers had given him a big promotion. He's not a grunt anymore. My guess is that the promotions will continue to come quickly for him. That's what he wants desperately."

"When was the last time you spoke with him?"

The breeze picked up and the butterfly left its perch. Yusuf looked away. "It depends on what you mean by 'spoke.' We sat at the same dinner table last summer and we said a few words to each other. I'm not sure you could call that speaking, though. A couple of months later, I called to ask him to come to the house for his brother's birthday. He told me he was too busy and I said some hurtful things about his priorities and his dependence on money." Yusuf turned to Alex with an expression of self-recrimination. "That was the more polite half of the conversation. You can imagine what the other half was like."

"Nothing since then?"

"Not even a snarl."

"Maybe it's time for you to reach out to him."

Yusuf regarded Alex more fully. "I've thought about that. More lately, actually. But I'm not a masochist."

"Maybe he'll surprise you."

"Maybe I'll sprout wings like that butterfly."

Alex offered a soft chuckle. "It's fine to feel that way. As long as you can live with it."

"The funny thing is that I thought I was. Recently, though, I've been having other thoughts. Some of that has to do with you."

"Wow. I'm not sure I like the sound of that."

Yusuf smiled at him. "I wasn't trying to blame you, if that's what you thought and I'm certainly not trying to burden you with this responsibility now. What I meant was that when I heard you were coming, I read a little more about you and I couldn't help but think about my son. Now that I've gotten to know you this little bit, I have a feeling that I might have undervalued where he was going."

"Then my work here is done."

Yusuf nodded. "Your work? Yes. My work? I think most of it is ahead of me." He patted Alex on the knee. "You have a session to attend, and the staff isn't accustomed to my disappearing in the middle of the day. Thank you. You're a good listener for a corporate baron."

∾

L unch had been like flirting with a beautiful woman who gets up and leaves in the middle of the conversation. It was like this at every meal. The food was delicious as always, fragrant, nuanced, and balanced, but there wasn't nearly enough of it. Because Alex was conscious of maintaining a rigorous exercise regimen, he never worried about what he ate. At the ashram, though, while his spirit's appetite sparked, his stomach felt unsatisfied.

"I think these guys are underselling one of the benefits of coming here," he said to Sloan as they walked up the hill toward their rooms. "They're not just providing us with a greater appreciation of our souls; they're also providing us with a greater appreciation of huge bowls of pasta."

Sloan held up his hands. "Please don't mention pasta. There are certain words I avoid contemplating when I'm here. Blackberry, for instance. Glenlivet. Pasta is one of those words."

"I guess I'll have a better grasp of this when I become a vet like you." They took several steps in silence, Alex suddenly feeling a bit apprehensive about talking to his newest friend. He forced himself to get past it. "It's probably better that I'm not eating much right now, anyway. I'm not sure how much I'd be able to keep down."

"Is your stomach feeling strange? It probably has to do with anxiety release. It happens around here a lot. You'll get over it."

"Actually, that's not it."

Obviously, the tone of Alex's voice drew Sloan's attention, as the younger man looked at him confused.

"I've had some disquieting experiences up here. The craziest was this thing yesterday with Valerie Sears."

They'd reached Sloan's building, but rather than peeling off as he usually did, Sloan gestured Alex toward a wall, leaning against it. Alex proceeded to tell him about the hypnotic exercise in which he saw the jagged darkness that Valerie perceived so gravely.

"What the hell was that thing?" Sloan said, affected by this more than Alex had expected him to be.

"I've been trying to figure it out ever since I saw it. When any vision of your life involves a black gash, though, you can be pretty sure it isn't good. There's something else, though."

"Please tell me you aren't seeing your body at the bottom of a pit."

"Not quite, though the effect is similar. I think I have a ghost haunting me."

"Like in a Stephen King novel?"

"I don't know; I've never read Stephen King. Are his ghosts old lovers who died tragically?"

Sloan slid down the wall until he was sitting on the grass. Again, this seemed like a strong reaction to Alex. "The ghost is an old lover?"

"Someone I knew a long time ago. Someone I'd worked very hard to get out of my mind."

"Holy shit."

"Exactly."

"No, I mean 'Holy shit, I've met that ghost.'"

"What?"

Sloan splayed his legs outward, staring off at the mountains for close to a minute. When he didn't speak right away, Alex sat against the wall as well.

"I told you how my coming here this time was a spur-of-the-moment thing, right? Well, ever since I made that decision, I've been having these weird dreams – except I'm not always sleeping when they happen. Sometimes, I'll just be sitting quietly. Sometimes, I'll be walking. I did one meditation session and quit after that because I could swear someone else was in my body. I've gotten this, I don't know, *ghostly* sense of the woman a few times, and whenever I do I feel sad, and guilty, and confused. But I swear I've never met this woman in my life. I mean, I've plowed through a bunch of women over the years and I should probably feel sad, guilty, and confused about several of them – but I wouldn't have forgotten one that makes me feel this way."

Alex put his head in his left hand, massaging the temples. "I need to get a grip."

Sloan chuckled. "What I just said made you think that *you* need to get a grip?"

Alex looked over at Sloan, who was regarding him with disbelief. "Actually, I think we both need to get a grip, but I didn't want to speak for you."

"This is profoundly bizarre. Or bizarrely profound. I'm not sure which."

They sat together on the grass for several minutes longer, neither saying a word. Alex studied the mountains, feeling as though he could see all the way to Yosemite if he tried hard enough.

Then he stood, swiping stray grass from his pants. "I'm going to stop thinking about this now."

He offered Sloan a hand up and the man took it, rising to stand next to him. "Really?"

"At least I'm going to try."

Sloan looked down at his feet and then quickly back up to Alex. "Yeah, me too."

14.
SOUTHERN CALIFORNIA, 2010

By two o'clock in the morning, the idea that Alex could "stop thinking about this" was mocking him. Throughout the afternoon, past dinner, and well into the hours he lay prone on the thin mattress; the implications of his conversations with Sloan and Valerie – and the regular interruptions from his "ghost" – played on Alex's mind. Even the talks he'd had with Yusuf gave off echoes. Alex had anticipated that the work he was doing at the ashram might cause some feelings he'd buried in his subconscious to bubble up. To some degree, he welcomed this, believing it would be a link to the work he'd abruptly ended more than a decade and a half ago. He did not imagine, though, that the people he met here would leave him feeling at once a part of some spiritual continuum and consistently uneasy. Perhaps if he'd buddied up to the talk show host rather than Sloan, or chosen to take more yoga sessions with the group rather than solo meditations with Valerie, he would have experienced fewer pin-pricks on his soul. Perhaps if he'd accessed the computer via the man who'd checked him in, he would have allied himself with one less psyche in turmoil. Then this could have been nothing more than a spur-of-the-moment exercise in relaxation whose anecdotes would have entertained his friends at Soho House for weeks after his return.

Instead, he had this night. This night where his thoughts owned him. They didn't simply avoid elusion; they demanded his focus. Valerie's jagged drop into the abyss. The ghost he shared, somehow, with Sloan. Yusuf's son, whose face Alex could visualize clearly, the face of a distant cousin, though he was sure this was exclusively the product of some form of projection.

He realized how confining this room could feel under the wrong circumstances. At home, if his middle-of-the-night ruminations became too active, he could always work, or lose himself in any number of electronic diversions. He had books. He had Angélica, though he had no idea whether that would continue to be the case when he got back. Here, though, he had the silence and the darkness, both of which abetted the thoughts he would have preferred to keep away.

He tried meditating, but he experienced the most intense case of "monkey mind" he'd ever had. If anything, the meditative process seemed to intensify his sense of siege, making him feel more vulnerable to his thoughts. When that failed, he decided to get out of bed. While there might be no useful form of distraction in his room, simply being upright made him feel like he was controlling his environment in some way.

Pulling out the family history he'd brought on the trip, he reread the author's introduction in which he referred to Alex's ancestors as "a singular combination of mercantilism and mysticism." He started to read about the Soberanos in the nineteenth century, but he quickly found himself skipping to the end of the book, to the passages about his great grandmother, Alejandra Soberano.

> Vidente did not see the way other seers did. Though she could access images of the future if she wanted, Alejandra found colors much more telling. She could summon these by closing her eyes and concentrating intensely on her subject. When asked to explain how the colors spoke to her, she would only answer that it was a matter of instinct and that it varied from case to case. Royal blue could mean a sudden instance of wealth for one person and the onset of emotional difficulties for another.

> On occasion, though, Vidente felt the need to look elsewhere for her vision of what was to come. Sometimes, she would need to "see beyond the colors...."

Alex looked up from the page. He'd read these words before, of course, as recently as five days ago. Their familiarity, though, came from another source. Valerie had spoken to him about seeing beyond the colors when she took him to that jagged precipice, that place where he could find nothing but absolute darkness. She'd mentioned that her method was

unconventional and relatively untried. It was difficult to imagine that it was a coincidence that she
chose to introduce him to a method a member of
his own family had perfected half a world away and
nearly a century earlier.

Now I understand.

This was one of the first things Valerie had said
to him – with great solemnity – when they met. Alex
had chalked it up to the instructor's famous quirki-
ness, assuming she greeted all of her students with
some expression of deep-eyed portent. What if that
wasn't the case, though? What if she'd found something of distinct consequence in their meeting?

Alex shut the book and stood up from his chair,
uncertain of where his legs should take him, but
utterly certain that they needed to take him somewhere. It was as though the remainder of his body
had caught up to the sense of restlessness that his
mind had been experiencing since the early afternoon. He looked out his window, finding a bare
sliver of moon in the sky. There was very little light
available and he couldn't see much other than vari-
ations in the darkness that indicated trees and the
valley below the ashram. He probably wouldn't have
even been able to see that much if he hadn't already
memorized this view.

He realized that he needed to go outside. Though
the path would be very dim and would require extra
caution, a hike up the mountain might be exactly
what he needed to calm his restless mind. He'd done
his share of late-night walking in Manhattan. He
could recall employing this form of therapy as far
back as his days at school in Cambridge. Of course,

he'd always had the advantage of streetlights and the diversion of shop windows when he'd done this in the past, but he was sure that the physical expenditure alone would help. Lacing up his sneakers, he felt for the first time all day that he was moving forward.

As anticipated, there was very little light outside his door. His room was no more than fifteen paces from the path up the mountain, but that was barely visible. He had an app on his Blackberry that turned the screen into a flashlight – something Angélica had downloaded when she was toying with his phone one night. He decided to go inside to get it, figuring any additional illumination would be a help. While he was there, he wondered if maybe he should simply stay inside entirely. There were, after all, many things about these California woods he didn't know. Instead, he checked his pocket for his room key, stepped out the door, and headed toward the path.

Looking down the hill, he could see that the path to the main building had some muted lighting, and looking out over the valley, he found some lights in the distance. The ashram intentionally kept the light low at night, believing this aided sleep and contemplation. He certainly couldn't argue with the latter, though it was contemplation that had him standing outside in the first place.

As he started his hike, his eyes adapted to the dark to some degree. He could discern more trees in the distance and the path itself gained form. Within a few minutes, he began to think less about how empty the space seemed around him and more about his stride and his rising heartbeat. The physical sensations of scaling this rise were both familiar and welcome. If he'd learned nothing else during these days, he'd learned that exertion was a palliative.

The silence was the biggest surprise. He'd expected to hear any number of wildlife sounds, but beyond the occasional bit of scurrying in the woods, only his footfalls broke the quiet. Did the animals in this area honor the same middle-of-the night request for stillness that the ashram asked of its human visitors?

The thought of those animals chilled him. There were coyotes out here, weren't there? Didn't bears sometimes roam this area? He hadn't really thought this through entirely. Alex was fine with domesticated animals, but wildlife – especially wildlife with fangs and claws – tended to make him uneasy. How ironic would it be for him to come here for some peace and wind up being mauled by a vicious beast instead? Again, he thought about foregoing this hike. And again, he pushed through his reservations.

At a bend, Alex walked toward the cliff face to look out across the valley. As was the case when he looked out his window, he saw very, very little. The headlights of a lone car wound the road near the limit of his eyesight. Another restless soul, in all likelihood, with a more propulsive method of transportation. He turned to get back on the trail. Before he did, though, he stopped to look in the direction of the northeast edge of the cliff, the direction they didn't go on their hikes. There were no lights from cars here. Even the trees were sparser at this angle. He couldn't see anything but the jagged line of the cliff leading out to deeper darkness.

That jagged line was a shape that had become very familiar in his mind in recent days.

Certainly, Alex knew better than to accept at face value what his eyes showed him while he was at this ashram – especially in the middle of the night. But it was difficult to avoid thinking there was some significance to his seeing the exact jagged shape right now that he had been seeing inside his head. Even if this were nothing more than his subconscious sending him a message about this trek in the limited moonlight, it had to mean something.

That was when he saw the others, or at least a suggestion of the others. At first, they appeared to be standing in the void, simply floating in the deepest darkness. As Alex willed his eyes to see more sharply, though, he noticed that the cliff face wound to meet them. Yes, if he followed the jagged line all the way out there, he could see that the relatively lighter darkness of the earth reached to where these people stood.

Three people, little more than shadows, probably more than a quarter mile away. Yet he knew who they were because he had come to know their shapes in the last five days. Sloan's broadly athletic silhouette was facing him directly, practically making eye contact, though he was much too far away and it was much too dark. A quarter-turn downhill stood the softer form of Yusuf, and facing out toward the valley was the wispy outline of Valerie.

Why had they all decided to go out on a hike during Alex's restless night? And why had they all decided to go out *together*?

Prodded by curiosity, Alex raised a hand to wave at the collection of his ashram colleagues. None of them waved back. Were they unable to see him? It was so dark where he stood that Alex could barely see the ground, so this was certainly possible. He carefully stepped back on the path and moved in their direction, hoping they wouldn't choose this time to go further up the trail.

That eastern trail was more twisty and the footing was less steady here. Maybe this was why the instructors avoided bringing hikers this way. With a destination in mind, and with a desire to catch up to the others, Alex found the difficult conditions frustrating. As he continued on the path, he thought about how odd it was that the three people he'd gotten to know the best at the ashram were all together on this night. This was especially odd because he'd never seen any of them together before. Surely, Valerie and Yusuf had met, since they both worked here. Sloan had told him that he hadn't taken any of Valerie's individual meditation classes, though, and he had little reason to have ever met the general manager. Alex was no stranger to irrational juxtapositions in his life, but this one seemed particularly unusual.

At last, the path leveled and bent toward the cliff line. Alex heard a shuffle and, given how silent the wildlife had been, guessed that he'd come to the place where the other three stood. Again, he stepped off the trail and headed into the woods. He'd walked no more than twenty feet when the light began to change. It wasn't bright by any means, but the darkness was thinner here and grew more silvery as he took his next steps.

In another twenty feet, the tree line ended. As he came out to this clearing, only a short distance from the cliff face, he saw the others. Yusuf must have heard his approach, because he turned toward him. Except that it wasn't Yusuf. The man here had the same body type as the general manager, and like him his dark features spoke of Middle Eastern lineage. But his face was not Yusuf's. Even in the tricky light, Alex could tell that this man's brows were thicker, his eyes larger, his jaw squarer.

He'd never met this man, yet his face seemed familiar. He reminded Alex of the distant cousin he thought of when he thought about Yusuf's son.

The woman came to stand next to the man-that-wasn't-Yusuf. Now that Alex was this close, he could see that this wasn't Valerie Sears. This woman was somewhat younger and, while still built on a small frame, she had the bearing of someone considerably taller. As the improving light settled around her, Alex got a clearer look at her features. He knew those features. He'd seen them as recently as an hour ago.

The woman standing no more than ten feet away from him now was Alejandra Soberano. The great Vidente.

"Now I understand," Valerie had said to him when they first met. What was going on here?

Alex was so fixed on the vision of his great grandmother that he didn't notice the third figure approaching until that person was standing behind Alejandra. At this point, he'd already assumed that this would turn out not to be Sloan. Even still, he could never have anticipated who he was going to find here.

It was himself, in his early twenties, back when everyone called him "Dro," a truncation of his formal name, Alejandro.

Alex had trained himself to be prepared for anything. He was not prepared for this.

He stared at his younger self, unable to pull his eyes away even though Dro was hardly the only remarkable sight present.

"You look good," Dro said after Alex had been gaping at him for several seconds. "I've wanted to compliment you on how well you've held up, but I thought you would think that was a little strange coming from Sloan."

Alex couldn't speak. His eyes flitted between the man he once was and the woman who'd been a legend in his household for as long as he could remember. He contemplated many scenarios, including one that had his subconscious playing out all of this while he lay in his bed deeply slumbering on the cheap mattress. None of these scenarios even began to feel comfortable.

At last, essentially in an attempt to cleanse his thoughts for a moment, he looked at the other man. Not-Yusuf took a step forward, as though he'd been waiting for Alex to acknowledge him again.

"My name is Khaled Hebron. I am your mother's father's father."

Khaled extended his hand and Alex shook it, half expecting to touch nothing but vapor. Under different circumstances, shaking hands with his long-dead great-grandfather would qualify as unusual. Right now, though, it seemed perfectly sensible. Alex regarded the man with curiosity. He knew so much less about this side of the family than he did about the Soberano side. He'd always been aware that he had some Palestinian blood running through his veins, but it was only a tiny contribution to his genealogy.

Alex found he still couldn't say anything. He was feeling less stunned by the second, but that didn't mean that he had any idea what to say upon meeting a collection of this sort on a dark path in the woods.

"We're supposed to take you for a walk," Khaled said.

"I'm already on a walk."

Khaled tilted his head sideways. "Not like this one."

Dro had moved back toward the cliff, kneeling at the edge of it. Now he patted the air and turned in the direction of the others. "It's solid over here."

His great-grandparents, two people who'd probably never met in real life, headed toward the cliff. Alex stood his ground until Vidente reached in his direction.

"Come walk with us," she said.

Alex gestured toward the trail on the other side of the trees. "The path is in this direction."

Dro stood and took a step beyond the edge of the cliff, standing on air. "We have a different path."

Alex was willing to accept many things. He was willing to accept that he had much to learn about himself on this trip to the ashram. He was willing to accept that his understanding of the metaphysical world was far from complete. However, he was not willing to accept an invitation to jump off a cliff, regardless of how solid his former self seemed to be while suspended over the chasm.

Khaled walked out to stand next to Dro and then turned to Alex in anticipation. Alex held his ground, particularly thankful at this point that he could *feel* the ground. Vidente walked closer to the edge, but she still hadn't joined the others.

Though she was perhaps twenty feet from him and though the light was limited, she had no trouble making eye contact with Alex. Her gaze made him feel lighter, as though this connection between them had made him less subject to gravity. If he kept looking at her, would he float away?

"I've come to give you something we need, Alex," she said. "I'm not going to let anything hurt you."

With that, she too stepped on the invisible path. Nearly without volition, Alex moved toward the cliff's edge.

He stopped less than a foot away. From here, if he stretched, he could touch Vidente's shoulder. The sudden temptation to do that became very strong. Until he looked down at her feet. It was dark everywhere, but it was especially dark beneath the three standing in front of him.

He looked up and once again found his great-grandmother's eyes.

"Alejandro, come with us."

Reason made one final effort to prevail. *Accept that you're actually seeing who you believe you are seeing,* it said. *Accept that they are standing on thin air. Consider this, though: two of them have been dead a long time. How could this hurt them anyway? As for Dro, I have no idea what to think.*

When reason fails to make a complete argument, faith needs to take the lead. Alex looked from one face to the next.

And then he stepped off the cliff.

He didn't immediately plunge to his death. He didn't even stumble. The air on which he now stood seemed as steady as the path had been. Steadier, actually, because it seemed entirely smooth.

Gingerly, he took a step to the side, noticing no difference. "How wide is this thing?"

"You're thinking too much," Dro said. "Come on; let's walk."

They walked for several minutes in the darkness. It took Alex this long to notice that no one was talking. Fascination with what was happening to him and curiosity about where they were going had preoccupied him. He took a look back toward "shore" at that point, noticing that he could only barely make out the jagged shape of the cliff face. When he turned again, the air around them changed form. He began to make out vague shapes, and when he looked down, he noticed that they no longer seemed to be walking on air. Instead, a street was emerging at their feet.

A fruit-and-vegetable cart scuttled past them on the left. Alex needed to step away briskly to avoid contact with it. They stepped up onto a curb where a cluster of men were sitting at a table playing cards while others bustled past. Though everything was very old-fashioned, there seemed to be a sense of energy here, a sense of vibrancy and newness.

Khaled took the lead and gestured them toward a doorway. Alex expected his great grandfather to open the door, but instead the man raised his palm and the setting shifted. They were in a modest living room now with tile floors and a richly colored tapestry on the wall.

A teenaged boy was sitting on a rust-colored couch with a toddler on his lap. The older boy had Khaled's Arabic features while the child's face bore distinct Latin traits and surprisingly long eyelashes. The teen was showing the little one two sepia-toned photographs of a woman whose spirit emerged in spite of the stiff nature of her pose. To the teen's side were several folded sheets of paper. They seemed to take no notice of the arrival of four people in their living room, which made as much sense as anything else did to Alex at this point.

"This is your mama, Leandro," the teen said in Spanish. "Her name was Lina." The teen studied the photograph. "I have to admit that she was quite a beauty. It's almost possible for me to understand how my father would have wished his family dead so he could marry her."

The teen's expression grew darker and he seemed on the verge of saying something venomous. But then he pulled the boy closer to him and kissed the top of the child's head.

"According to the letter Father wrote Aunt Leila, your mother believed she had a magical touch. She also seemed to know a great deal about flowers. Father wrote at length about the gardens she created. It's hard to imagine that a garden could be like this, but everything does seem to grow very well in this country. Certainly better than anything did at home."

The toddler seemed to be paying rapt attention to what the older boy was saying. Alex guessed that the child wasn't absorbing much of this, but he seemed to be enjoying this moment.

The teen picked up the papers, which Alex assumed was the letter he'd just been talking about. He read these papers for a short while, and then put them down again.

"I'm sorry I don't have more to tell you, Leandro. We will try to find out more about your mother, I promise. You should know about her."

Alex heard a sob to his right and turned to see tears running down Khaled's face.

"I can't believe Tarek is doing this," Khaled said as he cried. "He walked in on me once showing Leandro the pictures and he sneered at me as he always has since we've come to Legado. He hates me. I can't believe that he's doing this for me."

Alex turned back toward the two boys. Tarek was now tickling Leandro, causing the toddler to squeal with laughter and fold in on himself.

"That little one is your grandfather," Khaled said, wiping his eyes. "I promised myself I would try as hard as I could to keep the memory of his mother alive for him. I had no idea that Tarek would help me in any way."

Alex made a note in his mind to search more deeply into this side of the family when he got back to New York. Assuming, of course, that he didn't fall into the abyss when this journey was over. Unlike the Soberanos, no one had written a book about these ancestors. Maybe someone should have, though.

He felt Khaled's hand on his shoulder.

"Your great grandmother Lina was truly magical. You have much of her inside of you. She changed everything she touched for the better. Nothing more than me. I didn't understand love before I met her, but I will have her love with me for all eternity." He turned back toward the scene. "And maybe other love as well."

Alex had heard talk about a Palestinian ancestor who'd married a woman from Legado while he was still married to the wife he'd left behind, but he hadn't immediately connected this ancestor with Khaled. The few stories Alex had heard had always been tinged with salaciousness, the kind of thing that reinforced the hopelessness of all romantic commitments. The way Khaled spoke of Lina, though, suggested something entirely different, and Alex found this surprisingly warming. Though he knew neither of them, he wanted to believe that Khaled and Lina had found love on another level.

Two girls came into the room at this point and Tarek started tickling them as well. The conversation about the toddler's mother was obviously finished for now, though there was no question that the older boy would return to it for the toddler's benefit in the future.

Vidente took a step forward and the others followed her. Alex did so reluctantly, wanting to spend more time with these distant relatives about whom he'd heard so little. Still, he obviously needed to go wherever this was taking him and the last thing he wanted was to be stranded in the distant past.

They reached the door through which they'd entered – if that were the right word – and Vidente held her palm outward this time. Instantly, they were in a very different living room.

This one was ornate, with color and decoration everywhere. Alex recognized the ample display of worldly goods. His mother and grandmother from his father's side had decorated their homes in Anhelo in a similar way. He even thought he recognized a painting on the wall as one that sat to this day in his mother's home.

He glanced over at Vidente. This was obviously her house and he watched as she admired her things as though she hadn't seen them in decades. She wandered from the group to gaze at a glass case, the contents of which Alex couldn't see, then moved to a china cabinet.

As she did, a man in his mid-thirties came into the scene from another room. He was counting what appeared to be a stack of British pounds, stopping in mid-stride to calculate the total. He nodded to himself and then continued on.

"We'll have dinner on Saturday, yes?" The voice came from the room the man had just left.

The man paused again. "Dinner...yes. I think so. I have to check." He left without another word.

Vidente called over from the china cabinet. "That was Mauricio, my *other* son. Sometimes our best efforts bring us very little. He did do one thing right, though."

"What's that, Vidente?" Alex said.

"He fathered your father."

Only a few seconds later, a knock came at the door. A second Vidente came from another room, causing Alex to flinch briefly at the vision of two versions of his great-grandmother in the same place. The maid answered the door while the first Vidente watched the second with a look that appeared to be filled with envy.

A woman came into the house carrying a basket that she handed to Vidente. Vidente pulled back the napkin that covered the basket to admire the baked goods within. She thanked the woman and brought the basket into the kitchen. When she did this, the spectral version of Vidente came back to join the others.

"My hair does not look good today," she said. "I'm not sure how that is possible."

She pointed to the woman who'd entered and now sat at the dining room table. "That is Ana. She comes often so I can see her colors."

The trio watched as the other Vidente returned and sat across from Ana. She then closed her eyes and concentrated while Ana watched. Alex found Ana's expression fascinating. This wasn't simply a form of entertainment for her or a wistful game of "what-if." Ana fully expected to learn about her future here.

Vidente opened her eyes. She smiled warmly and reached across the table to clasp Ana's arm. "I see a great deal of crimson, my Ana."

Ana recoiled. "Crimson is bad, isn't it Vidente?"

Vidente folded her hands in front of her. "Not this crimson. This is the crimson that you and I have not had the chance to discuss before – the crimson of deepest passion."

Both of Ana's hands went up to her face. "Passion, Vidente? Love passion?"

"There is no doubt about this. As you know, sometimes the colors are indistinct. Sometimes I need to interpret them in some way. This is not one of those times."

This news seemed to fluster Ana so much that she had trouble speaking, her mouth opening and closing rapidly. This would have seemed comical to Alex if not for the unabashed joy that came with Ana's gestures. Alex wasn't sure he'd ever seen anyone happier than Ana seemed right now.

Vidente leaned toward the woman. "Have you met a man, Ana?"

Ana's eyes searched the room, as though she might find the man sitting on the couch in the corner. "Maybe I have. Maybe...at the bakery today someone came in who I'd never met before. He had just moved to Anhelo and he was very handsome. We talked for several minutes and he said he would be back tomorrow."

"Maybe you should bake something special for him in the morning."

Ana stood up, her excitement uncontainable by the chair. "I will. He came for pastries yesterday. I'll make him my quince turnovers. They usually require a special order but...but what could be more special than this?"

Ana pulled Vidente to her breast so tightly that Alex worried the woman might break his great-grandmother's back. Then she kissed her on the cheek and scurried from the house without another word. Vidente watched her go with deep satisfaction on her face.

"That hasn't happened yet," the Vidente next to him said. When Alex turned toward her, he saw that she was wearing the same expression as the version of her in the chair. "I guess I have at least one more job to do in Anhelo."

She stood in front of Alex and put her hands on either side of his face. "There's a reason to have this sight. It has benefitted many people over the years. It has benefitted me especially much. Do you understand that?"

How many times had Alex disparaged the "vision" in his family, even after he'd learned to utilize it himself? "I'm beginning to understand that Abuela Vidente."

"Our magic is a gift. It is also a privilege. If you have it, you must share it not only to enrich yourself, but also to enrich those around you. Otherwise, there are few things more wasteful."

"Yes, abuela."

"And you must pass it along. Something happened in the generations that led to you – something I never would have anticipated. I realized the second I saw you that this was what brought me here. Never forsake this gift, and make sure that you let future Soberanos know what a precious thing this is."

"I promise, abuela."

She nodded toward Dro and they began to leave the room. As Vidente passed the other version of herself, she scoffed. "I don't like what is happening with my hair at all."

Dro got to the front door, put out his palm, and the trio entered another room. This one was considerably more modern than the other two. It took no imagination for Alex to realize that they were in America now. No imagination at all, because he knew this room.

The Presidential Suite at the Four Seasons Hotel in Boston.

The living room of the suite was empty when the four of them entered, but only seconds later, a remarkably beautiful woman in a short bathrobe entered. The sight of her nearly caused Alex's knees to buckle, even though he knew to expect her from the moment he recognized the room. Viviana Emisario, the "ghost" who'd been haunting him since he arrived at the ashram, was so much softer, her lines so much more delicate, her eyes so much brighter than Alex remembered. His gaze drifted to her calves and bare feet and he found the sensation dizzying. The rush of emotions he felt at once – hunger, stimulation, affection, melancholy, and too many others to recognize – threatened to overwhelm him. He felt the urge to look away and found that he couldn't.

A somewhat younger version of the Dro that was with him followed her onto the loveseat, attempting to undo her robe. Viviana guided him to sit next to her instead. She wanted to talk to him about his employment future, she said, but Alex knew that she really wanted to talk to him about something else.

He knew where this conversation was going. He'd refused to think about it after he'd learned of Viviana's death, but it still showed up in his dreams on occasion. If he'd understood the implication of this next half-hour back then, he could have changed everything.

The Dro on the couch was practically invisible to Alex. Viviana alive and animated in front of him was all he could see. He'd forgotten how her eyes narrowed when she said something about which she'd given considerable thought. He'd forgotten how her head tipped forward when she dispensed wisdom. He'd forgotten the little uptick in her lips when she paused between sentences, a gesture that always made him want to kiss her.

As he watched her now, though, he saw something he hadn't seen around a personal acquaintance in so long that he assumed he never would again. He saw the colors of Viviana's electromagnetic field. The vision of this reminded him of the days when he took such vision for granted, when he assumed that he could read the demeanor of anyone he met. He could still do it in business settings, of course; he made all of his deals contingent upon such readings, and he'd cancelled the deal with Sandbank Media because he didn't like what he saw in Tom Waxman's aura. But he hadn't seen an aura around a friend or lover in nearly two decades.

Not since he learned why Viviana died.

What surprised him more than his ability to see the aura, though, was what he saw there. He'd always envisioned Viviana's aura as red, only natural for someone as passionate as she, especially since they were usually in some sexual situation or other when they were together. Now, though, he saw that her aura had much more orange in it than he'd ever recalled.

Reddish-orange. She was broadcasting to him that she was in love with him. And he'd completely missed it.

With effort, he pulled his eyes away from Viviana to look at the Dro standing next to him. The spirit – if that's what it was – of his former self seemed to be expecting this and Alex wondered if Dro had been staring at him the entire time.

"I can't believe how much of an asshole I was," Alex said.

"She was remarkable."

"But we knew that, didn't we? I thought she was just playing with me."

Dro dropped his head. He didn't look back up when he spoke again. "We should have understood, but we didn't."

Alex turned back to the scene in front of him. Though he hadn't changed all that much from his Cambridge days – a thinner hairline, perhaps, a slightly thicker face – he found it extremely difficult to place himself on the couch. He tried to remember what he felt that day and why he'd avoided Viviana's entreaties to join her in DC. Everything would have been different if he had. New York was where his career exploded and London was where he gained the polish and experience necessary to build the empire he was building. That never would have happened the same way in Washington. And being the much younger lover of his country's most famous figure was unlikely to have survived the rigors of endless media scrutiny. What was undeniable, though, was that if he'd understood Viviana's love for him – something he should have been able to do given his vision – he would have approached this discussion of their future in some other way entirely. If he had, there was every reason to believe that Viviana would still be alive today.

And that his soul would have remained intact. He recognized at last the deep darkness that he'd seen in his session with Valerie/Vidente. Again, he looked to the Dro standing next to him, but Dro was watching the couple on the couch mournfully. Alex kept looking at him, surprised at how long he could stare at his younger self without the other acknowledging him.

Finally, Dro turned toward him. Their eyes met and Alex captured all the regret and grief of his former self. Again, Dro dipped his head. In response, and not of his own volition, Alex did the same. For several long seconds Alex contemplated the floor. He'd always failed to give the women in his life what Viviana needed. She'd just been the first to suffer from this.

The only solace he'd ever been able to take in this was that the way Viviana killed herself had had a huge positive impact on Legado. In her letter, she'd asked Alex to keep her secret, and of course he had. Gordillo went ballistic over the thought that his deputies had shot down Viviana's copter. He assassinated several of them in the following weeks. It turned out that he was very fond of the ambassador even though they sat on opposite sides of the political spectrum. None of that mattered after the fact, though. Public opinion turned so strongly against La Justicia that the movement lost all momentum. Without a sympathetic following, especially in legislative and military circles, La Justicia's most powerful generals found themselves behind bars. And while the authorities never caught Gordillo, he'd gone so far underground that he'd become entirely impotent.

Viviana had imbued her life with meaning, a meaning that carried far past her death. He'd been blessed by her presence in his life, by the opportunity to know her as few others ever did, and he'd squandered that blessing. He'd turned a vibrant, irreplaceable woman into a symbol and he only realized now that this was an entirely unacceptable trade. Yet the symbol was all that remained. That symbol had revived his homeland.

He could only hope it would do the same for his spirit.

The emotional ache Alex felt at this moment seemed physical. It was as though something was moving around his insides, prodding and poking, pulling away at scar tissue, revealing rawness and bringing long-deadened pain sensors back online. It was enough to bring him to his knees, but his legs didn't threaten to wobble. Ironically, the vision he had in his head of Viviana – the full, unfiltered vision he'd failed to see for so long – seemed to be making him stronger. He understood something now, something that he could carry home with him.

When Alex looked up again, he was no longer in the hotel room in Boston. He was back at the edge of the cliff. Standing on either side of him were Yusuf and Valerie. They no longer looked like his great-grandparents.

Dro was nowhere in sight.

Alex looked down at his hands, flexing them as though making sure they still operated the same way. Then he took a deep breath and held it in, closing his eyes at the same time. Exhaling slowly, he opened his eyes again. He was ready to go back to his room. He looked at the others and they said nothing, so he assumed they'd already shown him everything they could.

He turned back to the path, Yusuf and Valerie next to him. They walked silently. It was difficult to think of a conversation starter after what they'd been through. The path seemed lighter now; Angélica's flashlight app wouldn't be necessary at this point. He didn't think they'd been out there very long, but it seemed that dawn was breaking.

When they got to his bungalow, Alex stopped. "This is where I get off."

"I think we're all getting off now," Valerie said.

Alex looked at her carefully. "Are you still in there."

Valerie nodded. "It's time for me to go. Valerie has been a very pleasant host. I think she's kicking me out now, though."

Was it possible to mourn someone who'd died nearly four decades before you were born? "Thank you for your help."

"I have something for you," Valerie/Vidente said. She reached into a pocket and pulled out a ring, handing it to him. Even in the dawning light he could tell that it was quite a treasure.

"Platinum," he said, rolling the ring between two fingers.

Vidente scoffed. "Oh no. It's just a tin trinket I picked up on a trip. It did very good things for me, but I realize now that I got it for you."

Alex examined the ring more carefully. "This is definitely platinum, abuela."

The body of Valerie shrugged. "Imagine that."

She pulled Alex toward her and kissed his face, keeping their cheeks together for several seconds. "Remember what I said."

"I can't forget it."

"You have even more gifts than you realize. Promise me that you'll explore all of them and that you'll be generous with them."

"I promise, abuela."

She stepped back, looking at him as intently as Valerie had the first time they'd met. "You can reach me if you need me."

Alex held up his Blackberry and smiled. "I don't have you in my phone."

Valerie/Vidente looked at the device confusedly for a moment and then she locked eyes with him again. "You can reach me if you need me."

At that point, Yusuf stepped toward him. "I have something for you as well," he said, handing Alex a polished piece of wood.

Alex turned the wood in his hand, unsure what to make of it.

"It's a grounding charm."

Alex looked up at the general manager, trying to find his great-grandfather in there. "Grounding might be good."

"As long as you are grounded in the right ways."

Yusuf put a hand on Alex's shoulder, squeezing it tightly. "I hope my sons grow up to be like you. All of them."

Alex reached for the hand and held it to him. "It was a true pleasure to meet you. I wish we'd had more time together."

Yusuf/Khaled nodded. "You never know. Maybe we will." Then he released his hand, patted Alex's cheek, and turned away. He extended an arm to Valerie and she took it. Alex watched as they headed down the hill. No more than fifty feet down the path, Valerie disengaged her arm, looking at Yusuf awkwardly.

Alex returned to his room, convinced now that he would sleep at least a little before he faced the new day.

15.

ANHELO, 1928

Videnté didn't know how long she had left to live after her return to Anhelo. Until today. The colors were very clear about this. She didn't need to go any further to discover their meaning.

She'd come to accept it. Before her journey to California she wasn't sure, but she was sure now. Seeing Alejandro and realizing that moving him would secure her family legacy had given her a sense of completion she didn't realize she could have on the dawn of an event of this magnitude.

She had seen Ana yesterday, playing out the scene that she'd already watched with both Alejandros and their great-grandfather. She glanced at the clock on her night table, wondering if Ana's man had already come to the bakery for his quince turnovers. Before Ana left yesterday, Vidente gave her one of her most beautiful tablecloths, asking her to use it to set the table for her first dinner after her marriage. This morning, she decided that she wanted Ana to have a pair of candlesticks as well. Vidente had always told everyone that the candlesticks were silver, though she had good reason to think that they really weren't. Who knew, though? She thought the ring she'd given Alejandro was tin and he insisted it was platinum.

She left a few more things on the dining room table for Javier to distribute to friends, putting their names on cards next to the items. Considering how much money she'd given Mauricio yesterday – money that had nothing to do with the sum she was leaving for his children – she should have handed this task to him; Javier had so many real responsibilities, after all. However, Mauricio would only have made a mess of things, so she had no choice but to entrust this to her trustworthy son. This would confirm to Javier that she was aware of her fate, and he would probably be angry with her that she hadn't told him about the vision, but she couldn't do that to him. Javier took everything too seriously.

Vidente slid underneath the covers of her bed, gaining comfort from their familiar embrace. She gazed up at the ceiling and said a prayer. Then she thought about the Anhelo she was leaving behind and the America that her spirit visited to touch the future of her family.

Distantly, she felt a clutch at her chest, but she was only dimly aware of what was happening to her body. She had already begun to take flight.

❧

JOYA DE LA COSTA, 1921

K haled stood outside of his front door for several minutes before entering. He'd been back from his unimaginable journey for probably an hour now and his legs still felt weak. He'd returned to the spot in the shop where he'd been when he suddenly transported to California. Brayan, the shop owner, quivered at the sight of him when he'd walked over to that part of the store with a customer. After he finished with the customer, Brayan explained that Khaled had simply disappeared from the store while Brayan was in the back getting him a glass of water. He later heard that Khaled couldn't be found anywhere and he feared the worst. Khaled tried to make up an excuse to explain what happened, but his mind was too hazy to do this well. Incredibly, Brayan had his sample case in the back room and he brought this out to him. The shop owner mentioned the price of the grounding charm Khaled had taken and Khaled tried to pay him for it. However, Brayan waved his money away. "I know you understand its value," Brayan had said before Khaled left the store.

It was now time to walk back home. Khaled did this especially slowly, needing the time to gather his wits. Fortunately, he didn't run into anyone he knew along the way; he had no idea what he would have done if he'd seen Nahla coming toward him on the street.

The time in California had been remarkable on so many levels. Seeing America in the twenty-first century was astounding. The machines were magical, yet everyone there took them for granted. The people were so different as well. Everyone seemed to have vast amounts of money there to go with high levels of education. It was chastening for a man of modest upbringing such as Khaled. Fortunately, Yusuf, the man whose body he shared, seemed as sophisticated as the others; Khaled just let him take over whenever necessary.

Khaled had no idea why he'd been chosen for such a journey until he met his great-great grandson. Alex was an estimable man even in the company of the others at the ashram, and meeting him gave Khaled tremendous hope for the future of his bloodline, the bloodline he'd started with Lina. Still, it didn't make sense that he should be catapulted nearly a century into the future just so he could shake the hand of one of his descendants.

The truest purpose didn't reveal itself until the very last night.

Khaled's head still wasn't clear, but he didn't think he could stand in front of the house much longer. How much more awkward would this be if one of the neighbors saw him standing here? Surely all of them knew about his disappearance.

A high-pitched giggle from inside the house finally spurred him to reach for the doorknob, the sound of Leandro finally reminding him of how much he'd missed his son while he was away. He'd been so nervous about reentering this world that he'd forgotten the most wonderful part about being home.

He stepped through the doorway to the sound of playful commotion. From the foyer, he could hear Tarek threatening in Spanish to torture Mona with tickles, which caused Khaled's younger daughter to protest and chuckle at the same time. Khaled put down his sample case and approached the entryway to the living room. As he suspected, he'd returned home to the very scene he'd witnessed just a short while ago ninety years in the future.

For several moments, no one noticed his presence, occupied as they were by tickling or being tickled. Then Tarek looked up, saw him standing there, and immediately stiffened. The girls hadn't realized the game had ended and jumped their older brother simultaneously. Tarek stumbled, but didn't break eye contact with his father.

At that point, May and Mona noticed that their brother was no longer playing and turned to see what had drawn his attention. Khaled looked at each of them as they sobered and watched him without moving. Leandro got up and tugged on May's leg, still oblivious to his father's presence.

Khaled stepped into the room very slowly. His presence seemed to have mesmerized the girls; Mona's jaw hung slackly. Tarek was hardening by the second, though. The boy took one glance down at the chair where the pictures were, and then locked eyes with his father again.

Leandro finally realized that Khaled was there and began toddling over to him. Khaled reached down to pick up the child, but he never took his eyes off Tarek. When he stood just a few feet from his oldest son, he reached his hand toward Tarek's face. At first Tarek flinched, but Khaled persevered, caressing the boy's cheek and then pulling him forward to kiss him on the forehead.

The bluster fell from the teenager's expression at that point and his eyes grew misty.

Before he could start crying himself, Khaled pulled Tarek, Leandro, May, and Mona into his embrace.

୬

NEW YORK, 2010

A lex boarded a plane the next day. He could have remained at the ashram for the duration of his planned stay. The hiking, the yoga, and the stress-relief exercises would still have had medicinal value. That was, of course, the reason he'd gone to the ashram. It might have even been entertaining to get to know Sloan, Yusuf, and Valerie now that they were *only* themselves. After what happened out beyond the cliff, though, anything else would have seemed anticlimactic (though he did have all of their contact information in his Blackberry). More to the point, though, he felt a compulsion to get back to his life. Part of it, at least.

He thought about calling ahead to make sure that Angélica was going to be home at her apartment. It would have been frustrating to attempt to surprise her only to discover that she was out for the night or that she was entertaining friends. He decided against doing so, though. She would want to know why he was leaving the ashram early, and he didn't want to have part of that conversation on the phone. There was also the issue of how they'd last separated. If he was going to make things up to her, he needed to do it in person without any preamble.

His driver took him first to his apartment so he could drop off his bags. On his way upstairs, he got his mail from the concierge, flipping through it quickly as he rode the elevator. His flipping stopped abruptly when he came upon a hand-addressed envelope with the name "Roemer" in the return address. He'd stayed in close touch over the years with the now-retired associate admissions director at MIT. They spoke on the phone at least a couple of times a month, e-mailed regularly, and even stayed abreast of each other on Facebook. He wasn't sure he'd ever gotten a physical letter from her before, though.

As the elevator reached his floor, he opened the envelope. Inside was the sheet of paper upon which he'd written the differential equations for Susan the first time they met. Attached to it was a Post-It that read: "I saw this while meditating today and knew it was time for you to have it."

Alex entered his apartment and tossed down his bag. Carrying the rest of the mail to his coffee table, he sat down to regard the paper. His handwriting had been sloppier back then, but he could easily imagine the boy who'd hastily jotted this math in an attempt to impress his way into one of the most vaunted educational institutions in the world. He shouldn't have been able to understand differential equations back then; not with so many moving parts. And in some ways maybe he didn't. Maybe only now was he beginning to grasp their intricacy.

He put the paper down on the coffee table for a moment, wondering what he should do with it. His first thought was to frame it. This was, after all, in many ways his admissions essay to MIT, and MIT was where everything had begun. But as he thought about it some more, he realized that this wasn't really the case at all. Going to his backpack, he retrieved the copy of his family history he'd brought to California. He placed the sheet of equations between the title page and the first page of text and then put the book on the coffee table, where he intended to keep it.

Then it was time to go to Angélica's place in Tribeca. Though Angélica and he had spent very little time in this building together, the concierge knew him and granted him permission to go up to Angélica's apartment without notice, in the process confirming that Angélica was there and that she was alone.

On the ride up the elevator, Alex toyed with the platinum ring he had in his pocket. He smiled at the memory of the expression on his great-grandmother's face when he informed her that the ring was much more valuable than she'd imagined. Family legend had it that she'd gifted many people with treasures of questionable value and authenticity. How ironic that she would give him something worth exponentially more than she'd anticipated.

Alex knocked on Angélica's door and stood back several feet. He wanted to see all of her at once when she answered it. Ten seconds later, he heard her peephole slide sideways, and then her door opened a moment after that. Angélica was in a simple white shirt with the kind of loose-fitting jeans she wore when she wasn't planning to go out. As always, she looked sensational, but as she cocked her hip sideways and looked at him confusedly, Alex wasn't paying attention to her dress or her demeanor. Instead, he was looking around her.

At the aura that blazed a rich orange no more than a second after she opened the door.

"What are you doing here?" she said gently.

"I came back early. Do you mind if I come in?"

Angélica stepped away from the door to let him enter. He kissed her softly on the lips and the way she kissed him back told him that she'd neither forgotten how they'd parted nor fully processed it. The orange aura, however, told him everything he needed to know.

He faced her and put his hands on her shoulders. "I'm sorry. I completely screwed up our last night together. I did it for a stupid reason and you deserved much better than that."

Angélica's posture softened under his hands. "I just wanted you for myself."

He moved his hands to the sides of her face. "You have me for yourself. I came home early to tell you exactly that."

Angélica kissed one of his hands and then moved into his arms. For several minutes, he just held her, reveling in her warmth, feeling his passion for her building, but knowing that he needed to do something else before he could act on that passion.

At last, she took a half-step back. "You didn't like the ashram?"

Alex shook his head quickly. "I loved the ashram. I definitely want to go back. We can go there together sometime. I think you'd enjoy it."

"Then why did you leave?"

Alex wondered how much he wanted to say now. He didn't want to get into a long diverting conversation. "Something happened that made it important that I come back to you as soon as I could. I met two of my great-grandparents."

Angélica's eyes glittered with amusement. "I didn't realize you had family in Southern California."

Alex chuckled. "I don't, but I did for a few days."

He reached into the breast pocket of his jacket and pulled out the wooden implement that Khaled had given him. "This came from my great-grandfather. He told me it was a grounding charm."

He handed the piece to Angélica and she examined it. "What do you do with it?"

"I'm not sure, but I'm going to keep it someplace important and reach out for it when necessary."

While he was talking, he dug into his jeans pocket for the ring, putting it into his palm and presenting it to Angélica. "My great-grandmother gave this to me."

Angélica looked down at the ring and then back up at Alex, seemingly unsure how to respond. "It's beautiful," she said. "So intricate."

"It's for you."

Angélica tipped her head to one side and he wanted desperately to kiss her for hours. "You're giving me a ring?" she said with a small smile. "Does this mean something?"

"I certainly hope you think so. I'm giving you a family heirloom. Our family heirlooms stay in the family forever."

Angélica took the ring from his palm and examined it carefully, her eyes growing teary as she did so. Then she pulled him toward her and kissed him with a hunger that seemed nearly as large as his own.

Alex Soberano felt a sense of wholeness he thought he'd lost forever.

EPILOGUE
NEW YORK, 2010

Alex had managed to convince Angélica to request an extension on a story so they could spend two days at home together with the only interruptions coming from takeout deliveries. After that, though, she had to get back to work, which meant that it made sense for him to do the same.

He picked up four followers on the trip from the elevator to his office, all of whom were exercised over a pending decision. His nine-day absence had not done nearly as much to spur independence among his key staff as he had hoped, though he was pleased to hear that Sarmistha had gone very deep into the Lansing negotiations. Even better, it appeared that they would be able to make that deal for less than he'd authorized her to spend.

Alex lost count of the number of people who came to his office when they learned he was back early. Curiously, the one person who hadn't stuck his face in the doorway was Mark. His Executive Assistant had resisted the urge to accost him, presumably because he knew better, or perhaps because he'd even learned something while Alex was out of touch.

After an hour of dispensing advice and direction, still feeling the palliative effects of the week at the ashram and the two days in Angélica's arms, Alex sent his staff away, asking Kathy to keep his office clear at least until lunchtime. He turned to his hundreds of e-mail and phone messages and attempted to get his head back into the game.

Forty-five minutes later, Kathy buzzed him to ask if Mark were exempt from his no-staff dictate. A minute after that, Mark slipped in, closing the door behind him to assure that no one followed.

"Okay, so if I promise never to question you ever again, can we dispense with the I-told-you-sos?"

Alex chuckled. "I would be better equipped to answer that question if I had any idea what you were talking about."

Mark's brows knitted. "You haven't heard about Sandbank?"

"Mark, it surprises me how delighted I am to say that I'm completely out of the loop on this one."

Mark paused, as if waiting for Alex to tell him that he was joking and that he knew exactly what was going on. When it became clear that this wasn't going to happen, he continued. "Tom Waxman is gonna wind up in jail."

Alex smiled, remembering the yellow and gray he'd seen in Waxman's aura that had counseled him to walk away from the Sandbank deal. "What did he do?"

"Embezzlement, identity theft, and intellectual property theft among other things. He was very clever about disguising this, which is why none of it came up in our due diligence."

"Then how did the government find out?"

"It appears that Waxman let his guard down after you stood him up at the altar."

Alex was amused, but his mind was already working.

"You knew about this, didn't you?" Mark said. "Somehow, you knew about this."

Alex held up his hands. "Truly, I didn't. Not the specifics, anyway. As you can imagine, though, this doesn't come as a shock to me."

Mark looked down at the floor, shaking his head. "We really dodged a bullet there. As I said, I'll never question you again."

"I'm going to pretend I didn't hear that. Stop questioning me, and you're fired. Let's buy Sandbank."

Mark's eyes darted up toward Alex's. "What?"

"Under the circumstances, we'll get it for twenty percent of what it's worth."

"For good reason. They're hemorrhaging members right now. At twenty percent, we'd be overpaying."

By this point, the idea was nearly fully formed in Alex's head. "They have an infrastructure we can use."

"An infrastructure for what? We were buying them because of the ad revenue they were generating."

"They also had an excellent number two man over there. That guy Plum. He's the right person for this."

Mark leaned against the door. "You were less cryptic before you went to California."

Alex motioned Mark to sit, though he started to talk before the man had even settled in his chair. "We're going to use the Sandbank infrastructure to create a company called Vidente. Social media with a specific goal: to help people see their future. This is literally coming to me as we speak, but I see it as a way for people to form connections with others who can help them envision their best outcomes. We'll put together a huge team of mentors and visionaries and then let crowd-sourcing take over."

"How do we make money on this?"

"I'm not concerned with making money on it."

"See, now you're just frightening me."

Alex laughed. He'd trained Mark well. "We *will* make money on it. I'm sure you'll even help me to figure out how."

Mark looked off into the middle distance. "This could be a great story to tell at future board meetings."

"Get Plum on the phone. I'm sure this'll be the last call he's expecting today."

Mark bounded from the chair and moved toward the door. As he put his hand on the knob, he turned back to Alex. "How was your vacation, by the way?"

"Illuminating. I'll tell you more later. For now, go change the course of history."

෴

NEW YORK, 2015

Alex reached into the yellow bag and pulled out a cardboard circle, announcing, "Snake" to the three children sitting around him on the floor with playing cards in front of them. He used the piece to tickle his son's neck while making a hissing sound. Year-and-a-half Cal, still too young to play Animal Bingo, giggled and folded in on himself.

"I have a snake," three-year-old Allie said, proudly placing a game piece on her card. The only piece Alex's daughter still needed was a lobster, while her cousin, eight-year-old Christina was waiting for a snail in order to win. The third player, Christina's four-year-old brother Paul, still needed three animals on his card, so he didn't stand much of a chance. This seemed unlikely to disturb Paul, who at that moment was laying on the floor staring up at the ceiling and wagging his tongue from side to side.

It would be easy enough to set things up for Allie to win. Neither of the girls could see the pieces before Alex pulled them from the yellow bag, and he could make sure he brought out a lobster before the snail. He knew from experience, though, that if Angélica caught him doing this, she'd scold him for cheating. Alex could barely help himself, though. He so loved the way Allie's eyes glimmered when she was happy. This was likely to cause Alex all kinds of trouble from his daughter as she got older, but for now, if he could manipulate things to augment her happiness, he didn't consider this beneath him.

As it turned out, the next piece Alex pulled from the bag was a lobster, which meant that Allie could win without Alex having to rig the game for her. His little girl squealed with delight and he gave her a congratulatory hug before complimenting Christina on a game well played. Paul didn't seem to notice that the game was over, as he had now flopped over onto his stomach and was pretending to be a turtle. The boy had goofiness down to a science.

This had been a welcome day of simple fun. It had been an especially intense week at the office, with the media buzzing over the announcement from an emerging Third World leader that he'd gotten his inspiration and direction from the Vidente social media site. Alex had done easily two dozen interviews while dealing with all of the normal business associated with the end of the quarter. The site was taking so much of his time now. Fortunately, the staff had finally learned to operate as self-starters.

Alex swept up the playing pieces and put them back in the yellow bag, preparing for another game. They'd played three times already, with Allie winning twice and Paul winning once, back when he was paying more attention. Alex switched out the kids' cards and was getting ready to start a fourth game when Angélica came into the room.

"How's the World Animal Bingo Championship going?" she said, rubbing Cal's hair and giving Allie a kiss on the top of the head.

Alex reached out for her hand and squeezed it gently. "The competition is fierce. You really should be witnessing this from a front-row seat."

Angélica rolled her eyes. "I wish I could. This deadline is driving me crazy. I'm very, very sorry to be missing out on all the fun."

Alex pulled her hand closer and kissed it. "I'll let you have some fun later."

Angélica looked at him with an expression that always managed to get his imagination going. "That sounds very nice," she said dreamily. Then, seemingly remembering why she'd joined them in the first place, she added, "Your sister called; she'll be by in about a half hour to pick up Christina and Paul."

Alex rustled the yellow bag and turned toward the kids. "It sounds like the competition is entering its final stages, boys and girls. Are you ready for some action?"

Angélica leaned over to kiss him. "I'd better get back. Fun later, though, right?"

Alex kissed her again before letting her stand back up. "Definitely fun later."

His wife offered him a tired smile and then exited the room.

"Mommy's red and grey," Allie said as Alex watched Angélica leave.

"Totally red and grey," Christina said. Paul focused long enough to concur.

Alex turned back to the kids and locked eyes with his daughter.

"Is Mommy okay?" Allie said.

Christina leaned forward. "There was a *lot* of grey there."

It had been a little more than a year since Alex had taught the three kids how to read the electromagnetic fields of others. Christina had been ready for a while, but he wanted to wait until Allie was a little older. The process was incredibly easy. It was clear to him that all the kids had the Soberano gift, because they were quickly seeing the colors vividly. While many assumed that he'd named his daughter after himself, he'd really named her after Vidente, who would no doubt love seeing how much her great-great grandchildren had already learned.

"Mommy's fine," he said to his little girl. "She has a really tough writing assignment and it's making her very tired. She's almost done, though, and Daddy is going to take her to a very special place afterward and we're going to have a really nice night. I'll bet she'll be good and pink when you see her tomorrow morning."

"Pink," Paul said absently, already losing interest in the conversation and finding fascination with a piece of lint on his shirt.

Allie relaxed with Alex's assurance. Christina's brows drew closer together, though.

"My mom is coming to get us soon? Aunt Angélica promised she was going to braid my hair today. Will she still be able to do that?"

Alex tipped his head to the side. "I'm not sure that's going to happen today, Chrissy," he said delicately. While he was not above fixing a game to let his daughter beat his niece, he hated letting Chrissy down. "Aunt Angélica really needs to get her work done."

Christina looked down at the floor. "It's okay," she said, unable to prevent disappointment from seeping out of her voice. Then she looked up at him. "Even though I don't like what is happening with my hair at all."

As she said this, she threw her eyes toward the ceiling. Alex did the same, but for a very different reason.

You're always with me, aren't you Vidente? he thought gratefully before gathering the kids together for one last game before his sister arrived.

ABOUT THE AUTHORS

Julian Iragorri lives in Manhattan. He has worked onWall Street since the early nineties.

Lou Aronica is the author of the *USA Today* bestseller *The Forever Year* and the national bestseller *Blue*. He also collaborated on the *New York Times* nonfiction bestsellers *The Element* and *Finding Your Element* (with Ken Robinson) and the national bestseller *The Culture Code* (with Clotaire Rapaille). Aronica is a long-term book publishing veteran. He is President and Publisher of the independent publishing house The Story Plant. You can reach him at laronica@fictionstudio.com.

Made in United States
North Haven, CT
14 May 2023

36576520R00211